DANGEROUS

LESLEY FIELD

Book one in the Duchess in Danger Series

Shortlisted for Historical Novel of the Year 2016 by The Romantic Novelists Association

HISTORICAL NOVELS

Next in the Duchess in Danger series

DANGEROUS DECEPTION

Published as an e-book on 29th November 2016

by MuseItUp Publishing

Follow Lady Caroline Sutton as her idyllic life turns from heaven to hell. Can she survive and recapture the life she desired.

* * * *

CONTEMPORARY NOVELS

Coming 2017 the first book in the Saunders Series.

Set in the beautiful town of Banff in the heart of the Rocky Mountains in Canada.

Book One - "Saunders - Lies and Deception."

Book Two - "Saunders - Endings and Beginnings."

Book Three - "Saunders - Sisters and Lovers."

Dangerous
Entrapment.©

by

Lesley Field

First Print Edition April 2017
Published as an e-book on 11th August 2015
by MuseItUp Publishing

For Neil for his complete faith in me,

and his patience and understanding when talking was banned. And his perseverance in preparing this print edition

For my friend and mentor Val Wood

for setting me on the right path, and for her continued support.

In memory of Cindy,

who would have loved to share this day with me.

And now of her husband Peter.

Friends are people who are always there, but one day you have to let them go.

DANGEROUS
ENTRAPMENT

Chapter One

London 1810

Lady Isobella Rothbury was tired with the ball already and it had barely begun. She wished she had stayed at home pleading a headache but cousin Juliette was desperate that she accompany them if only to offer protection from the unwanted attentions of Lord Edward Carlisle.

At one and twenty, Isobella was almost ready to consider herself to be on the shelf and she was little impressed with the young bucks of the day. Juliette, or precisely, Lady Juliette Rothbury, sister to the young Duke of Rothbury, had, at the age of eight and ten, come out this season and was enthralled with the whole experience of balls and musical events. The family were delighted when she caught the eye of James, the young Earl of Preston, and her mother, Eleanor Duchess of Rothbury, was fully expecting him to offer for Juliette before the season ended.

Isobella sighed. She had been here before filled with hope and dreams. She could not help but let her mind drift back to when she had come out, a time so much like Juliette's. Having caught the attention of Harry Duke of Exmouth, she had been smitten by his good looks and the attention lavished upon her. Aunt Eleanor was excited, anticipating him offering for her hand but just over half way through the season it all dissolved. Mostly in tears shed by Isobella, tears of humiliation.

She could remember quite clearly the moment she lost him; or rather he lost interest in her. It was at the Cavendish Ball. They had just finished dancing when there was a flurry near the entrance. Heads had turned. It was almost past the hour of being fashionably late but the newcomers took no heed of bad looks. Indeed, they looked down on the crowd and Isobella heard someone whisper.

"It is the Duke of Cumberland and his family. Look at Lady Cordelia, has she not grown into the most delightful young woman?"

Looking in the direction of everyone else as Exmouth led her from the floor back to her party, she had not failed to notice the petite Lady Cordelia, sweet, pale skinned with golden curls that fell about creamy shoulders. The dress she wore was the palest pink in contrast with the tiny deep pink rosebuds sewn onto the skirt and bodice. The low top and off the shoulder sleeves showed just enough pale flesh to be fashionably decent, and even Isobella had to admit that she was a beauty.

How much of a beauty became apparent when she heard the gasp from Exmouth and looked up to see him gazing in wonderment at the vision in pink. Handing Isobella into the care of the Rothbury party, and with the fleetest of bows in her direction, he was gone, striding across the ballroom to join the other bucks clambering for an introduction. That was the end for Isobella; Exmouth was smitten, and before long he and Cordelia were the talk of the ton. Isobella was left to face the sympathetic glances from people for the rest of the season, and she swore that she would never again let herself be caught up in silly romantic thoughts.

She had enquired of her aunt at the time why Cordelia failed to come out with the rest of the young debutants, and discovered that the family had been on holiday in Italy, but the Duchess was indisposed and too ill to return home for the start of the season. Isobella wished at the time that she had stayed sick a bit longer. At least until she and Exmouth were betrothed, but then if he had still fallen for her she would have been in an even more embarrassing position than she found herself in.

The following season she had excused herself as much as she could from attending the balls. Cousin Charles, thoughtful for her feelings, had taken the family to the country estate when Exmouth and Cordelia married. He had wanted to call Exmouth out but Isobella begged him not to. She was shamed enough by what had happened and wanted nothing more than to forget what had happened. Honouring her wishes, he had not done so, but had spoken to Exmouth and left him in no doubt as to what he thought of his behaviour.

Now it was two years later and a new season, but this time it was Juliette's turn to be the belle of the ball. Drawing her thoughts back to the present Isobella watched as the Earl of Preston whirled Juliette around the room, a smile touching the corners of her mouth as she gently swayed to the music. She hated waiting for someone to request a dance so stood back near to one of the columns, watching the dancers. The Earl escorted Juliette back to the family and bowed low over her hand. Her cousin dropped the deepest courtesy to him, and Isobella saw his lips gently brush over Juliette's hand.

Hurrying back to Juliette, she saw Lord Edward Carlisle approach their party and then bow to Juliette before leading her onto the floor. Isobella cursed herself for not reaching them in time and saw Juliette throw a look of panic in her direction. Not able to do anything at present she gave an encouraging smile, but watched like a hawk as young Carlisle swept her cousin around the floor. Seeing them nearing the edge of the dance floor she quickly excused herself to her aunt, and skirting through the crowd was just in time to see him pull Juliette into a corridor.

As she turned into the dimly lit area she saw the fear in her cousin's eyes. Lord Edward's back faced Isobella so he had no knowledge of her presence.

Offering reassurance to her cousin with a smile, she hurried forward. "Oh, there you are, Juliette. Your mama is looking for you," and with that she put out her hand and took hold of her cousin's. Without a backward glance at Lord Edward, she pulled Juliette back towards the dance floor.

"Oh thank you, Izzie. I was at a loss as to what to do. He twirled me round so much I was beginning to feel dizzy, and then took advantage and led me away. Is mama really looking for me?"

"No, of course she is not, silly, but I needed to say something to get you away without causing a scene."

"Izzie, you are so wonderful and clever. If I had been caught with Lord Edward I have no doubt James would have withdrawn his favour and I would end up a spinster," she said woefully.

Isobella laughed at her cousin's remark. "There is only room for one spinster in the family and that position is most likely already taken, Juliet."

"Oh no, Izzie, you will find someone who will love you much more than Exmouth did."

"Perhaps I do not want to be loved. It all seems much over rated to me."

By this time the girls had reached the side of the Duchess, and there they stayed chattering until the Earl came and claimed Juliette again.

By the time the ball was over, all Isobella yearned for was the calm of her bedchamber. She had just finished being undressed by her maid, Anna, when Juliette came rushing in. Once the girls were alone she confided in Isobella that James had requested an audience with her mother and Charles the day after tomorrow.

"Why not tomorrow?" enquired Isobella.

"It would seem his presence is needed at Preston Hall, so he will be out of town but will return for the ball at Arlington House the following day, and is to see mama and Charles in the afternoon before the ball. Oh, Izzie, I believe he is going to offer for me," she said, twirling round in excitement.

She looked at her cousin's face and the dreamy look in her eyes. "I take it that you have feelings for Preston and are not adverse to marrying him?"

"Izzie, I love him. I get all breathless and tingly when he is near."

"Are you sure you have not just got the vapours?" replied Izzie with a laugh.

"Of course not," replied Juliette stamping her foot to make a point.

"Oh, cousin, I was but jesting with you. I can see how you are smitten and I am so happy for you." With that, she hugged her, and the girls jumped up and down with excitement before collapsing on Izzie's bed in a fit of giggles.

The following morning, both girls were in the library when the footman brought in a note for Juliette. Tearing it open in the belief it was from James she let out a gasp, a hand flying to her face as she turned to Isobella with a cry.

Jumping out of the chair Isobella rushed across the room, and took the offered piece of paper and began to read. She felt her cheeks start to burn. How dare he ask Juliette to meet with him clandestinely this afternoon? It was not signed except for a large E and they both knew it was from Lord Edward.

As Isobella took in her cousin's unshed tears, she knew something needed to be done to stop this horrible person from ruining her cousin or at best, exposing her to gossip. Telling Juliette to forget about the note and to leave the matter to her, she finally persuaded her to sit back down and return to her reading.

Calling for Anna to attend, Isobella rushed up to her bedchamber and pulled out an outdoor day dress and cloak. She instructed Anna to fetch her own things, as she needed a chaperone to attend with her outdoors. Fastening a matching bonnet onto her curls, she checked the mirror to ensure that she looked the epitome of a young lady going out for a stroll. Having requested that the carriage be brought around, she climbed inside followed by Anna. Driving close to, but not up to Carlisle House, she asked the driver to stop and instructed him to return in half an hour, hopefully giving the impression she intended to walk in the park opposite.

Waiting until the carriage disappeared from sight she quickly pulled up the hood on her cloak, careful not to dislodge her bonnet, and turned, much to Anna's surprise, and walked along the street until she came to Carlisle House.

Instructing Anna to wait outside for her, she approached the door and lifted the knocker, hearing it resound inside the house. If she felt a moment of panic she knew it was too late to turn back as the door swung inwards and an elderly butler stood there.

"I wish to speak with the Duke of Carlisle," she said, clearly presenting her calling card.

Taking the card, the butler placed it on a silver tray and stood to one side, motioning Isobella to enter. Casting a quick glance back at Anna, who was watching with pursed lips and a stern look on her face, she stepped inside before the last of her bravery left her.

Standing in the hall, she looked round at the opulent furnishings and the figurines adorning the entrance. She did not have long to wait before the butler returned and indicated for her to follow him. Allowing her to pass into the room, he turned and closed the door, leaving her alone with the Duke Carlisle. If Isobella had felt nervous before she found she was now more frightened than she had ever been. Whatever had possessed her to come to the home of a man whom a lot of the ton considered to be somewhat of a rake. But then remembering the look on her cousin's face and the unshed tears, she pulled herself upright and walked into the room.

As she entered, she carefully removed her hood and saw the object of her visit sitting at a desk. He rose and started to walk towards her. She had never really seen him at close quarters and was quite startled by how young he looked. She had imagined him to be at least some one score years older than herself, but he looked to be closer to her own age, and surmised he was not yet one score and ten. His dark hair intrigued her; it was not caught back and tied as was the fashion, but was shorter and touched on the collar of his coat.

She found the darkness of the colour startling and the light from the lamp caused it to shine. His skin was clear, and his straight nose was quite beautiful, she thought to herself, before pulling her thoughts back to the task in hand.

Sitting behind his desk, Richard Duke of Carlisle watched as this young lady of breeding came unattended into his domain. He had entertained young ladies here before but rarely of the ton, and even then it was by invitation. Curious as to what would entice her into his lair, he waited as she crossed the room towards him.

Rising, he approached and bowed low over her hand as she dropped into a deep courtesy in front of him. A hint of her scent drifted up to him and he found it quite pleasant. Usually his ladies smelled of heavy scent that had a tendency to linger on the person, but this was a scent of delicate flowers that just teased the senses.

"Lady Isobella, this is a surprise," he said, rising from his bow. "Can I offer you some refreshment?"

Straightening from her courtesy, she assured him that she was not intending to stay long enough for refreshment. Escorting her to a seat he waited until she was seated before sitting in a chair opposite.

He was intrigued at her presence and the direct way she had said she did not intend staying long. He could not think of anything he had done to warrant a visit from the lady in question, particularly un-chaperoned, so wasted no time in enquiring as to the purpose of her visit. He watched as her tongue ran across her lips giving away her nervousness. He smiled at her discomfort but his smile quickly disappeared when her words registered in his head.

"I would wish very much, my Lord, if you would speak to your brother Lord Edward and ask him to desist making a nuisance of himself to my cousin, Lady Juliette." The words came out in somewhat of a rush but Isobella kept her head up and her eyes on the Duke as she spoke.

"My brother, a nuisance, my lady? In what way?"

Taking a deep breath she continued, "By paying unwanted attention and sending inappropriate notes to my cousin," and to press home her words she held out the note that had been delivered earlier to Juliette.

Leaning forward, he took the note from her and read the contents. His lips narrowed. Edward was a bloody fool and he was sick of getting him out of scrapes.

"How can you be sure that my brother's intentions towards your cousin are not entirely honourable?"

"It is well known, my Lord, that the Earl of Preston is about to offer for Juliette and that alone should deter any gentleman," she replied, emphasising the word gentleman.

"Ah...but what if my brother intends to offer for your cousin?" He watched as his words reached her ears and saw her start.

"I would hope that he does not, sir. My cousin has made it quite plain to me that she does not entertain any feelings whatsoever for your brother. In fact, quite the opposite. He begins to frighten her with his whispered inappropriate words when he is in her company."

"What inappropriate words?" He sat upright, his eyes narrowing.

"I cannot say, sir. My cousin would not repeat them, save to say she was afraid of what would happen if the words were overheard."

Carlisle felt his anger growing. That a young woman of breeding had felt it necessary to come to his home alone to complain about his brother's actions fared ill for Edward when he eventually found him, for he knew he had not been home since yesterday dinner. Standing, he indicated that the meeting was over, and Isobella taking her cue from him, stood to her feet. He walked across the room to the door and put his hand on the handle before turning back to her.

"Lady Isobella, I will speak to my brother as soon as I find him. Please assure your cousin that his behaviour will not be repeated at any time in the future."

"How can I be sure?" she queried.

Carlisle raised an eyebrow. He was slightly amused that she was questioning his word. "Are you doubting my word, my lady?"

He watched her cheeks flush as she became conscious of her mistake.

"Oh no, my lord. I was simply wondering if it were possible to let me know when you have spoken to your brother, so that I can put my cousin's mind at peace."

The confusion that crossed her face when she realised what she had implied made him smile, but her words made sense. "I presume that you are attending the Arlington Ball tomorrow eve?"

"Yes, my lord, we are."

"Then I will seek you out and confirm the conversation I have had."

"Thank you, my lord. I would ask that you do not mention my intervention in this matter?"

He chuckled softly. "Are you worried for your reputation, Lady Isobella? If so, it is a might late having spent this length of time alone with me." He heard the soft gasp and could not prevent his laugh. "Fear not, my lady, your intervention and reputation are quite safe."

She sank in a deep courtesy, softly thanking him again. Taking her hand he raised her, and instructed her not to worry, as he would resolve matters.

Once she had left, he called for a footman to find his brother wherever he was and to instruct him to come home. The whole meeting with Lady Isobella had surprised him. He knew of her vaguely, the daughter of the late Duke of Rothbury's younger brother. She had been raised in the country where her late father was a clergyman. She had been living with the Rothburys since the untimely death of her parents, and had come out some three years since. The story of her treatment at the Duke of Exmouth's hands had reached his ears and, having now formally met the lady, he was at a loss as to why Exmouth would have wanted such a pale creature as Cordelia Cumberland, when he had such a strawberry and cream delight already in his hands. Sometimes he was at a loss to understand his own species.

More surprising were his own thoughts about the lady in question, to think of her as strawberries and cream had him wondering what it would feel like to touch her skin. Would it be as soft under his fingers as it appeared to be? He had been in many intriguing situations in his nine and twenty years but had never been so intrigued as he was with Lady Isobella Rothbury.

Dangerous Entrapment

* * * *

The library door was thrown open and Edward Carlisle walked somewhat unsteadily into the room. "What is the problem, Richard, that I am dragged away from a card game I could quite possibly have won, and brought home like a puppy on a leash?"

Looking across at his brother, Richard could clearly see the irritation in his face and shook his head at Edward's slightly intoxicated state. "Behave like a naughty puppy and you will be treated like one."

"What is that supposed to mean?" replied Edward, flopping down in one of the large chairs.

"Let us just say it has been brought to my notice that you have been making somewhat of a nuisance of yourself to a certain Lady Juliette Rothbury."

Edward laughed. "Well she is mighty pretty and I have no doubt that she would be an asset to any bedroom."

"So you have intentions towards her. Do you intend to offer for her?" Richard put the question and waited for the reply and was not disappointed.

"Good god! Offer for her? Why would I do that? I have no wish to be saddled with a wife."

Hearing the astonishment in his brother's voice confirmed his own suspicions.

"I thought not. So you are just toying with the lady?" he said coldly.

"Well toying is not perhaps the right word. I would like to do more than toy, but I reckon I could bed her given time," he answered, failing to notice his brother's change of tone.

Richard stood, almost knocking the chair over. "You will cease your attentions to the young lady. You will not attempt to see her again or communicate with her, and you will *certainly* not attempt to bed her," his voice thundered around the room.

Edward sat up with a start. "Good god, Richard, what's got into you? Fancy her yourself perhaps?" he quipped.

Moving quickly so he towered over his brother, he bent down. "No. I have no intentions towards the lady in question but I understand that Preston does. The lady is most distressed at what she considers to be your inappropriate attention. So if you wish to continue enjoying your allowance you will stop this dalliance forthwith and find someone else to play with. I hear Lady Gwendolyn Ashton is on the lookout for another lover. Perhaps you might find her more acceptable of your interest."

"I thought you might be considering taking on Gwendolyn yourself since you are without a bed companion at present, brother?"

Raising an eyebrow, Richard looked at his brother. "I may have no mistress but it does not mean that I would be looking in the direction of Gwendolyn Ashton. Anyway, I hear she prefers men of a younger age so you would serve her well."

Edward appeared to consider his brother's words. "Why this interest in protecting the Rothbury girl if you have no interest in her?"

"I am more interested in protecting the Carlisle name than that of Rothbury," answered Richard, tiring of the conversation. "Anyway, you have said you have no interest so let that be an end to it. Go and find a mistress and keep yourself occupied."

With that, he turned and walked out of the room, leaving his younger brother considering the possibilities of a new mistress.

* * * *

Returning home, Isobella forbade Anna to mention to anyone where they had been, telling her it would have grave repercussions for her and her cousin if word got out. Entering the library, she found Juliette pacing the floor.

"Oh, Izzie, you have been such a long time. I was beginning to despair."

"Fear not, Juliette, all is well. I have spoken to the Duke of Carlisle and he will speak to his brother and tell him to cease his unwanted attentions."

Juliette clasped her hand to her mouth. "You have been to see the Duke?"

"Of course. How else could we stop this awkward situation from becoming much worse?"

"Oh, Izzie, you are a darling," she cried flinging her arms around her cousin and hugging her.

Chapter Two

The following day, there was a buzz of excitement in the Rothbury house. The Duchess was in a tizzy at the thought of the Earl hopefully coming to offer for Juliette. As the appointed hour approached, Juliette and Isobella took themselves into the drawing room, and awaited the outcome of the meeting that was to take place in the library. Anna slipped in to inform them of the Earl's arrival, and Izzie found herself being spun round the room by an over excited Juliette.

Juliette paced the floor while Isobella sat watching her from one of the large chairs. Eventually the door opened and her brother came in, to inform her that the Earl of Preston awaited her in the library. Not needing a second bidding, Juliette almost ran out of the door, her brother's words echoing behind her.

"Decorum, Juliette, decorum."

Sitting in the drawing room with her cousin, Isobella could only imagine how the scene in the library was unfolding. She imagined Juliette running in and the Earl taking her in his arms. Then he would get down on one knee and propose marriage. This was all that she had expected three years since with Exmouth but it had turned from the promised dream into something she did not wish to remember. She was her own woman now and would not tolerate that treatment again.

That night, as they travelled in the Rothbury coach to the Arlington Ball, Juliette was almost jumping up and down with excitement. Tonight the ton would know that she would be the future Countess of Preston and tomorrow she and James were to choose a ring.

Looking at her cousin, Isobella could not keep the smile from her face. She had never seen her looking so happy, and if the Duke of Carlisle had spoken to his brother then there would be nothing to mar the evening.

News of the betrothal spread quickly through those present and Juliette and James found themselves the centre of attention. James, having already claimed every dance on her cousin's card, had no fear that he would lose his betrothed from his side for the remainder of the evening. Isobella's own card was decidedly empty by comparison and she came to the realisation that she would again spend the evening sitting with her aunt and the other somewhat older ladies, something that held no appeal to her.

Watching the dancers on the floor she saw the Duke of Carlisle and his brother arrive, and wondered how he would let her know the outcome of his conversation with his brother. As if he knew she was watching, he looked in her direction and inclined his head to acknowledge her presence. Looking away quickly, she felt a flush rise to her cheeks.

As soon as he entered the room, Richard's eyes cast around until he espied the Rothbury party. He had already been informed of the impending marriage of Rothbury's daughter and Preston. Hard to avoid the news when it was the main topic of conversation. Having already warned his brother not to make a scene and to let the young lovers alone, he had been relieved to be informed that causing trouble was the last thing his brother intended.

"I have every intention of seeking out Lady Gwendolyn Ashton and bestowing my attentions upon her."

"Good," was his brother's reply.

Richard took note of Isobella standing to the side of her aunt. *What the devil is wrong with the bucks of today?* She was far above some of the young ladies who had just come out. Catching her gaze, he gave a faint smile, watching with amusement as she quickly turned her head. Unlike the young ladies of this season, she was dressed in a gown of shimmering dark blue. The low square neckline was decorated with pale blue flowers and the short sleeves sat just off the shoulder. For the first time Richard took note of her, taking in her slim figure with the gown falling to her feet and the pale blue gloves stopping short of her elbows. As he watched, he felt a stirring in his breeches that surprised him. He was not in the habit of reacting like this with one of his own kind; this was usually reserved for his mistresses. *Maybe that is the problem. I need a new mistress.* It had been almost twelve months since his last dalliance and clearly that has been too long.

Moving around the room as the night wore on, he realised that he would have to speak to Lady Isobella soon, to inform her that his brother had been spoken to. Seeing her leave her aunt's side and move towards the refreshments room he took the opportunity to follow her. Losing sight of the object of his attention for a moment he strode into the room and glanced around surprised to see no sign of her. Back tracking his steps, he heard voices from one of the alcoves. Stopping, he listened.

"Please, my lord, let me pass. I have no wish to speak to you now or in the future."

"Oh come now, Isobella, you were only too happy to spend time with me three years since."

"Yes, sir, but then you were not a married man and about to become a father. So again I say, let me pass."

Before Exmouth had a chance to answer Carlisle stepped towards them, speaking as he did. "Lady Isobella, I do believe this dance is promised to me."

With flushed cheeks, and grateful for the opportunity to escape Isobella did not stop to think but walked forward, and after a brief curtsey, accepted the duke's outstretched hand.

"Thank you, my lord," she said quietly as he led her back to the ballroom

She made no mention of what he might have heard and so he chose to ask no questions for fear of embarrassing her further.

It had been Richard's intention to escort her back to her aunt but he felt the trembling as she took hold of his arm. Instead, he led her out onto the floor, and bowed low as the music started up. He had no intention of returning her to her party until he was certain that she was recovered.

Isobella's nerves began to calm. The encounter with Exmouth had been frightening and her relief when the Duke appeared was overwhelming. Now as he held her she felt safe. As he guided her through the dance, she could clearly see the eyes of many following them, and for once they did not show pity. For Isobella this was a welcome relief as she had long since tired of the consoling looks and understanding pats on her arm. Now she was being eyed as a woman held, even though briefly, in the arms of a handsome man. That she thought of him in that way pulled her senses up sharp.

She lifted her head slightly and glanced at her companion from beneath her long lashes. He was concentrating on the dance but she could not fail to see that he was handsome. Even acknowledging that fact made her heart flutter. But she also reminded herself that she knew of his reputation of being somewhat of a rake where the ladies were concerned. Not wishing to dwell on her thoughts, she waited until the steps brought them close and then asked, "Did you speak to your brother, sir?"

"I did, my lady, and he has promised that he will not cause more mischief. Indeed, I think his intentions have now turned to another who should keep him suitably occupied for some time."

"Thank you, my lord," said Isobella, having some idea as to what 'suitably occupied' meant.

Finishing the dance, he ventured to enquire if she was recovered from her unwanted encounter. Being assured that she was, he escorted her back to her family, and with a low bow left her. Shortly after, he made his excuses and left. He had no stomach tonight for the intrigue of affairs between husbands and mistresses and wives and lovers. A night at his Club seemed a more enticing prospect. Also, he found he wanted to escape the temptation of watching Lady Isobella Rothbury, and remembering how she had felt in his arms as they danced. Holding her close for those brief moments he could not fail to see the flawless skin and her hair held back with pins before being allowed to fall in soft waves over one shoulder. Hair that was the colour of rich chocolate. He dared not think further as to his thoughts on her lips, and shook his head as if to dispel an unwanted thought of a large bed and tangled limbs.

The following morning, Juliette spun around Isobella's bedroom much to her cousin's irritation. Seeing her cousin's excitement she vowed to keep the encounter with Exmouth to herself. "Oh, Izzie, I am so happy I could cry."

Juliette's chatter pulled her from her thoughts. "Well that is wonderful, Juliette, but some of us would wish to lie abed a while longer."

"Oh tosh, you never lie in bed. Come, get up, and let's go walking in the park. James is to call after lunch and I do so hope you will act as chaperone instead of mother?"

"Why ever would you want me instead of your mama," said Isobella, with a laugh.

"You know fine well why. You will not make us sit apart and do nothing else but talk."

"Whatever else would you wish to do, cousin?" she said teasingly.

"Something that perhaps mama would not wish to see," said Juliette as she picked up a small cushion from the chair and threw it at Izzie.

Laughing and twirling around the room in her night rail she disappeared out of the door and back to her own bedchamber.

Throwing the cushion in the direction of the chair, Isobella settled back down underneath the covers, but it was to no avail. She was wide awake and her mind was on the events of the night before.

Slipping out of bed, she pulled on her robe, and then rang for her maid. She stood looking out of the window for a while before going into the bath chamber next door. Anna was already there supervising the hot water for Isobella's bath. Waiting until the serving girl had left, Isobella slipped out of her night rail and sank into the warm jasmine scented water, letting it sooth away the worries from the night before.

Returning from a walk with Juliette shortly before lunch they quickly freshened up before joining the family. Sharp at two, James was announced and Isobella found herself as acting chaperone for the rest of the afternoon as James and Juliette sat in the jewellers selecting a ring. Returning to Rothbury House, they took tea in the library, and although Isobella turned the pages of her book endeavouring to read, it was extremely difficult concentrating when she was aware of what was happening about her. She could hear the whispered sweet talk between the betrothed couple and felt her cheeks flushing on several occasions.

After James left, Isobella took her cousin to task telling her that in future she would have to ask her mama to chaperone or she and James would have to restrain themselves until they were wed.

"I was blushing, Juliette, and you were very wicked to put me in that position. I am sure that James was uncomfortable although I note he did little to restrain himself." Although she spoke the words with affection, she needed her cousin to know she had been embarrassed.

"Oh, Izzie, I am sorry. I've never been betrothed before and it is *so* exciting. And I cannot stop looking at my ring." She flashed the single stoned diamond at her cousin. "I get such a desire to kiss James, and when I do my stomach curls with pleasure."

"Enough, Juliette." Isobella held her hand up before she burst into laughter. "You will have to restrain your urges or you will be undone before your wedding."

"I do not think I would care, Izzie."

"You would if James walked away and left you," said Isobella softly, attempting to bring some reason to her cousin.

"Izzie, James is not like Exmouth. Anyway, you were not undone by him. He was simply a cad and turned his affections to someone else. You were not undone by him, Izzie, were you?" She asked turning suddenly to face her.

"No, of course I was not. I have no intention of being undone by anyone other than my husband. And since that looks most unlikely I shall probably die an old maid and still intact," she said with a flourish.

Both cousins looked at each other and then burst into laughter.

"Come, Juliette, we need to dress for dinner, and you can tell me all about how you plan to be wed."

Chapter Three

With the season well underway the Rothburys were in demand as were most of the ton, attending a number of society events. For Juliette, the time was wonderful as she had James to accompany her to all of the celebrations. For Isobella, the tedium of the season was only appeased by the fact that every house party they attended the Duke of Carlisle seemed to be in attendance also. He requested one dance from her every time and then returned her to her family. His attendance brought forth gossip since he was not one to accept invitations, and it was bandied about that he had his eye on someone.

Watching the Rothbury family from a discreet distance Richard was still attempting to make some sense of his sudden attraction to Isobella. He had accepted more invitations that he had ever done this season. Why, he asked himself on more than one occasion. *So I can see her or rather watch her from a distance.* He restricted himself to requesting only one dance from her and did the same with several other ladies not wishing to draw attention to the object of his apparent growing interest.

As Richard watched Isobella, he was not the only person with his eyes upon her.

Standing in the background, Exmouth watched her every move, his insides burning with lust for her. He had followed the family to every house party they had attended but, since the first encounter, had kept his distance. He cursed Carlisle for his intervention at the Arlington Ball and was just waiting for another chance to get the lady in question on her own. His greedy eyes were watching her now, and he noticed her head lift as she looked across the room but not at him. As his eyes followed her gaze he saw Carlisle was the object of her interest.

Watching the pair, he saw Carlisle's almost discernable inclination of the head and the slight smile he gave to her, and he seethed inside. He had seen this interaction between them on several occasions and suspected Carlisle was interested, but the gentleman was playing his cards close to his chest. Returning his gaze to Isobella, he saw the blush that rose in her cheeks, and quietly cursed under his breath. If Carlisle thought he was going to steal his prize he was very much mistaken, but this interest of his could prove to be of use. He smiled to himself as he considered his next move.

* * * *

Dangerous Entrapment

It was two weeks since the Arlington Ball and nothing of note had been heard from the Duke of Carlisle or his brother. Isobella was thankful for the latter but somewhat disappointed that the former had not made any attempt to seek her out, apart from the one dance he claimed from her when they attended the same house party, and then his conversation was limited. She had spent many an hour remembering the way she felt as she danced with him. The way he held her, and the tingling she felt when his hand touched hers. She was loath to admit to herself that she had been re-enacting his rescue of her from Exmouth in her head, and making the ending much more than it had been, or indeed should be. A fantasy that was encouraged by the discreet looks he cast in her direction while in the same room. Looks that made her blush and have thoughts that were most unladylike and belonged more in the pages of her women's journals.

* * * *

Richard had made discreet enquiries about the night's entertainment and discovered that the lady of his sudden interest was not to attend. For him it was a relief as it meant he could spend at least one night away from the demands of society. Leaving Carlisle House, he was minded to go to his club but instead chose a tavern in a quieter part of the city. Sitting in one of the booths sipping his wine he waived away the attentions of the serving girl. She looked no more than ten and four and had more flesh exposed than was decent. Besides, he did not want to bed anyone and his thoughts of a few weeks ago of acquiring a new mistress, had been long cast aside.

Lost in thought, he was brought back to the present by a party entering the adjoining booth. Their loud laughter and bawdy speech disturbed his solitude. He was minded to leave when he recognised one of the voices as Exmouth. Settling back in his seat he listened to the conversation.

"By gad, Exmouth, you took that filly at a fair pace. Never seen breasts move at such a speed."

There was a roar of lewd laughter and Richard's mouth set in a grim line.

"Oh, and what breasts, Levington, Did you see the size of them? Could hardly get my mouth around the end. But what a ride, gripped me tight as a coil, thought I was going to bloody explode before I had taken my full pleasure."

"So what next? Do we go to the Cumberland's or seek out some more game?" asked one of the other voices.

"Well, I for one have other plans," said Exmouth.

"Oh, got your eye on another filly? Perhaps you might need some help with her. I enjoyed the last one, once you had finished with her."

Richard heard Exmouth laugh.

"No, this one is strictly for me. A thoroughbred, and when I have ridden her she will know what it is like to be bedded by a man." "A new mistress?" asked one of the voices.

"No, not yet but she will be."

"What if she refuses?"

"Then I will fuck her senseless until she agrees, and agree she will. She will be glad of my protection."

"What, you mean to keep her?" said an astonished voice.

"Keep her and breed her," replied Exmouth with a laugh.

His words sent a chill through Richard's body. He knew whom he was talking about, and the thought of him with his hands on Isobella caused a rage to boil within him. It took all of his control not to make himself known to the party but he needed to be discreet. The fact that Exmouth was unaware of his presence gave him the advantage. Sitting in the booth until the other party had left he then departed for Carlisle House.

* * * *

Her aunt and her elder cousin, the Duke, were attending a soiree tonight at the home of the Duke of Cumberland, and Juliette, and Isobella had pleaded to be excused. Juliette had hastily arranged for James to call and once again Isobella had been persuaded to act as chaperone.

Izzie and Juliette were in the library when the footman brought in a note for Isobella. Taking it from the tray, she broke the seal and found it contained a simple message, *"I need to speak to you on an urgent matter. I will send my coach at nine,"* and it was signed *"C."*

"Who is it from, Izzie?"

"I believe it is from the Duke of Carlisle."

Peering over Izzie's shoulder, Juliette squealed.

"If it is from the Duke do you think his brother is proposing to cause mischief again? Oh, I could not bear that; not now James has offered for me and Charles has agreed."

Hugging her cousin, Isobella told her it was probably nothing to do with his brother.

"Well if it is not why is he wanting to speak urgently with you?"

Isobella felt her cheeks flush as she remembered the encounter with Exmouth and how he had saved her, and wondered if it had anything to do with his note, or perhaps it was the fact that he had sought her out for dances. Her pulse raced at that thought.

"I do not know, cousin. Maybe his brother has found out it was I who told the Duke about his being a nuisance to you."

"Are you going to go?"

Shaking her head Isobella looked at her, "I do not know, but I cannot leave you. James is due shortly and you cannot be alone together...well, not yet anyway."

"Oh but, Izzie, it must be something really important for him to request your attendance and to send his carriage. You must go if only to put my mind at rest that his brother is not proposing to cause more mischief. I will receive James on my own but we will not let anyone know that you are not here. That way, you can slip out, see what the Duke wants, and then slip back in and nobody will be any wiser."

"James will," declared Isobella.

"Oh, James will not say anything. Anyway, he will benefit from the pleasure of my un-chaperoned company and I am sure that will be more than enough to ensure that he keeps the matter to himself."

"Oh, I am not certain, Juliette. It is not quite proper for me to go alone but I cannot think that the Duke would openly risk my reputation for something trivial. If you are really worried about Lord Edward then for that reason alone I will go.

You stay here and I will fetch my cloak and wait for his carriage."

A short while later, Juliette watched from the window as her cousin slipped unseen out of the door and climbed quickly into the waiting coach. She clapped her hands in delight. She had this notion that the Duke of Carlisle was interested in Izzie and they would certainly make a splendid match. She was just about to start some needlework when the butler announced that Lord Preston was here and wished to see her. Flustered suddenly at being on her own and, trusting that the dim lighting hid the fact that Izzie was not there, she could only instruct that his lordship be shown in.

Striding into the room, Lord James Preston took Juliette's breath away. He was smartly dressed in the most up-to-date fashion. His blonde hair was slightly ruffled from his recently discarded hat, and the ends rested on the collar of his fitted coat. Rising from her chair, Juliette dropped a quick curtsey as he took her hand and raised it to his lips.

"You look beautiful tonight, my love. Please forgive my early arrival but it has seemed such a time since we were last together, and the Cottingham Ball is two nights away and..."

Whatever else he was going to say she stopped by placing her fingers against his lips.

"No need to apologise, James. You were expected and I, for one, am delighted you are early." She saw him look round and then noticed the frown.

"You are alone...*we* are alone?"

She smiled mischievously at him. "Yes, my lord." She bobbed a curtsey.

She had hardly risen when he laughed, clasped her to him and quickly claimed her lips.

Sometime later, as she sat upon his knee in the large chair, they heard someone at the outer door. Jumping up, she moved to a separate chair and waited until the knock came at the library door. Bidding the person to enter she was told that the Duke of Carlisle wished to see Lady Isobella. Thinking quickly, she told the footman to give them a few moments and to then show his lordship in. *Did one keep a Duke waiting,* she wondered, but at this moment she did not care. As soon as the door closed she spoke quickly to James.

"The Duke of Carlisle is here."

"That is no problem, my love. He is a gentleman and I am sure he will not say anything about you not being chaperoned."

"No...no you do not understand," she cried. "The Duke sent his carriage for Izzie shortly before you arrived. But if Carlisle is here...where is Izzie?"

Before James could reply there was a knock at the door and then it opened, and Carlisle strode into the room.

Dropping into a deep curtsey, Juliette murmured, "My lord."

Bowing over her hand, he replied, "Lady Juliette, please excuse my unannounced intrusion but I have need to speak urgently to your cousin." As Juliette rose to her feet James walked across the room.

"Carlisle."

"Preston," replied Richard as the men shook hands.

Finding her voice she told the Duke that his carriage had arrived for Izzie almost some two hours since.

"What carriage, my lady?"

"Your carriage, my lord. Just as you said in your note."

"Note?" said a bewildered Carlisle. "I am sorry, my lady, I am somewhat confused. I sent no note and certainly did not send a carriage as my carriage is outside."

Juliette's hand flew to her mouth and she turned to James with tears in her eyes. "Someone has taken her. Someone has kidnapped Izzie."

"Calm down, Juliette," said James, leading her to a chair and throwing an appealing look to Carlisle.

"Where is the note, Lady Juliette," asked Carlisle.

His mind was already heading down a dangerous route. If indeed the lady had disappeared he knew who was behind this so-called abduction, and the thought of her in his hands and unprotected brought a chill to him.

Putting her hand into her sewing box, Juliette held out the note to James and he in turn handed it to Carlisle, who moved slightly away. Standing at Carlisle's shoulder both men read the note.

"Damnation," said Carlisle under his breath.

"Do you have any idea what it is about or who is behind it? Surely nobody would have the audacity to kidnap a Duke's cousin?" said James quietly so as to avoid Juliette overhearing his concerns.

Moving away across the room and motioning for James to follow, Carlisle briefly told him that Lady Isobella had been receiving some unwanted attention from Exmouth, and he had been fortunate enough to come to her rescue a few nights since. He hesitated deciding not to tell him about the conversation he had overheard, which was the very reason for his call.

"I suspect Exmouth is behind it."

"But he is a married man, and his wife is with child."

"Married men take lovers, Preston," said Carlisle, "as I have no doubt you know."

"Well yes, but not usually unmarried ladies, and not those of a certain class. More likely than not they take married woman who are bored, and anyway, I am sure Lady Isobella would not consent to become his mistress."

"Agreed, but Exmouth is clearly not happy with his lot and perhaps he wishes to capture the one he let escape."

"What are you whispering about?" came the impatient question from Juliette.

Looking at Carlisle's face, Preston asked the obvious question "What can we do?"

"We must find her before it is too late," came the stern reply.

Juliette crossed the room and stamped her foot in displeasure. "Will one of you please tell me what has happened to Izzie?"

Taking her hand, James quickly explained Carlisle's fears about Exmouth.

Her features paled and for a moment appeared as though about to faint.

"We have to find her," she pleaded, looking from Carlisle to James. "If she is not found she will be ruined."

"Quite," said Carlisle, "and perhaps I should not question why you are here alone with Preston, my lady?"

Before she could answer, James spoke. "Lady Isobella was supposed to be here, but I can assure you, sir, that nothing inappropriate has taken place."

"Preston, I could not care if it had. What I do want to know is does anyone know Lady Isobella is not with you?"

"No," replied Juliette. "She slipped out without being seen and as far as the servants believe; she is in here with me, with us."

"Good, let us keep it that way. Could I ask that you allow me to speak privately with Preston for a few moments?"

She inclined her head, turned away, and walked back to her chair.

Drawing Preston to the far side of the room, he said, "Do you have any idea where Exmouth might have taken her?"

"I do not know, Carlisle. He has a town house here although I cannot believe he would take her there. His country estate is too far away but his wife is in residence."

"Does he have a place he takes his paramours to that is close enough to town, but far enough away for privacy?" Carlisle watched as the younger man glanced across at his intended.

"Well there is his mother's house on the outskirts of the city. It does have a hunting lodge and I believe it is frequented by Exmouth when he is in need of a private place."

"Do you know where this lodge is?" He waited as the younger man looked uncomfortable.

"I have been there before. Not with anyone, just for, well...let us say a somewhat out of the ordinary party."

"I see. I trust Lady Juliette knows nothing of this?"

"Good God no! I would not like her or anyone to think I frequented that kind of establishment other than to satisfy a natural curiosity."

"Duly noted, Preston," said Carlisle, "but I do need to find this place and since you know the way I feel I have no choice but to ask you to accompany me and give me directions."

"You do not need to ask. Of course I will go with you. I will just explain to Juliette and then we can leave."

"Perhaps not, it may be preferable if the lady came with us."

Preston looked aghast at Carlisle. "Why?"

"If we are to keep this matter private then we must make out that the four of us have been together all evening. So to that end we need to take your intended with us."

Seeing the sense in the argument James crossed the room to explain all to Juliette.

Waiting impatiently while the couple spoke, Richard contemplated ahead. What was going through his mind had his anger and his fear growing by the second. That Exmouth could actually contrive to carry out such a dastardly plan. For he had no doubt as to whom had taken Lady Isobella. He had come here tonight to inform her of the conversation he overheard but also to speak to her, to try and put some sense to the feelings that had been wrought in him during their encounters. Now, the thought of her at Exmouth's hands made his blood boil, and he did not wish to think beyond this moment. He just needed to get on the road.

Walking across to the couple, he asked, "Are you able to come with us, Lady Juliette, for I have a fear that your cousin may need your assistance?"

"Of course I will. I just need to get a cloak and I will be right back down. Wait here, please?"

Running up the stairs Juliette was thankful not to encounter anyone. Grabbing a heavy cloak out of the closet she ran to Isobella's room and retrieved a similar garb. Pulling the cloak around her shoulders, she slipped back down the stairs only to meet the butler at the bottom.

"My lady?"

"Oh, Smithson, Lady Isobella and I are stepping out for a short while with Lord Preston and Lord Carlisle. We should not be too late."

"Very good, my lady," said the servant, bowing.

"You can retire, Smithson. We can see ourselves out when we are ready to leave."

"If you are sure, my lady."

"I am. Goodnight." She passed by him making sure to display Isobella's cloak over her arm.

Opening the doors she went back into the library and sighed with relief. She was quite pleased with her little act. Waiting a few moments until the hall was clear, she and her two accomplices slipped out of the front door and into Carlisle's waiting carriage.

Dismissing his groom and sending him back to his house, Carlisle kept the horses at a brisk pace until they were clear of the city. Then he let them have their heads and drove at as fast a pace as he could, conscious of his passengers, but even more conscious of the danger Lady Isobella was in.

Following Preston's directions, it was not long before they approached the gates to the home of the Dowager Duchess of Exmouth. Turning at a junction part way along the drive he slowed the horses and allowed Preston to guide him until the hunting lodge came into view.

In the darkness, both men could see lights on in the rooms. Pulling the horses to a stand some distance from the lodge, Carlisle asked Preston to describe the building to him if he could recall its layout.

"The building is one storey as you can see. From what I remember there is a small entrance hall and the two main rooms are entered by doors that lead off from there. The door immediately in front of you opens into a small lounge. The door to your left leads to a bedchamber. I do not believe there are any other residence rooms. There may be some servants quarters but the two rooms I have described are I believe only those habited by Exmouth."

"Thank you, Preston. I think I should proceed alone. If you will stay here with Lady Juliette and the carriage. Try and keep the horses quiet so I can surprise Exmouth, hopefully before any damage has been done," he said under his breath.

Nodding, Preston pointed Carlisle in the direction of the front door to the lodge, and both he and Juliette watched as he ran silently across the grass towards the building.

Chapter Four

Inside the lodge, Isobella paced the bedchamber. It had not taken her long to realise that they were not travelling to Carlisle House, but the carriage was moving at such a pace she was trapped inside until it stopped. Fear had gripped her when the city began to disappear and the open fields of the countryside became more frequent. She had no idea who was driving the carriage. She had assumed it was Carlisle's groom on the seat when she got in, but now there was no certainty at all whom it was. It seemed impossible to imagine Carlisle having them meet this far out of town, and all she could think of was what was going to happen when they reached their destination, and who was waiting?

Before long, the carriage turned through large gates and then bore off to the side and down a small track before coming to a halt. She could just make out the shape of a low house but was unsure to whom it belonged, or indeed where she was. As she sat on the edge of the seat she could feel her heart pounding with fear.

The carriage rocked as the driver stepped down, and she heard the crunch of footsteps on the gravel path moving towards the carriage door.

As the door flew open, Isobella backed away into the corner. She was too scared to say anything but her fear turned to anger when Exmouth appeared in the open doorway.

"Welcome, my dear Lady Isobella, to my private residence," he said with a laugh and a mocking bow.

Drawing herself upright, Isobella glared at him. "Take me home at once, my lord, before my family realise I am missing."

"What, after all the trouble I've gone to in bringing you here? No, my lady, I think you owe me a night of your company." As the words were spoken, he dove into the carriage and grabbed Isobella's wrists, pulling her through the door. Laughing, he hauled her over his shoulder and strode off towards the house with Isobella pounding him on his back with her fists.

"Unhand me, sir, or you will be sorry." He made no reply and continued to mock her with his laughter.

Exmouth was in his element. He had his prize and intended to enjoy it to the full. Turning the handle on the outer door he flung it open and marched into the bedchamber, dropping Isobella onto the bed. As soon as she was freed and realised where she was she jumped off the bed. He was too quick for her and reached the open door first, slamming it shut. Turning, he took in her appearance for the first time. She was in an evening dress...not the ball gowns he was used to seeing her in but nonetheless she looked stunning. As if feeling his eyes on her she pulled her cloak across her front covering her green silk gown.

"So modest, Isobella, but a night in my arms will change that."

If Isobella was scared before she was now terrified. He meant to seduce her.

She would be ruined and there appeared to be no way of escaping.

"My lord, I beg you to take me home." She attempted to plead with him.

"Oh I will take you, Isobella...but not home. I will take you to my bed and you will enjoy what I give you, then you will be ruined. No man will want you, and your family will disown you but not I. I will set you up as my mistress. You will bear me many children...all of them bastards of course, but you will have all you desire. I will not deny you anything...except of course your freedom."

Isobella felt faint hearing his intentions. "You will not put a hand on me, sir. I would rather die."

He laughed again. "That would be a loss, Isobella, but I am not an unreasonable man. I will leave you to consider my proposition. You can come to me willingly or I will take you anyway. The outcome will be the same; you will be my mistress. You will serve me better than the pale skinny wife I have at home."

"Your wife is carrying your child, sir. You do her a great disservice acting this way. You chose to marry her."

"Yes I did choose to marry her and in doing so I let you slip through my fingers. I have tried to court you these last few weeks and seduce you into becoming my mistress but you would have none of it. Then Carlisle came to your rescue and I saw the way he looked at you that night and I am damned if he is going to have you."

Isobella could not answer, there was no answer to what he had disclosed so remained silent.

Looking at the defiant face, Exmouth turned on his heel and walked to the door. Opening it, he turned back. "I will give you time to think. I will return so be ready to receive your lover, madam."

With a smirk he left the room closing the door firmly, and Isobella heard the key turn in the lock.

Leaving her to ponder her fate, Exmouth strolled into the sitting room and was pleased to see that his instructions as to wine and food had been obeyed. This decision to take Isobella had been forming in his mind since the evening he had failed to capture her. He had seen the way Carlisle watched her, and was damned if he was going to let him have her. A messenger sent to his mother's house were enough to ensure that the lights at the Lodge were lit and ready for a visitor. This was not the first time he had cause to use this residence. Indeed, it was a useful place to bring his mistresses. His mother, if she was aware of its use, made no mention.

Sitting and drinking the wine allowed him time to ponder on the pleasure he was about to receive from the delightful Lady Isobella. Oh, there was no doubt that she would put up a fight, but that would make the battle all the more exciting. Just thinking about it made him hard, but he forced himself to allow her a little more time to consider his proposition.

The prospect of seduction by Exmouth was nothing short of revulsion. Once on her own, she frantically searched the room for something to use as a weapon but she found nothing. All that was in the room was the four-poster bed that seemed to get larger every time she looked at it, and a dressing table on which was a comb and brush. Apart from that the only other things in the room were two armchairs near a fire burning in the hearth. There was not even a poker for the fire since that would have been a sturdy weapon. All that appeared to be of use was the hairbrush but she doubted its effect.

Despairing, she picked up the hairbrush and was surprised at its weight. Looking at the paddle she realised it was made from ivory something she knew to be of substance. Drawing the cloak around her shoulders like a shield she held the brush tightly in her right hand, hidden inside its folds. If she had to wait for him to return at least she felt some comfort in the feel of the brush in her hand. A weapon of kind but if she could strike a lucky blow she may be able to escape.

By the time Exmouth returned, she was sick with worry and fear. She pulled herself upright and faced him as he unlocked the door and entered. Kicking the door partly shut behind him, he moved slowly into the room.

"Well, my lady, have you considered my proposition?"

"I most certainly have not. I would not entertain any such suggestion, sir, and I demand that you return me home...at once," she added, trying to sound braver than she felt.

"Oh, Isobella...Isobella, will you not learn that you cannot escape."

The words made her feel sick. She could see him gloating; see how pleased he was with himself. She may be afraid but she had her wits about her. He knew she would not agree, he wanted to make this encounter exciting and knowing she would run he had left the door partly open offering her an escape route.

She waited and watched. He did not speak but started to advance towards her. She knew what he was thinking was she going to run to his left or his right... because run she would, she had no choice if she wanted the chance to be free.

He was the hunter and she was his prey and it was little comfort to her that the chase would only serve to increase his ardour.

If her heart pounded any louder she would not be able to hear herself speak. The open door was enticing her towards it. Her gaze darted from it to Exmouth. *Could I run past him and escape into the night and then try to find a way home?* She was past caring. She knew she had to try. Moving quickly to her left, she made as if to run that way but the moment he moved she turned and ran as fast as she could to the right. She could see the door getting ever closer and believed escape was within her grasp when her cloak was suddenly pulled violently backwards, causing her to pitch forward, her body crashing heavily onto the floor.

He was on her in an instant, hands clawing at her, pulling at her cloak. She managed to turn to the side and get her right hand free. It tightened around the brush. She stilled for a moment to catch her breath. As soon as she stopped struggling he spun her over and rested on top of her. The smell of alcohol on him was repelling, and as he moved his head down towards her she swung her hand up with all her strength and caught him on the side of the head. His cry of pain echoed round the room, and he momentarily rolled to the side. Seizing this opportunity, Isobella sprang to her feet, and gathering her cloak and dress up made a dash for the door.

She got as far as the outer door before he hauled her back by her hair. She let out a scream, struggling to free herself, but he did not stop. She was dragged back and across the bedchamber, then thrown towards the bed. Losing her balance, she struck her head against the corner post and fell to her knees.

"Not so feisty now, my lady. Well a good fucking will sort you out." The words seemed to be coming from some distance away.

Then she felt hands lift and push her backwards onto the bed.

Terrified by the violent actions and of what was about to transpire, she tried to lash back with her feet. Her vision was obscured with a grey mist, and strength seemed to elude her. She felt his hands on her bodice and the buttons being undone. Then his lips brushed one of her breasts and a hand fumbled trying to get beneath her skirt. The blackness was descending again, but for a moment she felt him free her and she made a desperate effort to raise her hands and kick. Finally she made contact with his leg...enough to make him curse. Then there was a voice she had not expected to hear.

"Isobella, it is Carlisle. You are safe. Stop fighting me. I am here to take you home."

"Richard," was all she managed to say before she gave herself up to the blackness that descended upon her.

Carlisle had covered the ground between his carriage and the front door in record time. He knew Exmouth would not wait long before carrying out his intentions. He was near the entrance when he heard the scream, and his blood ran cold. Running the last few feet to the front door, he was relieved to find it unlocked. Stepping silently into the hall, he heard noises from the room on the left. The bedchamber, he thought, remembering Preston's description of the Lodge. Approaching the door quickly, he was incensed by what he saw. Exmouth throwing Isobella towards the bed and her crying out as she hit against the bedpost.

Before he could move, Exmouth had dragged her up and was pulling at her bodice. By this time, Richard was half way across the room, moving silently to give him the advantage of surprise. When Exmouth's hand moved under her skirts Richard sprang at him, dragging him away, landing a right hook to his chin. Exmouth collapsed on the floor in a heap, his mouth gaping open in surprise.

Ignoring Exmouth, Richard attempted to cover Isobella's breasts but, assuming it was Exmouth, she lashed out at him. He spoke to calm her, and then she slipped into unconsciousness. Pulling the cloak about her he lifted her into his arms and looked at Exmouth who was attempting to get up from the floor.

"If I were you, sir, I would stay where I was. I have not come alone and unless you wish to have a beating, I would suggest that you let me leave unhindered." He watched as Exmouth glanced anxiously towards the door. "I have only to call out, sir, and they will come."

Exmouth glared at him. "Take the bitch. She is not worth it."

Richard's nostrils flared at the insult to the lady in his arms. "No, it is you who are not worthy...not worthy of your rank, your title, or indeed to be called a gentleman."

With that, he walked purposefully towards the door. "This is not over," Richard called back as he walked through the hall and out the front door.

Cradling Isobella in his arms he made the journey to his carriage only to be met part way by Preston.

"Saw you come out in the light from the hall. Thought we heard a scream.

Is Lady Isobella all right? Did he...well, you know?"

"No, he did not have the opportunity, but I fear the lady has sustained an injury to the head that will require attention."

By this time, they had reached the carriage and Carlisle saw Juliette standing by the horses, holding them steady. As soon as she saw him carrying Isobella she cried out.

"It is all right. Your cousin is only in a faint," he said quickly, glancing at Preston to prevent him from saying anything further.

"I will hold the horses while you get Isobella and Juliette in the carriage," said Preston, taking over the reins from his intended. Once they were all settled, Carlisle turned the carriage and headed back to London.

Going directly to Carlisle House, Richard instructed his butler to fetch a physician. The journey home had given him time to work out an acceptable story for Isobella's injuries. He instructed Juliette and Preston they must all stick to this story if Isobella's reputation was to remain unblemished. So after a short discussion they all agreed that they had been walking through one of the parks when some urchins had run out and knocked into Isobella, causing her to fall and strike her head on a nearby pillar. Putting Isobella down on the chaise longue in his sitting room gave him the first opportunity to see the injury.

He had been so intent on covering her up and getting out of the Lodge that he had not paid much attention except to note that there was some bleeding. Now in the light, he could see the bruise forming on top of her forehead, and the small gash that was still bleeding slightly. Looking at her pale face he felt a tugging in his chest and a fury that he had never known before. Exmouth would pay for this as soon as the opportunity presented itself.

Juliette, distraught at the injury to Izzie, pressed Carlisle several times to confirm that Exmouth had not violated her. Assuring her that he had not had the time to do so Richard had no intention of disclosing how close Exmouth had come to achieving his goal. How close he had come left him in a fury and his need to protect Isobella came as something of a shock to him.

He did not usually expose himself to the ladies of the ton and managed to avoid most of the invitations set up by his mother, in her attempts to see him married and with an heir. He was quite content with his life and with a mistress when he felt the need for one. These thoughts kept him occupied while they waited.

The physician arrived, by which time Isobella had been revived with the help of her cousin's smelling salts. The men withdrew while the physician examined Isobella, who then told her that she had been very lucky indeed not to have sustained more serious injury. The cut to her forehead had stopped bleeding and was close to the hairline, and partially hidden by her curls. Unfortunately, the same could not be said for the bruise that showed quite clearly on her forehead.

"Oh, Izzie, you will not be able to venture out for days looking like that."

"Thank you, cousin, that makes me feel a lot better."

"Oh I am sorry. I did not mean it to sound that way."

"I know, Juliette, I am only jesting with you."

Thanking the physician for his attendance they watched as he left the room. They then heard him talking to Carlisle in the hall while Preston came back into the room.

"If you feel up to it, Lady Isobella, Carlisle will see you and Juliette home." "Will you not come with us, James?" cried Juliette.

"Of course I will. We all need to return together to give credence to our story."

"What story?" asked Isobella, and listened intently while they explained everything to her from the moment Carlisle had turned up at Rothbury House.

"So you see, Izzie, you have to remember the story of how you came to be injured otherwise we will all be in bother, and you will be disgraced."

"But what of Exm..." Isobella began to say when she was interrupted by a voice from the doorway.

"Do not worry about Exmouth. Leave him to me. He will not say anything if he knows what is best for him."

"Oh," was all Isobella could say as Richard walked across the room towards her.

"Lady Juliette, Preston, if I could impose upon you to let me have a few moments alone with Lady Isobella before we depart."

"Certainly, Carlisle. Come, my love, we will wait in the hall." Taking Juliette's hand, he led her out of the room.

Once they were on their own, Isobella thanked Carlisle again for what he had done.

"I could not leave you in Exmouth's clutches. Do you remember what happened after you fell?"

Isobella tried to think back feeling a shudder go through her as she did. "I remember trying to run to the door and him pulling me down. Then I hit him with the brush and managed to get away. I nearly reached the front door but he pulled me back...pulled me back by my hair." She felt tears welling as she remembered but continued. "Then he pushed me, and I fell and struck my head. Then everything started to go grey but I could feel his hands on me. Pulling and undoing buttons." The tears now trickled down her cheeks, and she put up her hands to brush them aside. "Please tell me he did not...he did not expose me?"

Richard longed to say he had not but knew he could not lie. She deserved the truth. "Not fully."

"Oh no!" Her hands immediately covered her face with shame.

He could not stop himself, and gently pulled her hands away. Tilting her chin upward, he looked into the tear-filled eyes

"What was exposed I do not think he even saw. And if he did he will not remember, he was well in his cups."

He saw the relief flood into her face and thought it as well she did not know that he was the one to have covered the creamy breasts, and fastened every one of the buttons on her bodice until she was presentable again. She had suffered enough tonight without knowing that he had seen the delights that she would one day offer to a husband.

"I am only thankful that Juliette was with you, my lord, for I think I have suffered enough shame tonight to last me a lifetime."

"Quite so, my lady," he replied, allowing her to believe that Lady Juliette had re-dressed her.

Chapter Five

It was two weeks before Isobella was able to return into society, by which time the story of the urchins who knocked her down was lost in the latest scandal of the Earl of Sheldon's affair with the sister of his brother's wife. That both parties were married to other persons was distraction enough from Isobella's encounter. Having spent a further week in town, the Rothburys were decamping to their country estate for a month. Juliette was unhappy at this turn of events since it took her away from London and her betrothed.

"Oh why do we have to go to the country, Izzie, and for such a long time?" complained Juliette.

"Because it is customary to go to the country in the summer for a month as you well know, and no matter how you beg or plead Charles will not change his mind.

You know how much your mama loves spending time there?"

Juliette sighed. "I know but it is such a long time for me not to see James."

Isobella hugged her cousin. "The time will pass and I am sure that James will come visit while we are there."

They left the following morning in three coaches. Isobella, her aunt and two cousins travelling in one while the luggage and staff travelled in the other two. Some staff had already gone ahead to open up the house and ensure that all was ready for their arrival. It was well into the afternoon when they arrived, and for Isobella it was like coming home. She loved being in the country and if she had her way she would spend more time here. Racing Juliette up to their rooms, they were soon changed out of their travelling clothes into day dresses and went downstairs to have tea in the drawing room.

Richard was still trying to work out how his mother had managed to persuade him to accompany her and his brother to the house party at the Arlington's country estate. It would seem that his mother had become very friendly with the Dowager Duchess and that had resulted in the invitation. Believing that his mother was happy with his brother joining her, thus leaving him free to follow his own pursuits, he had been caught off guard when she insisted that he join them if only to stop Edward from entangling himself with that floozy Ashford. He had bitten back a smile at his mother's words, but had no intention of telling her that her younger son was already ensnared between the legs of the floozy. So to keep his mother happy he was suffering a long and hot coach journey to the Arlington Estate.

Having been shown to his room, Richard quickly freshened up and took himself off to explore the outside of the house. Coming across the stables, he found them well stocked with good blood animals and decided that at least he could ride out while they were here and escape the chattering females.

Walking back to the house, he encountered his host and complimented him on his bloodstock and enquired if it would be possible for him to ride out. Having been assured that the stable was at his disposal Richard returned to the house in slightly better spirits.

Entering his brother's room, he was confronted with a scene that would have sent their mother into vapours. Gwendolyn had her back against the wall and Edward was, well...for want of a better description standing breeches down and fucking her senseless. Richard groaned, and as the sound reached their ears they both stopped, and his brother turned his head. He at least had the grace to go red, thought Richard.

"If you want me I will be in my room. Carry on," and with that he turned and left the pair to continue with their dalliance.

It was some time later when his brother appeared in his room dishevelled and with a grin on his face that Richard wanted to slap away.

"You could at least have waited until the luggage was unpacked," he said

"Sorry, old thing, did not expect an audience. In fact, did not expect that at all. Was not sure they would be here. She was waiting when I got to my room and well...when it is offered it is un-gentlemanly to refuse. And how could I refuse such a wonderful little...."

"Enough, Edward. I do not wish to know the details. Be thankful it was I and not mother who walked in. I take it that you intend to enjoy the offerings of Gwendolyn over the next week?"

"I most certainly do. That old fart of a husband of hers does not know what to do with her."

"That old fart as you call him is a powerful Earl and if you embarrass him with your entanglement with his wife, you will find you are no match for him or his power. So be warned, little brother. Keep it in your breeches whilst here or at least be very discreet."

Richard recalled this conversation the following morning as he rode out across the Arlington Estate. His spirits were somewhat raised having learned something of interest at dinner last evening. The Rothbury Estate adjoined the Arlington's and apparently the Rothburys were in residence. That information pleased him. He had not seen Isobella since the day after the incident with Exmouth, and then he had simply called to see how she was recovering. But that did not mean he had not thought of her since the night of her abduction.

He had been inclined to take another mistress before Lady Isobella Rothbury crossed his path, but somehow that idea did not hold such appeal to him now. Pondering on the delights a mistress would bring him caused his mind to go back to the perfectly formed breasts he had gently covered up before carrying their owner away from Exmouth's hands. He wanted to see Isobella again but had cried away from calling on her. Now she was here and if what were spoken was correct the family would be joining the Arlington's for dinner two nights hence. That would give him the opportunity to speak to her.

Riding through the small wooded copse, he was thankful for the means to escape the house. He hated being away from his own home and his own comforts. Suddenly, his horse stopped and gave a soft whinny. Holding the reins in one hand he patted his neck. "What it is, boy?"

The words were barely out of his mouth when a horse and rider went at full gallop along the field adjoining the wood. Moving his horse forward, he reined in at the edge of the clearing. The horse and rider could clearly be seen at the bottom of the field to his left. He watched the rider pull the horse to a standstill and then reach down and pat its neck. Judging by the rider's attire this was a stable lad enjoying himself at the expense of his employer and his horse. It was very early in the morning and Richard did not doubt that the lad had crept out and borrowed the horse before anyone noticed.

Having no wish to spoil his enjoyment, he was about to pull back into the wood when the rider lifted his hand and pulled something from off his head. It was then that Richard realised that the lad was in fact a lady. Long dark hair tumbled down about her shoulders, and as he watched bemused she swung the horse around and kicked it into a canter. By the time they passed Richard they were in a flat out gallop, the rider's hair streaming behind her. Hair that Richard recognised; the last time he had seen it up close it had been spread across his shoulders. *Well, Lady Isobella Rothbury, what are you up to?*

Any thought of quietly withdrawing was immediately forgotten. He moved slightly out into the clearing watching as she pulled her horse to a standstill at the other end of the field. Kicking his horse into a gallop he rode after her.

Isobella was thoroughly enjoying the morning ride. This was her secret while she was on the estate. Well, hers and the head groom. She hated riding side-saddle and had ridden astride like a man since she first learned to ride. As a youngster, she would sneak out wearing her father's old breeches and ride like the devil across the fields. Now the only chance she got to do this was when they were in the country. She loved to feel the wind blowing through her hair as she galloped; it gave her a feeling of freedom and wild abandonment. However, she was careful not to let anyone see her and kept her outfit in the stables changing only when she got there.

Pulling the gelding to a stop, she caught her breath and listened to the stillness of the morning. But then a sound caught her attention. Turning her mount, she espied the rider galloping towards her. Her immediate thought was to escape and she kicked the horse into action with the intention of outrunning the intruder. She was part way across the field when she realised she was outrun, and had no choice but to slow and bring her mount to a halt as the other rider approached.

Keeping her head down she was acutely aware of her attire. Old breeches with long riding boots, a silk shirt and an old waistcoat were not quite the attire for a morning meeting with a stranger. As the other rider reached her she raised her head and found herself looking into the laughing eyes of Richard Carlisle.

"Well, my lady, I certainly did not expect our next meeting to be in such delightful circumstances," he said, a grin playing across his lips.

Isobella was shocked to see him. "My lord" She answered his greeting more demurely than she felt. She was angry at being caught out like this; especially by someone whom already had rescued her twice from embarrassing situations. She tried discreetly to pull the edges of the shirt down over her thighs but it did little to hide their shape.

Richard saw her action and it drew his gaze to her thighs and then to her shapely legs. Again he felt a movement in his breeches and this time he did not intend to ignore it. There was something about Lady Isobella Rothbury that was stirring him and he intended to explore it some more.

He watched her face. It was flushed from the exertion of the ride and he realised in that moment how beautiful she was. She was delightful, charming, a perfect lady, but at the same time there was wildness about her. How had he not recognised this before? Even before he could stop himself he thought how she would look the same when she had just been made love to. He had no intention of letting this lady slip away from him until he found out exactly what was pulling him to her.

"Perhaps we should ride together one morning, my lady. I think I would find that a most delightful interlude."

He said the words with a hint of mischief that he hoped she would recognise and was not disappointed when he saw her lips twitch, trying to conceal a smile.

"I do not think that would be a good idea."

"Why not?"

"Well...I am sure you have other things to do. And it would not be proper."

"I think you and I are beyond caring about proper, and I am sure that your early morning ride is only one of many you have done before. So I can see no reason why we cannot meet here...say tomorrow at the same time, or I could of course come to the house to meet you?" He inclined his head, waiting for her reply.

He knew he was asking much of her. He had done all he could to protect her reputation but this suggestion could compromise her if they were discovered. Indeed it would compromise them both, but it was a risk he was prepared to take, but would she?

Her eyes narrowed, her features suggesting she was considering his proposal. Before a response was given, he took the advantage.

"So that is decided then. Tomorrow here, same time." Then as he turned to leave, he whispered,

"And please be wearing the same outfit." Then he was gone galloping across the field towards the wood.

* * * *

If anyone thought Isobella preoccupied at dinner nothing was said. Excusing herself to retire early, she was glad to reach the sanctuary of her room. She was still in a spin from her encounter with Lord Carlisle. Lying on the bed, she considered not turning up for their meeting. But then what if he did what he said and came to the house? The argument she was having with herself was making her quite vexed. In the end, she asked herself a simple question, *do I wish to meet with Carlisle?* Her head said no as he was too dangerous, but her heart was saying yes.

She had always tried to be sensible but for once she decided to follow her heart.

Having made that decision she finally drifted into a somewhat disturbed sleep. A sleep where she was in the arms of Carlisle, who was behaving in a most inappropriate way with her, and she was doing nothing to stop him.

She awoke in a sweat, with her heart beating fast. It took a few moments to recall the reason for this and, when she did, she felt the heat in her body. Frightened by the feelings, she threw back the covers and slipped out of bed. Going to the washstand she placed both hands in the cold water and splashed it on her face before quickly dressing and making her way to the stables.

Riding across the fields, she tried to act as though this were just another morning ride but she could not quell the excitement, and also fear at the forthcoming tryst with Carlisle. She wore the same outfit as he requested, although she had been tempted to dress correctly and ride side-saddle, but she simply could not forego the pleasure of her secret ride. The concession to her female status was that today she wore a cloak over her breeches and shirt so at least she was afforded some cover for her legs.

Reaching the open field from the previous day, she saw no sign of him. A feeling of disappointment swept over her at the thought he may have forgotten, so she kicked her gelding into a canter. She was half way down the field when she saw him ride out from the copse moving quickly towards her. Pulling up her horse she waited until he joined her.

"I thought you had forgotten, my lord, or at least decided against this risky meeting."

He gave her a wicked grin. "My dear Lady Isobella, how could you think that I would forget our meeting? I am deeply pained."

She could not help but laugh at his expression of hurt. "I am sure that your pain is not serious, my lord."

"No, you are right, Isobella, I have no pain when I am in your company, and that is something that perplexes me."

"Would you wish me to give you pain, my lord? For I could lash you with my tongue or raise my hand and strike you?"

Her words sounded harsh but the look on her face told him they were only words and a smile curved his lips.

Leaning across from his saddle, he took her hand and raised it to his lips. "If you were to strike me, Isobella, I am sure I would feel no pain at all."

Snatching her hand back, her cheeks blushed red. "Sir, you are presumptuous and your words are not gentlemanly."

"Maybe I do not feel like a gentleman this morning. Maybe the sight of you makes me forget I am one."

Laughing, she waved her hand in his direction. "Now I know you are teasing me, sir, and for that you can try and outrun me."

Before he knew what was intended, she swung her horse around and set off, galloping quickly across the field. Laughing, he turned and raced after her, catching up just before she rode through a narrow gap in the hedgerow. They rode in silence until she finally stopped at the edge of a small lake. Jumping down, she walked forward, leading her horse and then tied the reins to a small bush.

Following her actions, he walked after her and stood looking out across the lake.

"It is beautiful, is it not?" she spoke the words not really needing a reply.

"Yes, it is. Tell me, is this where you come each morning?"

"Yes. It reminds me of home. Well, the home I had when my parents were alive. I do not dislike the city but I love the country, and when we are here I feel as though I have come home again."

Richard watched her as she spoke. The softness of her skin was even more apparent by the flush to her cheeks from the race, and she again reminded him of strawberries and cream. He only wished she had not worn the damned cloak that she now held about her like a shield. Even as he thought that he felt a hardening in his breeches and took a deep breath to control himself.

Walking forward, Isobella sat down on a fallen tree trunk, and for a moment appeared to forget she was not alone. Leaning forward, she put her elbows on her knees and rested her chin in her hands. She looked so peaceful looking out at the lake until his approach startled her. He sat down alongside her.

"So, I have found your secret place, Isobella," he said softly.

She turned and smiled and simply nodded her head. He looked at her seeing her again in a different light. She was beautiful, and probably headstrong, but there was softness about her and somewhere there was passion. He kept seeing glimpses of it when something or someone annoyed her and it would flash in her eyes. She intrigued him and he found himself drawn to her more with each passing moment they spent together. He had never considered taking a wife, but now the thought was not so distasteful.

He looked at her as she gazed out across the water. Her chin resting on her hands made her look almost childlike. But the cloak that had fallen open displayed thighs and slender legs that were certainly not childlike. He swallowed hard at the thoughts rushing through his head. Thoughts of her at his side and in his bed every night. Riding like this and then making love in a meadow. The tightness in his groin reminded him that these thoughts were not going unheeded, and he pulled the tails of his coat around to cover the visible evidence.

Standing up suddenly, he walked to the water's edge to put some distance between them and gain time to compose himself. His heat began to ease until she came and stood next to him.

"I think it is time to leave. I cannot be out too long for fear of being found out."

Turning to her he only hoped that the thoughts he had been entertaining were not clear for her to see in his eyes. Smiling, he held out his arm and she placed her hand on it. Putting his other hand on top of hers he tucked her arm into his as they walked back to the horses.

Reaching the horses he released her hand and offered to assist her but she declined. Accepting her rejection he turned towards his own mount. Kicking himself for a missed opportunity he turned back towards her just as she undid her cloak and threw it across her saddle. He stopped mid stride at the sight of her slim figure perfectly off set by the close fitting breeches encased in long boots and a silk shirt fastened at the waist with a wide belt. His breath caught in his throat and he must have uttered a sound for she swung around to face him.

"Sir, please turn away?"

"Isobella, you ask too much of me to ask me that."

She put a hand up to pull the cloak back down but he was by her side before she could. Placing his hand over hers to stay the movement, he looked down into large green eyes. He could see the fear in them and smiled.

"Do not fear me, Isobella. I will not harm you."

"What do you intend doing, my lord?"

"At this moment in time I am not at all sure. I know what I want to do," and as he said the words he lifted his other hand and stroked a finger down her cheek. She shrank back.

"Please, Richard."

His name on her lips released him from his thoughts and he smiled broadly at her. "I like it when you call me Richard. You should call me that at all times when we are alone. And I will call you Isobella except on other occasions when I will call you Bella...my Bella."

Isobella was lost in a trance as she listened to his words. Never had anyone spoken to her like this before and it made her stomach curl. She could not have uttered a word if her life had depended upon it. She was mesmerised by what he was saying and could only watch as his head lowered and his lips closed over hers in the gentlest kiss she could ever have imagined. If she had been prone to fainting she was sure she would have done so but her legs did feel as though they did not belong to her. The kiss was soft and short, just enough to send her senses into a spin.

This was taking a risk and he was not sure if he was rushing matters, but the sight of her body was too much for him. He was holding himself away lest she felt his arousal. It was important that he take this slowly and had no wish to scare her away with his amorous feelings at the beginning of what he hoped would be a courtship.

How his thoughts were moved from considering taking a new mistress to contemplating matrimony in the space of a few weeks he was at a loss to understand. But considering marriage he was, and that was something that would no doubt please his mother. But would it please the person he desired as his wife?

Releasing her, he linked his hands together. "Let me assist you to mount."

Placing her foot in his hands, she held her breath as she was swiftly lifted upwards. Throwing her right leg across her mount she settled in the saddle and watched as he placed her left foot in the stirrup. His hand rested on her ankle a moment longer than was necessary and heat ran up her leg. Pushing back, he raised his head and smiled, a smile that was enough to melt her. Turning, he walked to his own horse and mounted then followed as she led the way back to the meadow where they first met. Stopping at the path near the copse that led back to the Arlington Estate, she waited while he drew alongside.

"Thank you, Isobella, for a delightful time. I would like to think we could repeat it again. Perhaps tomorrow morning?"

Smiling, she shook her head. "I am afraid my ride tomorrow will have to be cancelled. Lord Preston and his family are arriving at noon and I have no doubt Juliette will be in my bedchamber exceedingly early full of excitement. If I am not there it will lead to awkward questions. So I must stay indoors and abed until a respectable hour."

Richard appeared disappointed and gave a sad smile. "I am despondent at missing your company, and your cousin is a very lucky lady to share your bedchamber."

Isobella thought she had misheard him, but one look at the teasing glint in his eyes told her she was not mistaken. She felt the flush spread across her cheeks as a tremor ran through her body. No one had ever mentioned sharing her bedchamber.

"My lord..."

"Richard ...we are alone Isobella."

She started again. "Richard, I think you speak out of turn to mention my bedchamber."

He hesitated for a moment. "No, Isobella. It was you who mentioned your bedchamber. All I said was how lucky your cousin was to share it. How you wish to interpret my remark is entirely in your own hands."

The grin on his face caused her eyes to flash in anger and he threw back his head and laughed.

"Oh, Isobella, you look stunning when you are angry and it is wrong of me to tease you when we have enjoyed such a wonderful interlude. I will take my teasing away and sulk until we meet again."

This time it was Isobella who laughed. "I cannot imagine that you would ever sulk, sir, particularly over a female."

"You are right. I would not sulk over a female...but I would sulk over you.

Until tomorrow eve, Isobella."

She raised a brow questioning his comment.

"You are to dine with the Arlingtons, are you not?" he enquired

"Yes, we are all invited including Lord Preston's family. Are you invited also?"

"I hope so since I am a guest at the house along with my mother and brother."

Isobella's head jerked at his comment about his brother. "I hope your brother will keep any mischief to himself."

"Oh do not worry about him. He is more than occupied with his latest conquest to be of trouble to anyone. Apart from himself if her husband finds out," he added as an afterthought.

"Oh," said Isobella, not wishing to ask any further questions.

"So until tomorrow, my Isobella," he said, sweeping a low bow in the saddle and rewarding her with a wide grin before turning and riding away.

Watching him disappear she put her fingers up to her lips. Had he really kissed her...had she really allowed him to? Isobella's heart was fluttering like a fly caught in a trap. She could not believe what had taken place. She had cursed her cloak for hampering her mounting but then he had assisted her and had held her so close she was able to feel the heat from his body. The thoughts were dangerous. Pulling her cloak around her shoulders, she turned away and kicked her mount forward, quickly putting distance between herself and the occupier of her thoughts.

Chapter Six

Just as Isobella predicted, Juliette was in her bedchamber well before dawn, jumping into the bed beside her. Listening to her chatter she could not help her thoughts going back to Richard's words about her cousin being lucky to share her bedchamber. She wondered what his words would be if he saw them sharing a bed, and wondered even further what it would be like to share a bed with him. Her wayward thoughts shocked her. What was she doing daydreaming about sharing her bed with Richard? For daydreaming it was, he would never consider a liaison with someone like her. And yet he had kissed her, or was that just a dalliance? She was brought back to the present by her cousin's voice.

"Izzie, are you paying attention?"

"Of course I am. I do not have any choice but to listen to your words of praise for James and how you cannot wait for his arrival." She smiled to let her know she was only jesting.

By the time the Preston party arrived, Isobella had a headache from listening to her cousin's non-stop chatter. Excusing herself after lunch, she retired to her bedchamber and slept until late in the afternoon when Anna awoke her. Thankful that her headache had gone she waited while Anna saw to her bath and then dressed carefully, conscious that she was in her mind dressing for Richard.

Sitting by the dresser, she made a sudden decision to leave her hair down so instructed Anna to simply pin the sides up with small flowers but to leave the curls tumbling down around her shoulders. If Anna was surprised at the sudden change from her more formal style for dinner she knew her mistress well enough not to comment.

Looking at the reflection in the mirror, Isobella was pleased with the result. The dark green silk gown was flattering to her colouring. The low square cut bodice fitted closely and nipped in to show off a small waist before falling in soft folds over the underskirts that swished around her feet as she walked towards the door. The choice of small emeralds in her ears and matching necklace finished off the effect.

Proceeding down to the hall, she gathered up the matching stole and waited while

Anna fastened a matching evening cloak about her shoulders. Following Juliette and Aunt Eleanor out to the carriage and carrying the stole over her arm, she was conscious of the increasing beat of her heart as she counted the minutes before seeing Richard again.

Isobella thought her heartbeats would be heard by everyone, but she kept her head high and eyes lowered. Glad of the formalities to be almost over, she waited while the Duchess of Carlisle was formerly introduced and then her two sons. Dropping a deep courtesy to the Duchess she then gave a smaller one to her elder son. Before she had time to rise, he took hold of her hand and raised it to his lips.

"My dear Lady Isobella, how lovely to see you again...so soon," he added in a whisper.

She brought her head up sharply only to be greeted with a pair of sparkling blue eyes and a mischievous smile.

"My lord," was all she replied, and if he expected more she was certainly not intending to give it.

Turning, she dropped a small bob to his brother who barely seemed to realise she was there. His attention was wandering around the room and she was thankful that he appeared to have no further interest in her cousin who stood nearby talking with her future in-laws.

Moving away with her aunt and cousins, she found her sudden need to put some distance between herself and Richard disturbing. Her fingers still tingled from his touch and she knew his words were meant to tease her, but she found his presence overwhelming yet exciting at the same time.

Sitting at the dinner table, she was conscious of his watching gaze. Her attention was taken up with the conversation she was having with the elderly Duke of Arlington. He had been a rogue in his day and still retained the ability to charm but in a fatherly way. He was explaining the bloodline of one of his horses and she surprised him by commenting on the lineage of the sire. One thing she had an interest in was horses, and it often surprised her dinner companions when she was able to hold a conversation with them on the subject.

Sitting at the opposite end of the table to the object of his growing affection, he conversed fully with his companions while keeping a watchful eye on Isobella. He had known the moment she arrived, the skin had prickled at the back of his neck, and had been obliged to take a deep breath at his first sight of the person whose eye he was trying to catch. He had tried to engage her glance but she had kept her gaze lowered as the party entered the room, thus allowing him a small smile at the action. But he had waited patiently in the background until the main introductions were complete before moving forward with his mother. She had thought to escape him but he had taken her hand and that fleeting touch had been enough to settle his need for the moment.

After they had dined, the ladies left the gentlemen and he was obliged to stay for port and cigars. Not that he partook of the cigars but the port was welcome. When it was reasonable to do so he excused himself and made his way to the salon where he knew the ladies were. As he approached, Isobella and her cousin came out from the room. As soon as the door was closed they both burst into laughter holding their hands over their mouths.

Walking silently up to them he enquired as to the cause of their laughter but neither could give him an answer. Raising an eyebrow at Isobella he saw her swallow hard and try to compose herself. Just then there were footsteps from behind and Juliette rushed past them to be caught in the arms of her intended who was approaching. Swinging her round, he quickly set her back onto her feet.

"Oh, James, can we take a walk in the gardens? It is such a lovely night and I have hardly seen you since you arrived."

"I would love to, my sweet, but it would not be proper if someone were to see us."

Turning to her cousin with pleading eyes, "Izzie, you would like to walk in the gardens, would you not?"

Before Isobella could reply a voice at the side spoke out.

"I think that is a fine idea, Lady Juliette. I will escort your cousin and we will follow you and Lord Preston."

Turning, she flashed her eyes at him and spoke quietly, "I do not think that would be quite proper, my lord?"

"Ah, Isobella, will you not call me Richard," he teased, "after all, we are alone."

Looking around she saw Juliette and James had disappeared out through the open doors. Moving quickly she set off after them only to have her hand caught and placed on his arm. Walking silently at his side they moved out into the garden and followed the path until it came to a small clearing. She could hear her cousin's voice nearby. Looking at the different paths leading off from the clearing she was uncertain which to take. "I think we can leave the lovers for a while, Isobella, and you and I can talk."

"We have nothing to talk about."

"Oh I think we do, and you know we do. Unless you are in the habit of allowing gentlemen to kiss you?"

"Sir, you are being un-gentlemanly bringing up such a delicate matter."

"Perhaps, but then again I did say that I am not always a gentleman but with you, Isobella, I will be what you want," his words ended with a flourishing bow that made her laugh. Picking up one small hand, he held it to his chest, pulling her close as he did.

"I have no doubt that you will be exactly whom you want to be, Richard," she said his name tentatively.

Isobella hardly dared to breathe. With their gazes locked, his head dipped down. She knew what was about to happen, knew it should not, but she wished his kiss, so raised her head offering rose tinted lips to him.

He saw the movement and smiled to himself. He wanted so badly to take the offered lips but this was a long game that were being played, a game for keeps, so instead of the offered lips he kissed the back of her hand. That she was disappointed was clear to see and it was with the greatest difficulty that a smile was kept from his face.

"Come, Isobella, let us find your cousin before she is undone and discovered by someone other than us."

When she made no reply, he sensed she was not only disappointed but also perhaps a little angry with him. Her cheeks were flushed but sadly not from what was anticipated.

They heard the sound of soft voices and just before they reached Juliette and James, he lifted her hand, partly removed her glove and caressed the back with his thumb. He then placed his lips on the pale skin. Raising his eyes to look at her, he saw the look in her eyes, expectation and something else. Something much more to his liking. He could not resist trailing the tip of his tongue along the back of her hand before replacing her glove. He smiled. He had seen the flare of longing in her eyes and knew there was a passionate woman beneath the demure appearance. All that was needed was to release that woman and make her his wife.

Coming upon her cousin and James, they returned to the house together and it was not long before they were sitting in the coaches riding back to Rothbury Hall. Isobella listened to Juliette's chatter as the horses made their way through the darkness, but her own mind kept returning to Richard. He was playing some sort of game with her, of that she was certain. His teasing was enjoyable and his kisses were a hint of danger, and she was not at all sure she was ready to embrace that danger. But she could not forget the heat that rushed through her body as his tongue caressed her hand. She thought she had imagined it until she saw the look in his eyes, and had been so overcome by such a blatant act she had been rendered speechless.

Having spent an unsettled night she was glad to be sneaking out to the stables for her early morning ride. She had no fear that anyone would be up much before mid-morning or indeed noon and she needed to escape into the morning air to clear her head.

Riding into the meadow she admitted to a feeling of disappointment that it was empty but chided herself that this was what she wanted. To be alone with her thoughts without any distractions. For Richard Carlisle was a distraction she had no reason to doubt that. Sighing, she galloped back and forth across the meadow several more times. It was another lovely day, the sky was blue and already there was heat in the sun. Riding through the gap it was not long before the lake came into view along with a riderless horse tied to a tree.

She slowed looking about for the rider and then she saw him. Leaning casually against a tree trunk watching her approach. She wished in that moment she had brought her cloak, but she was half way to the stables when she remembered it and had no wish to risk being caught by going back.

By this time, she was close to his mount, and dropping the reins onto the gelding's neck she swung her right leg in front of her and prepared to slide down to the ground. She saw him move slowly away from the trunk as she approached. Slipping from the saddle she found herself caught in a pair of strong arms and lifted down to the ground.

"You can remove your hands, Richard," she said firmly, when several moments had passed and he made no move to release her.

"Ah, but, Isobella, I have such a warm feeling when I hold you. Surely you would not deny me that pleasure?"

It was more than she could do not to burst out laughing at the woeful look on his face. He linked his hands behind her back, holding her now in a familiar loose embrace, but he made no attempt to draw her any closer.

"Well, Isobella, what shall we do now. Would you wish to walk, or sit and talk.

Or perhaps I could steal another kiss since we are so close to each other?"

She was not sure what was right anymore, but the feeling of being held by him did not feel wrong. Indeed, it felt quite right. And it was not like her to be so confused. Uncertainty in a moment when she should be certain. Lifting her head the teasing look expected in his eyes was not there and his face was set so serious.

"I do not know. I have no wish to act in an improper or inappropriate way."

"Yes, but you do not dislike me, do you, Isobella?"

"No. I do not dislike you."

"So, one could say that you like me?"

"One could."

"Good, because I like you, Isobella, and I think I might just steal that kiss, unless you wish me not to?"

She had no intention of answering his question. But thought if he did not kiss her soon she may well kiss him. They were both playing with words. Each eyeing the other to see who would concede first. She was not that naïve. She knew well what went on between men and women her Ladies Journals were all informing on that subject. It was just that she had never experienced it...well not since a few stolen kisses with Exmouth before his betrayal. She placed both hands on his arms and waited.

He took the silence as consent and brought his lips down gently on hers. He felt the tremble, and before he could stop himself, pulled her into a close embrace and deepened the kiss. There was a desire to taste the inside of her mouth but caution held him back. Time enough for that later, he told himself. Releasing the embrace, she fell back against his arms giving him chance to take in the deep flush to her face and the dreamy look in the green eyes. She was compliant in his arms so he turned, drawing her with him and walked towards the edge of the lake. Sitting down on the fallen tree he drew her down beside him and placed his arm around shoulders, soft beneath his hand, and held her close to his body.

He could not deny his feelings nor could the hardness in his breeches be ignored, but there was no wish to rush her. His plan was to gently coax her out of the demure state in which she had been held for too long, and into the full passionate woman that was inside. If this were one of his mistresses she would have been taken here, on the ground, relieving the hardness in his shaft, but he had no intention of taking Isobella, not until their wedding night. Something she was yet to be made aware of.

They stayed a while at the lake talking of minor matters and he told of his brother's latest conquest. Although perhaps this was something one should not relate to a lady but he felt at such ease, and conversation with her came easy. All too soon it was time for them to leave. He helped her mount, delighting in the sight of the small derrière as she swung a slender leg over the saddle. This time no effort was made to move his hand away from the slender ankle, and long fingers strayed up the shapely calf, gliding over the gentle curve of her knee to her thigh. It was the gasp that brought his wandering hand to a stop. Looking up he grinned

"Apologies, my lady," he said with a flowing bow. "I was completely mesmerised by your delightful leg."

"You, sir, are a tease. You should not even see my leg or indeed comment on it."

"Ah, yes, but it is such a beautiful leg and it cries out to be touched and caressed."

"Richard...enough or I shall leave you here and ride back alone."

Laughing, he walked to his own mount and within seconds was alongside her.

"Come, my lady, let us return to our respective abodes."

As she lay in the bath later that morning, she thought back to the assignation they had shared, remembering his words and his touch and kiss. She had been content to be held against him, listening to his soothing voice. Even thinking of it now made her feel quite hot, and there was a strange sensation between her legs. Oh, she knew what it was, just thinking of him was arousing her, that much she had read in a very risqué Journal that she and Juliette had kept well hidden. She moved a hand beneath the water and touched herself just where the sensation was and her body jerked so much the water splashed over the side. She was shocked not only at her reaction but at what she had done. She had never touched herself there before, believing it a private place for one's husband. Pulling her hand back she called for Anna and quickly finished bathing, before allowing Anna to help dry and dress her.

The day was long and by the time dinner was finished Isobella was bored and tired. Excusing herself on the pretence of a headache, she retired for the night. Dismissing Anna, she sat in front of the fire in only a night rail and robe reading one of the Ladies Journals. Tiring of this after a while she ventured out into the corridor and along to Juliette's room. Seeing the door not fully closed she pushed it open. She was surprised to see the curtains round the four-poster pulled across and it was then that she heard the soft giggles. Moving further into the room she could see the reflection in the long mirror of Juliette lying on the bed and to her horror James was with her. Clasping a hand to stifle the cry she knew she should leave, but what if someone else came. Would she not be better waiting here to distract them? Even as she thought this, her eyes were again drawn to the mirror and to her dismay she saw Juliette's night rail pulled down, partly exposing small cream coloured breasts and James kissing her there. This was too much for Isobella. What on earth was her cousin doing, but even as she thought this she recalled her own actions of today. Was she not doing the same, well not quite the same, but at least Juliette and James were betrothed. Deciding to discreetly retire she crept back out of the room closing the door quietly as she did, slipping silently back to her own room.

The following morning, it was with some difficulty that she faced her cousin and James. Having been an unwitting party to her cousin's indiscretion, and unnerved by her own reaction to Richard's embrace, she was hoping for an uneventful day, and had deliberately not ridden that morning, but by noon she was regretting that decision. She had missed Richard's teasing and with no idea when she would see him again was restless. It was at luncheon that she discovered she would see him later that day, as the Arlington party were to visit for a picnic.

Dressing carefully in a muslin day dress of pale green, a straw hat was tied over the long curls and secured with a matching green ribbon. Her bodice was demure but just showing enough cream flesh to tease any interested party. She often wore a partial lace infill with the dress but today she felt daring so discarded this and allowed a small exposure of cleavage. She was excited at the thought of seeing him again, so her disappointment when he appeared escorting the Duke of Arlington's goddaughter was all the greater. She hoped this did not show as she cordially greeted the party.

Watching as Richard escorted his companion to the seating she took in the pale complexion and golden curls that framed a sweet face. The dress she wore was cream with delicate pink flowers embroidered on the bodice. Suddenly, Isobella felt underdressed and exposed and regretted the decision to discard the lace insert. There was also the unwelcome feeling of having been in this situation before; it angered her that she appeared to have been duped again.

As the guests mingled, Isobella soon decided that her duty for the day was more than done. She had been the perfect niece to her aunt's guests but now she wished for time to herself. Stealing away from the party, she headed off to the orchard where she knew it would be quiet and deserted. Settling down in the grass at the foot of one of the trees she chided herself for her stupid thoughts about the Duke of Carlisle. She refused to think of him as Richard any more. To arrive with another lady upon his arm confirmed he was the rake people said he was. She could feel the tears stinging at the back of her eyes but refused to acknowledge them.

Just as Isobella had watched his companion, Richard was watching her. She was not able to hide the disappointment in her face when he arrived with Sophia but there was naught that could be done about it. He was simply acting as escort and had no attachment to the young lady whatsoever, but that clearly was not what Isobella thought. "Damnation," he cursed under his breath before dutifully returning with a glass of cordial for Sophia. He found it impossible to catch Isobella's eye, and all he could do was watch as she sadly moved around the party attempting to give the appearance of enjoying the proceedings. By the time the food was eaten he could stand it no longer and persuaded his mother to take Sophia under her wing pleading a need to seek some manly company.

Leaving his mother with Sophia, Richard looked around for Isobella but could see no sign of her. Walking to the edge of the party he only just caught sight of her as she disappeared in the distance. Discreetly walking away, he followed, having no idea where she was going. When he came to the orchard it first appeared deserted but then a trail of pale green showed against the darker green of the grass. He had found his quarry but was in no doubt that she would not be pleased to see him.

Treading softly across the grass, he came to a stop just behind her. Standing above gave a perfect view of her bodice and beyond. And it was the beyond that made him tense. Forcing himself to move, he sat down alongside her, having no idea of how she would react, and only trusted she would resist an impulse to run.

Isobella started when he suddenly appeared at her side.

"Did you require something, my lord?" she said abruptly.

Richard winced at the tone. "Yes, my lady, and I am pleased to say I have found it."

Isobella remained silent.

"Are you angry with me, Isobella?" he said, somewhat teasingly.

"Why would I be angry with you, my lord?"

"Well, you are not calling me Richard and that would seem to suggest that you are angry."

"I do not think there is that much familiarity between us to speak in first names."

He could not help himself and roared with laughter. "Oh, Bella, you are wonderful when you are angry, but you are beautiful when you are in my arms and my lips are on yours."

She made to rise but he put out his hand and drew her back down.

"Sit, and listen. The lady I escorted is Arlington's goddaughter. I was asked to escort the young lady as a favour to him since the object of her affections has been delayed in London. I have now left the said young lady to the tender mercies of my mother while I attend to my own affairs."

"So you are having affairs, my lord?" The tone of her voice told him that his words had been misleading.

"No, damn it. I did not mean that kind of affair. You are too quick to judge me, Isobella. I meant only that I wished to spend the rest of the time with whom I wanted, and not someone chosen for me."

He saw the smile and also the relief in her eyes. She had thought that she was about to be treated again the way Exmouth treated her all those years ago. Well, he was not Exmouth, and he would prove this to her, if she would allow. When she looked at him, he also saw the glisten of unshed tears in her eyes.

"Oh, Bella, I did not mean to upset you. I would never do that or hurt you, my silly love."

Her eyes flew to his face at his words and made him wonder if he had pushed things too far. He was not quite sure what love was but what he felt for Isobella was something he had never felt for any other woman before. Leaning across, he pulled her to him and took the rose pink lips with his own. She yielded to his touch and before he knew what was intended, she was laid on her back and he was lying across her, deepening the kiss, his hands entangled in the dark curls. Pulling himself together, he drew her up whilst gaining his breath. Standing, he held out his hand, pulling her up to his side.

"Much as I would love to spend the rest of the day here with you I do not think I can trust myself to behave as I should."

She tilted her head and smiled sweetly at him. "Perhaps I do not want you to behave."

"Oh, you do, Isobella. Believe me, you do. I have no wish to deflower you in the grass in an orchard."

She blushed. "Richard?"

He saw her eyes drop and realised she could clearly see the evidence of his feelings straining against his breeches. Seeing the eyes widen, he pulled his coat down.

"I see you have noticed how you affect me, Bella, and it is for that reason that we must return to the rest of the party. Although, hopefully, by the time we have walked back the evidence will not be so apparent."

He picked up her bonnet and handed it to her, watching as she secured it on the tumbled curls. Then held out his arm and they walked back towards the house.

The following morning, Isobella slipped away to the stables, and before long was at the lake. Her heart was racing, knowing he would be waiting, but was saddened to find no sign of another horse or rider. Sitting on the fallen tree, she looked out across the water, but as the minutes passed, found it no longer soothed as it had previously done. Restless, she stood and walked to the water's edge before turning back to her mount. She rode home feeling disappointed, but also with a touch of annoyance.

She expressed a wish to remain at home that evening but her aunt and cousins would not hear of it. They were to attend the Cunningham's house for dinner and a musical evening and insisted she attend with them. Dressing in a deep blue silk gown with a high waistline and low cut rounded bodice, she instructed Anna to pin her hair on top and then let the ringlets fall down loosely. She did not paint her face or powder her hair. Picking up a matching shawl she stood while Anna fastened cloak, and then descended the stairs to meet her family.

The first person she saw when they arrived was Richard Carlisle. It was as though he were waiting for them. She mingled with the other guests keeping away from the Carlisle party and eventually found herself standing near one of the open doors leading to the gardens. Slipping outside, she was thankful to be away from the gossiping and out in the fresh evening air. It was dusk, and whilst the air was still warm she was thankful for the shawl about her shoulders.

Walking around the gardens, she suddenly came upon two figures, one tall and the other a slight female. She stopped suddenly, not wishing to intrude on this tryst. Then she saw the gentleman place his arms around the female as she rested her head on his chest. She felt a tugging in her own chest as she thought of how she had felt in Richard's arms and wondered if this unknown female felt the same. She must have made a sound because the male suddenly lifted his head and looked directly at her.

Richard!

She was sure she cried out and a hand flew to her mouth. The female turned around. It was Arlington's goddaughter, Sophia Stansfield, held so securely in Richard's arms.

Turning, she fled. Tears burned the back of her eyes and the sob was held firmly in her throat. She needed to get away. Her flight caused her to lose her bearings, but suddenly she found herself near the front of the house and there was the Rothbury coach. Throwing the door open she called to the startled coachman to take her home and then come back for the others.

By the time they reached Rothbury Hall, she was composed enough to tell the coachman to inform her aunt and cousins that she had felt unwell and left discreetly so as not to cause a scene. She watched as the coach set off back to the Cunningham's and then went inside.

She left instructions not to be disturbed and told Anna to inform the family that she was perfectly well and simply needed to rest and sleep. *Sleep,* she thought as she watched Anna's retreating back. *How am I supposed to sleep after tonight*? As she slid down under the covers she allowed the unshed tears to fall and cursed herself for being taken for a fool once again.

Chapter Seven

The following morning, she did have a headache and stayed in bed until noon. The rest of the family and guests left for a picnic and she was allowed the privilege of being left at home alone. Having enjoyed a long bath she dressed in a simple lemon muslin day dress and tied her hair loosely with a yellow silk ribbon. Having eaten a light lunch in her own small sitting room, she curled up in the chair with a Ladies Journal.

She was disturbed by a knock at the door. Putting down the journal she called for them to enter.

Smithson entered and announced that the Duke of Carlisle requested to see her.

Oh did he! "Tell him I am not receiving today," she said firmly to Smithson.

"Very good, my lady."

She watched as the door closed. *That will serve him right. How dare he come calling after being caught with another woman in a compromising situation?* She was incensed at his behaviour, she thought better of him. But then, of course, she had thought better of Exmouth all those years ago and look what he had done then, and indeed more recently. She shuddered at the memory of the kidnap but could not help remember it was Richard who had saved her. It was all too much to consider and she picked up her journal again and began to read.

She had read but a few lines when there was a further knock on the door. As she bid them enter she wondered what was amiss now. This time it was Anna who came into the room but she could see Smithson outside.

"Sorry, my lady, but the Duke of Carlisle insists on seeing you and will not take no for an answer."

"Well he will have to take no, Anna, and you can go and tell him so."

Anna cleared her throat, clearly in some discomfort. "Sorry, my lady, but his lordship says if you will not come down to him he will come up to your rooms."

Isobella's head swung up. "He would not dare?"

"I believe he will, my lady. His lordship appears in a very agitated state of mind."

Isobella thought for a moment. *So he is agitated, is he? Well perhaps I should prolong his agitation and make him wait. Let us see how patient you can be Lord Richard Carlisle.* Putting down the Journal she turned to Anna.

"Put his Lordship in the small sitting room and tell him I will be down shortly. Oh and, Anna."

"Yes, my lady?"

"Bring me a small port."

"To the small sitting room?"

"No, here. His Lordship can cool his heels a while."

She saw the beginning of a smile on Anna's face as she turned away to do her bidding. Slipping on house shoes she walked to the dressing table and tidied her hair. It was all very well to keep Richard waiting but she was also keeping herself waiting. Taking the small glass of port when it arrived she sat at the window and made herself sip this slowly. When she felt he had been kept waiting for long enough she made her way down to the sitting room.

As he waited, Richard reflected on the unfortunate appearance of Isobella the previous evening. He knew exactly what she thought she had seen and ruefully admitted it had all looked extremely compromising. All that were needed now was to convince her it was not as it appeared. He looked again at his watch and could not help but smile to himself. She was keeping him waiting, playing a game with him. Well, he was happy to wait. But would have been even happier to have gone to her bedchamber if she had not agreed to see him. That had been no idle threat.

He was intending to sort this matter out without further delay.

Eventually, he heard the door open and rose to his feet. Turning to face her, his breath caught in his throat. *God, she is even more beautiful without finery,* was his first thought. His second was that she was devoid of corset or underskirts and he knew what delights were beneath the dress she wore. She closed the door and turned to face him. He moved forward and picked up her hand before she could prevent him. Bending low, he placed his lips to it, enjoying for a moment the softness of her skin as he retained his hold.

"Isobella, thank you for seeing me," he said contritely.

"You left me little choice, sir."

He winced at the words. He was in real trouble and was in no doubt that he was going to have a lot of explaining to do before she would forgive him or trust him again.

"I am sorry for my forceful tactics, but I needed to see you, to explain about last evening."

"I do not think any explanations are necessary, sir. I have eyes and I saw all that I needed to see. If truth be told, I would rather have not seen it at all. You can let go of my hand now, my lord."

"Ah yes...but sometimes things are not as they seem."

Taking the silence as a good sign he ignored the request to relinquish her hand and led her forward, seating her on the small sofa. Still retaining his hold he sat alongside and smiled as she moved away, putting more space between them. He tightened his hold needing to keep some contact with her.

"I know what you saw looked compromising but I can assure you that it was not. I was in the garden trying to find the words to explain why I had not met with you yesterday morning, when the very person who prevented me from meeting you came running to me."

"The Duke of Arlington's goddaughter."

"Yes. Look, I will start at the beginning. I was about to leave the house yesterday morning when Sophia's beau accosted me and begged me to give him some pointers as to how to go about asking for Sophia's hand in marriage. I am not the person to ask about that kind of matter and I tried to tell him so, but the poor soul was in such a state I took pity on him and took him off for a stroll round the gardens. By the time we returned it was too late to meet with you."

"That does not explain last evening," said Isobella more softly than intended.

"No, you are right, it does not. As I said, I was in the garden last evening trying to decide how much of the young lovers tale to disclose when Sophia came running through the gardens in considerable distress. I managed to catch up but found her crying hard. I was attempting to offer comfort when you saw us."

"So why did she need to be comforted if she was about to be offered for?"

"Because her father has turned down the offer and has forbidden her to marry or to see the young man again. Last evening she was begging me to appeal to her godfather to change her father's mind."

"And have you?"

"Have I what?"

"Spoken to the Duke."

"No, not yet, but I do not know whether it is my place to do so. I know little of the young man in question. He is a second son, is hoping to practise in the law and whilst he will have an honourable place in society it is not the marriage her parents were hoping for."

"Does she love him?"

"I do not know. She is young and who knows; she may feel differently in a few years time. But she is not my problem, Isobella. You are, and whether you believe what I have told you." He only hoped his explanation were enough to convince her of the truth.

"I need a moment to think on it, sir." She rose and walked to the fireplace then rang the bell.

He waited, and when the door opened she requested tea be brought. Hearing the request gave him hope that she was no longer angry. If she were then no doubt he would have been standing on the driveway by now.

Rising from the seat, he walked towards the small window and looked out across the gardens. Turning, he saw her watching him and risked a small smile. He saw the frown appear and took a step forward.

"Surely you believe me, Isobella. Do not tell me that you believe I would want a child in my arms when I have already held the woman I want in my embrace."

"Sir, I have no idea what women you have had in your embrace. Nor do I know what woman you refer to wanting."

He began to laugh and was about to speak when the tea appeared, so held his tongue until they were alone again. He watched as she poured the tea for them both and pictured her in his mind doing the same thing in his London home or at Carlisle Hall. His thoughts were running away with him and he did not know whether to rein them in or let them go full gallop.

"I think you are teasing me, Isobella. I believe that you accept as the truth all that I have told you and are no longer angry with me. But you wish to punish me for letting you down yesterday, and making you think that I was no better than another, whose name I shall not speak."

He sat and took the offered cup from her, his gaze upon her face. She wanted to forgive him, but not too soon, she intended teasing him. He would wait a while longer. But he would not wait too long.

She sat back, sipped her tea and looked at him over the top of her cup. "Would you really have come to my bedchamber?"

He took a sip of his tea before answering. "Yes. I do not make idle threats, and that is something you should be aware of."

Watching the faraway look coming over her face he had a vague idea where she was. Oh yes, he would have gone to her bedchamber and what might have happened after that he dared not think.

"Yes, Isobella, your thoughts are correct," he dared to confirm his own thoughts believing she shared them. Not that she would admit to it of course.

She looked at him, unable to prevent the flush creeping up her delicate face. He grinned at the awareness in her eyes as she realised her thoughts had been read.

"I do not know what you mean."

"Oh, I believe you do." He put his own cup down as he spoke and took hers, placing it on the small table.

Moving closer, he let his hand stray up her arm until it reached her shoulder. She made no move to stop him, which he took as a good omen. Moving closer still, until there was hardly a space between them, he leaned forward intending to draw her to him but she pulled back and slipped off the seat, walking to the window. He was not prepared to allow the escape. He had spent a tormented night and was not intending to lose this opportunity. He followed, stood behind her and wrapped her in his arms. He felt her stiffen, and whispered in one delicate ear, begging that she really must forgive him. Then placed a soft kiss on the side of her neck, just above the curve of her shoulder. He felt the shudder and in that moment knew she had returned to him.

Turning her to face him, she was held in a loose embrace, the way he had held her at the lake. Then moving forward, placed his lips on hers, gently at first and then, as she responded, deepened the kiss, holding her firmly against his body. He needed her to know how much he desired her.

The pleasure to be felt by the lack of underclothing became quickly apparent as he held her. It was all he could do to keep his hands still. But still they needed to be or she would most probably flee and he would be at a disadvantage again. Slowly releasing the kiss, he held her close, resting his forehead against hers.

"Ahh, Bella, you drive me to distraction. I think you have cast a spell on me."

She remained silent. Moving slowly back, he looked into the deep green eyes, seeing nothing but a look that said she was enjoying this as much as he. The knock on the door made her jump apart from him. He saw her trembling as she hurried back to the sofa before calling enter.

He stayed by the window casually looking out, his face turned away from the room as he tried to compose himself.

Smithson entered. "Apologies, my lady, but the family have just returned and upon hearing that his lordship was present enquired if he wishes to stay and dine."

Isobella looked toward Richard's direction. "Lord Carlisle?"

As if sensing her panic, he turned and smiled at Smithson but declined the offer saying that he was expected back at Arlington Hall and to convey his apologies to the Duke.

As the door closed Isobella thanked him.

"For what, Bella?"

"For declining the offer."

"So you have no wish to enjoy my company at dinner?"

"I did not mean that. It is just that it would have been too much sitting at table with you knowing what has just taken place."

He smiled. "I know and that is why I declined. I have no wish to rush what is happening. I will take my leave now and hope that I will see you in the morning at our meeting place."

She smiled and rose, walking to meet him as he crossed the room to her.

Taking her hands in his, he pulled her close and gently placed his lips on hers in the lightest of kisses. "Until tomorrow, Bella."

She walked out into the entrance hall with him. Having collected his gloves, he bent low over her hand turning it so the kiss fell on the inner wrist. Then he left, climbing onto his mount with ease and riding away without a backward glance. Isobella watched him disappear into the distance from the window in the small lounge. As she walked up the staircase to her rooms she gently caressed the inside of her wrist and knew she would be besieged with questions from Juliette once they were alone.

Safely in her rooms, she dropped onto the chair that she had left but a short time ago, but which now felt like a lifetime ago. So much had happened and her head was in a spin, her mind recalling the events that had just taken place.

His threat to come to her rooms had left her bereft of speech. The thought of him charging up her bedchamber had taken her thoughts away from the conversation they had been having. She wondered what he would have done. She could picture him striding into the room and sweeping her into his arms and.... *Oh no,* she thought, *not again these fanciful dreams that have no hope of coming true.* She shook her head to dispel the thoughts but she could not; indeed, she could only recall the sensations she had felt as he held and kissed her.

Every part of her had been on fire and the longer she were held the more intense the heat had become. Sitting in the quiet of her room she could only hope that the heat in her body would settle before she was discovered.

Chapter Eight

Entering the small lounge at Arlington Hall, Richard was in fine spirits. His mother was seated in one of the alcoves talking with the Duchess and his brother, well, he could not see him anywhere, but for once he did not care. His mind was already hours ahead at a certain lake on the Rothbury Estate and just thinking of the hours to get through before then was painful. He took a sip of the wine that had been handed to him and glanced round the room. Whilst deciding which group to join that would give the best conversation a quiet voice spoke to him from behind.

Turning, he found the Earl of Ashford. Inclining his head to return the greeting was about to engage in conversation when the Earl spoke first.

"I see your brother is not present. Is he not to dine with us tonight?"

Richard was immediately wary. "As far as I know he is to dine and has simply not yet come down."

"Leaving it a bit late, is he not? Hope the fellow has not come down with the same sickness that keep's my wife from the table."

Richard looked at the elderly man's face and saw the steel in his eyes. Ashford knew his wife and Edward were lovers, but if they were both absent at the same time this was flaunting the relationship in front of him, and he knew the Earl was not about to allow that to happen.

"Might be best if you collected your brother and brought him down to dine, Carlisle."

Richard bowed slightly. "As you wish, Ashford. I have no stomach for anything that would upset the ladies."

"Good. Neither have I," replied the Earl, and with that walked away leaving

Richard more angry that he had ever been.

Turning on his heel, he handed his glass to the servant and took the stairs as quickly as he could without drawing attention. Going into his own room he paused a moment to calm himself. Then walking through the sitting room that separated his bedchamber from his brother's entered through the connecting door. Just as Ashford predicted, his wife was here. The drapes around the bed were drawn and Richard could hear the soft laughter from inside. Squaring his shoulders, he walked to the side of the bed and silently pulled back the drape.

The sight that greeted him he could have wished to avoid. Both parties were naked and his brother's rear was pumping into Gwendolyn at a speed fit only to be used in a brothel. That the lady in question was enjoying it was clear from the moans coming from the partly open mouth. Neither had seen him and it was clear they were in the final throws of their coupling. It was Gwendolyn that saw him first as she groaned through her pleasure and then opened her eyes. She let out a scream just as his brother withdrew and spewed his seed onto the floor narrowly missing Richard's shoes.

"Bloody hell, Richard, you might give someone a warning when you are intending to appear."

"Oh, believe me, I was not intending to appear as you put it, but I have been requested, or perhaps ordered, by Ashford to enquire whether you have the same sickness as his wife, and if not, to escort you down to dine."

Gwendolyn said nothing during this intercourse and made no attempt to cover herself. Sprawled on the bed, legs wide apart, she eyed Richard seductively.

"Perhaps you would care to join us, Sir Richard. I am sure I can accommodate you both. I have served two together before and it is great fun."

Richard felt sickened and sorry for Ashford that he was encumbered with such a wanton for a wife. There was also a feeling of guilt that it were he who focused his brother's attention in the direction of the Earl's wife. Nevertheless, Ashford was influential and he was not intending to offend him by offending his wife.

Tipping his head in Gwendolyn's direction, he said, "I regret, madam, that I have no need of a mistress, and when I bed a woman I do not share."

Edward looked at his brother's face and could see the barely controlled anger.

"Does Ashford really know we are together now?"

"Of course he bloody well does. The man is not a fool, and will not be made to look a fool in front of his peers. So I would suggest that you diverse yourself of your paramour, get dressed and accompany me down to dine." Having said all that was needed Richard turned on his heel and walked back to his own rooms.

It was several minutes later when his brother joined him, and after straightening his cravat, they descended the stairs and joined their mother. Richard caught Ashford's eye as they walked across the room and the Earl gave the slightest incline of his head. Richard returned the gesture. His brother had the grace to behave impeccably during the rest of the evening and remained with the other guests until after Ashford retired.

Finally having escorted his mother to her rooms he was able to return to his own bedchamber. Throwing his jacket onto the chair he pulled off his cravat and walked through the adjoining room to speak to his brother. Even before the door opened it became clear Edward was not alone. The female voice he recognised, and could only shake his head in disbelief.

"Oh come, Edward, do not let your brother scare you away. The Earl has partaken of his port and the old fart is snoring in his bed as we speak. Now I could go back to him or we could continue what we were doing earlier"

Richard did not hear his brother's reply but the thump and laughter from within told him that she was no longer alone in the bed. Turning away, he had no stomach for his philandering, and no wish to again entertain the sights revealed to him earlier. Returning to his own bedchamber he turned the key in the lock giving himself complete privacy from his brother's actions.

Galloping across the fields the following morning, he breathed in the crisp air and only hoped that he had not kept Isobella waiting. Arriving at the lake, the area was empty. As he paced the ground waiting, suddenly the welcome sound of hooves thundering across the ground could be heard, and then the rustle of bushes as she came into sight. Her hair was tied back loosely with a brown ribbon and to his delight she wore her usual attire. His heart leapt at the sight, and it was not the only part of him that was moved.

She was out of breath and that told him she had galloped all the way believing she was late. Moving quickly towards her holding out a hand, she surrendered the reins to him, and he secured her mount. Stepping back, he waited as she swung a leg in front and then he opened his arms. She hesitated for only a moment before sliding down from the saddle and being expertly caught in his arms. He lowered her slowly, allowing her body to slide down his own until his lips were close to hers. Then took the one thing he had wanted since awakening. His lips pressed to hers, feeling her arms move around his neck. He deepened the kiss, daring to go further, teased her lips with his tongue, until he gained access to her mouth. A small gasp escaped her when his tongue found her own, but he had no intention of ceasing what were taking place.

He was drowning in her. In her perfume, her lips, her body. He moved a hand to the small of her back, pressing her against him, knowing she would again feel his need for her. He had expected that she would pull back so his surprise when she pressed into him was all the greater. This time it was he who gasped. Taking his lips from hers he swept her into his arms, and walked near to the lake edge. Setting her down, he told her to wait, and returned to his mount, pulling a package from behind the saddle. Unfurling this to disclose a cloak he walked back to where she stood and spread it on the ground.

Pulling her gently down, they sat side by side, neither quite knowing where this was going. For Richard, this was purgatory; he wanted her so badly it hurt but knew he could not take the one thing he desired.

"I thought you were not coming." His words broke the silence.

"I was almost caught by one of the boys who for some reason came early into the stables, but the head groom dispatched him on an errand so I was able to make by escape. But it did delay me a short time and I was worried that you may have left."

"No, Isabella, I would never leave without seeing you. I would wait until noon if I needed to." He heard the intake of breath.

"Richard, what is happening? Are you intending to seduce me, because if you are I will not allow it?"

He laughed at the words. "I think it is you who is seducing me, Bella. I cannot think clearly when you are near and I am in a permanent state of arousal."

This time she laughed. "Yes, I am more than aware of your state, sir."

"As well you might be, minx, for it is all down to your doing. The question is what am I going to do about it. Do I seduce you, take what I want and then leave, or do I forego the one thing I want and leave your maidenhood intact for your husband."

"I cannot answer your question for you. That is something you will have to determine on your own."

"What would you wish me to do, Bella?"

"I cannot say, sir."

"But if you could. What would be your answer? Do I seduce you or leave that delightful task for your husband?"

"You know the answer I must give. You cannot seduce me for I will be ruined if you do. So you must leave me for my husband."

"Good, so that is settled. While we are here we will dally with each other but I give you my word I will not seduce you. However difficult that may be." If Isobella was disappointed at his words she gave no sign, and he was not sure whether that pleased or saddened him.

Lying back on the cloak, he pulled her down alongside him. Leaning over, he put his lips to hers. She came to him freely and his hands slipped beneath her shoulders, holding her close while he increased the kiss. She surprised him by giving him access to her mouth, and he took it greedily. Kissing was not enough. He moved his body covering hers. Rising up on his hands and looking down at the trusting face his conscience told him he needed to stop what was amiss.

"Isobella, I am sorry, I should not be upon you like this." As he made to move, her hands went around his waist holding him to her.

"Do not move just yet, Richard. Let me feel you a while longer." The blush to her cheeks told him it had taken a great deal for her to say the words to him.

If she was enjoying the feeling of him atop her then he was in heaven pressing into her body. He was so bloody hard it hurt and longed to release his breeches and set his shaft free. But if he did that they would both be lost and she would be ruined. So he stayed where she wished him for a while longer, until he was forced to tell her he needed to move.

Rolling to the side, he saw the disappointment in her eyes, and closed his lips over hers. His hand roamed across her stomach and up to the opening of her shirt. Moving the edges apart, he set his lips against the delicate throat and then traced a line with his tongue down to the swell of her breasts. He longed to undo the ties on the under-bodice and take a breast in his mouth, but that was too close to seduction, and he had promised he would not do that. Staying his hand he touched her on the cheek.

"I regret to say that we must leave. Much as I desire to remain here all day with you, the time is passing and you will be missed."

Pulling her up alongside him, he held the tempting body against the length of his own. "Feel how you torment me, Bella. I think I might have to cheat your husband if we stay much longer."

She smiled at him almost wickedly. "But I may never have a husband to know that he has been cheated."

"Oh you will, Bella. You will have a husband. No man could resist you and then I will be the loser, or perhaps the victor."

He tempered his words with a cheeky grin to take the serious meaning out of them. She would have a husband and it would be he, but the time was not yet right to tell her that. She was unfurling to him like a rosebud coming into bloom and he was enjoying the role of tutor, giving the nurture she needed to do so.

They parted at the path leading to the copse with a promise to meet again the following morn. Riding home, Isabella was more confused than before. She was aroused when with him and he was most certainly aroused by her. All she knew was that she had wanted to keep the contact with his body, to keep the feelings that were raging through her own for as long as she could. She had never felt a man that way before and could not believe how much she took pleasure from it. His shaft had been pressed so hard into her and the urge to squirm against it had been all consuming. It was only shyness that stopped her. The feelings were the same as those she had felt while bathing that short while ago. She had wanted him to touch her, the way she had touched herself that day. She did not understand how to manage these feelings but she needed to do so, if she were to remain intact.

But then, was he just playing with her; and if so, did she wish to let him? She could not find an answer to her question and if she were truthful did not know if she wished to. All she knew was that she enjoyed being with him and was most certainly enjoying his kisses. She may never marry so perhaps she should enjoy what was happening with Richard Carlisle for it may have to last a lifetime.

Returning to the Arlington's, Richard was surprised to find the Ashton coach at the front, and the Countess being escorted inside by her husband. Crossing to the entrance his way was blocked by the Earl.

"My wife has decided to adjourn to our country estate for a few months for her health. It may be as well if you brother returned to London for the same reason." The words held no malice but a strong warning.

"I have no grudge with you, Carlisle, but your sibling needs to take care in crossing me. I will not be made a fool of in my own household. Discretion, sir, is everything and something your brother needs to learn."

"I regret any displeasure my brother has caused. I am sure that none was intended. I will return him to London this night."

"Good, but I would prefer that you accompany him, sir, to make certain he does not follow my wife. I have no stomach for divorce and it would not sit well with either of our families."

"I will do as you ask, Ashton, and trust that you will not take any action that would make this matter more public than it would appear to be."

"I will not, sir. I have no wish to be made an even bigger fool."

As he turned to leave, Richard said quietly, "I have heard, sir, that a strong hand on a derriere followed by a hard rout between the bed sheets can bring even the most troublesome filly to heel, and a man of your standing and reputation should have no problem in re-branding his filly. I mean no insult but there were two parties involved, and whilst my brother needs little encouragement, he does need some before acting improperly. So I will deal with my brother and leave you to deal with your Countess."

Richard thought Ashford was going to retaliate but then saw that his words were causing some thoughtfulness.

"Perhaps you are right, Carlisle. I have let the filly run too loose for too long. Time she was bridled and brought to hand." And with that, the Earl turned and went outside, ordering the coachman to wait as he was intending to join his wife.

Richard's good mood of earlier was gone. He sought his brother out and found him sulking in his bedchamber.

"Bloody old fool has ordered Gwen to the country."

"So what have you done to bring this about?"

"Nothing. Well almost nothing. We were caught in a delicate situation by one of the housemaids. She must have spoken about it and then it would appear it got to Ashton's ears."

"Yes, well you knew it would happen. When I suggested you seek a mistress and mentioned that she was available I at least expected you to be discreet. You have made a fool out of Ashton, but in a way you might have done him a favour."

"Favour... in what way?"

"Well, she has not gone to the country alone. I suggested that to put her over his knee and spank her may bring about a solution to his problem. If he has any sense after that he will fuck the life out of her until she cannot move. When she sees what punishment she has at home she will not wish to stray again."

"She will not like that. Ashton has several mistresses and if she is not allowed the same privilege she will be..."

Richard finished the sentence for him. "She will be forced to seek her husband's bed and that may keep him from his mistresses. Anyway, Ashton requested that you return to London tonight to prevent you following his wife. Whilst there is no fear of that happening now since Ashton has joined her. I gave my word that I would escort you, so pack your bags, Edward, we return to London this eve."

Back in his own rooms, Richard was furious. Not only was he required to act as some kind of chaperone to his brother; he was now no longer able to meet Isobella tomorrow. Writing a quick note, instructions were then given to ensure that it was delivered to Lady Isobella Rothbury that night.

Having to lie to his mother over the reason for his immediate return to London and that it was necessary to take Edward with him was most uncomfortable. However, there was no choice but to fabricate a problem within the household but promised that he would send the coach back for her two days hence so she could continue to enjoy the time with the Arlingtons.

The Duke was most considerate, and though did not come outright and say he knew of the reason for their departure, his comment on, *the sad state of affairs within the Ashton household,* clearly told that he did.

The journey back to London was done in silence. Richard having no desire to converse with his brother, and for once the latter kept any complaints to himself. Their arrival caused a stir since the household was unprepared, but like a well-oiled machine it was soon running as if their return had been expected. Spending most of the following days at his club he still kept a tight curb on his brother. It was clear from the gossip within the ton that the events in the country had not reached London and for that Richard was thankful.

The coach was duly despatched to collect his mother and her maid, and he was tempted to return with it. But could not think of an excuse to call at the Rothburys. Nor indeed did he know if they would still be there. Instead, one of the footmen was sent to assist. Flicking open his fob watch, he calculated that his mother should be arriving shortly so gave instructions for refreshments to be made ready.

Hearing the coach pull up, he walked quickly outside to greet the traveller whom he knew would be extremely weary. He was more than surprised when the coachman jumped down and handed him a note, the writing on which was clearly his mother's. Opening it with some apprehension he could barely take in the contents for a moment.

"My dear Richard,

I find that I cannot face returning to London at this time. The philandering between Edward and the Countess of Ashton has reached my ears and I have no wish to see him at present. I have therefore travelled to Carlisle Hall and will abide there for several days until I feel able to deal with the disgrace that has been brought to the family name.

Your affectionate, Mama"

Looking at the coachman he enquired whom had gone with his mother and was relieved somewhat that her maid and the footman were with her. There was a skeleton staff at the Hall but he did not intend to leave her to worry alone. Turning back into the house, he took the stairs two at a time and burst into Edward's rooms without pause, crashing the door open and causing his brother to step back in alarm.

"Richard, what the devil is wrong. Are we under attack?"

Unable to speak, he threw the letter at him. "Read this. Read what you have done to our mother."

He watched as his brother read their mother's words and was gratified to see remorse in his face.

"I did not intend that mother would find out. I would not cause her hurt for anything. You know I would not."

"Well you have. And for what, a piece of something that belonged to someone else. There are ways of keeping a mistress, and flaunting the coupling is not one of them."

"I did not flaunt it. If anything, it was Gwendolyn who was reckless."

"Yes, well you should have had more sense. The harm is done now but at least news of the liaison has not reached London so there is no need for mother to hide away. I will depart in the morning and see if I can persuade her to come home and speak to you. If I cannot, then perhaps you should pay a visit to our uncle at the Manse in Cheshire. I am sure that some time spent in prayer and being instructed as to the ills of wickedness will do you no harm. But I will not have mother upset. Do I make myself clear?"

His voice thundered around the room as he finished speaking, and his brother stood silent. He had never seen Richard so angry before but the one thing he did not wish was to be exiled to the

Manse. He was prepared to do whatever it took to remain in London, and for now that was to keep his tongue still and let his brother rant.

Finally not able to find any further words, Richard turned on his heel and stormed out of the room and down to the library. Pouring himself a large brandy, he sank into one of the winged chairs and contemplated his next move.

He was not intending to go that night but was aware there was a musical event at the Preston's. Although an invite was delivered, he had not formally replied but turned up with the intention of eliciting from the Preston's when the Rothbury party would be returning to town. He was surprised to see James Preston in attendance, having thought him still in the country. Approaching, he enquired after Juliette and was able to find out that the family were to return in two days time. Having acquired the information needed he took Early leave and returned home. So he had two days or possibly three to persuade his mother to return. Well, he only hoped his persuasive tongue was up to the task.

Chapter Nine

The journey to Carlisle Hall seemed endless but finally the coach turned into the driveway. He always took pride in the house when it first came into view. The long drive curved round to the left into a large turning area in front of the main entrance. The two-story building was bathed in the afternoon sun and the light from the sun sparkled on the windows. The six tall windows at the front overlooked the drive and the parkland to the front, separated equally by stone steps leading to the oak front door. As expected, the drapes were pulled back from the six identical windows on the first floor which indicated his mother was in residence. She hated the rooms to be closed up even if they were not in use.

Waiting while the coach pulled to a halt, he then descended and walked towards the door. Before he reached the top of the steps the door opened and Thomas the caretaker bowed and wished him good day. Walking in, the waiting footman took his coat while the maid showed him through to the small sitting room where he found his mother. Ordering tea, he greeted her warmly then sat alongside her on the chaise longue. "Mama, you cannot hide away here on your own."

"I am not on my own, darling. I have Marie and that delightful young man you sent to escort me home."

"You have no proper staff and if you are away from town much longer people are going to talk."

"What, you mean they are not talking already?"

"No, they are not. News of what happened at Arlington Hall has apparently stayed at the Hall. There is no gossip and no scandal about Edward. But if you remain here on your own then they will start to gossip and who knows what they will find out then."

"Oh, Richard, do not tell me you have come all this way to blackmail your mama?"

"No, of course not, mother. But I have come all this way to take you home. You cannot miss the rest of the season. Everyone is starting to return from the country and it is time for you to do so as well."

If he had thought it would be easy to persuade his mother to return home he was mistaken. He had the same argument with her day after day. Now having been at the hall for six nights, his patience was wearing thin. Not only did he want his mother to return to town, he needed to return himself. He knew the Rothburys would have been home for four nights and he was aching to see Isobella again. Aching so much that he had to relieve himself on two occasions, much to his disgust. A mistress would have made the relief all the sweeter but he wanted no mistress. He desired a wife, and only one person fitted the position.

Finally, on the seventh day his mother agreed to return to London but it took a further day to gather her things together. By the time they reached London he had been away nigh on nine nights and was thankful that Edward was home when they arrived and in a contrite mood. Leaving his mother to remonstrate his younger sibling, he excused himself and dressed before going out. Looking through the invitations awaiting his return one stood out. There was a ball tonight at the Farrington's and taking the chance that the Rothburys would be there quickly ordered the carriage.

Having heard nothing from Richard since his short note, Isobella could not dispel the feeling of being cast aside again entering into her thoughts. She had done things with Richard that she would never have done before, and then suddenly he left. *"Have to return to London tonight will explain all when we meet again. R,"* the note had read, and it had made no sense to her. Having sat that night through what seemed an endless dinner with chatter about Juliette's betrothal ball, she had been glad to find some peace in her bedchamber. The following days had been long and painful and she had read his note over and over again in the hope that it might convey something else other than the few words he had written. But it had not.

He was absent from any of the gatherings they attended since their return, although information from James told that he was in attendance while they were in the country. To Isobella, that meant only one thing, that he had no wish to see her. How she could have been so stupid as to think he cared for her? She had been tearful most of the day and wished nothing more than to remain at home tonight but her aunt would have none of it.

Looking around the room, she saw her family engaged in conversation. Having no wish to join them slipped discreetly through the open doors and entered into the garden. Pulling the shawl around her shoulders she walked slowly along the path, lost in thought. Coming to a small clearing surrounded by tall hedging she sat down on the stone seat and thought back over the past weeks. So engrossed was she that she did not hear the footsteps until a figure stopped in front of her. Raising her head, she found herself looking into the face of Exmouth.

"Well, Lady Isobella, what a find I have made."

Suddenly afraid, and conscious of being on her own she spoke with more confidence than were felt. "I wish to be alone, sir, if you please."

"And what if I do not please?"

"A gentleman would heed my request. But then of course you are not a gentleman, are you, sir?" she answered, referring to his kidnapping of her.

He had the grace to shuffle his feet. "Ah, well yes. I must admit things did get a might out of hand. But had you come quietly then there would have been no trouble."

"I will never go anywhere with you, sir, quietly or otherwise." She rose as she spoke intending to return to the house.

"Oh no, my lady, not so fast. I am wondering if perchance you were waiting for someone out here. Maybe you are not quite the lady I thought you to be."

"I can assure you, sir, that I am such a lady and I have no planned assignation with anyone."

"Good, Isobella. I am pleased to hear that. I would not like to think that someone is going to beat me to the prize. And while I wait for you to come to me, for come to me you will, I might just take a tasting from you now."

Before she knew what was happening, his arms were around her and his face moved closer to hers. She struggled in his grip and thought all was lost until a sharp voice brought them both to a stop.

"Isobella Rothbury, is that you?" Isobella swung round thankful that Exmouth had released her.

"Lady Brentwood" said Isobella in a shocked voice, but before she could say anything further a smooth voice spoke from the side and Richard stepped out from the shadows.

Nothing in his bearing gave hint to the fury that was raging through him. He had seen Isobella leave and followed, intending to put matters right between them. But seeing Exmouth ahead of him, had circled the bushes entering the clearing from the side and reaching them just as Exmouth made his move. He was about to rush forward and pull him off when the Duchess of Brentwood spoke. Now all that were needed was to use his wits to remove Isobella out from this situation.

Moving quickly out into the open, he walked directly to Isobella and placed his arm around the slender waist, pulling her into his side and dropping a tender kiss on the top of her head. Then in a low voice told Exmouth to say nothing and make no move or he would run him through. Not that he had anything to run him through with, but he did not know that. Leaving Isobella's side, he turned towards Lady Brentwood, sweeping a low bow.

"Duchess, you look more enchanting each time I see you."

"Carlisle, you are either a fibber or a rogue and I am not sure which I prefer," she said, tapping him on the arm with her folded fan. "However, I am intrigued to know what is transpiring here. I find Lady Isobella Rothbury in the arms of a married man and wonder what I am to make of it."

Richard laughed, and drawing the Duchess aside, lowered his voice, "I can guarantee there is nothing to concern you. I was standing nearby and I can assure you I have no intention of allowing another man to make advances to the woman I intend to have as my future wife."

The Duchess almost exploded with shock. Carlisle, one of the most eligible men of the day was about to marry. And marry Isobella Rothbury. Oh she could not wait to spread the news.

"I had no idea that you were pursuing the young lady in question, or indeed that you were considering entering into matrimony. But that does not account for Exmouth's presence or his embrace."

"No indeed, you are right, it does not. I was but asking the question of Lady Isobella when Exmouth came upon us and overheard my words. He assumed I had received the answer I desired and was in the process of congratulating Lady Isobella when your grace appeared."

"So you have not received a reply from the lady in question?"

"No, sadly we were interrupted, but I have no doubt that I will receive the answer I seek. All I would ask your grace is that you keep this information private until I have sought the opportunity to present my suit to the Duke of Rothbury tomorrow and seek his approval to the marriage."

As he spoke the words, Richard hoped that his ruse had worked. His mind had been pushed to come up with a proper explanation. Whilst the story he told was close to the truth, it was not how he intended the news to be broken. Hopefully, the Duchess could be trusted to keep the secret until at least he initiated the opportunity to formally propose to Isobella, which was the very reason for his following her. Exmouth could be dealt with later.

Thrilled to be the recipient of such news the Duchess was subdued to find that she would have to keep this secret.

"Carlisle, you test me too much, but I will keep your secret. One condition attaches."

"And what is that, your Grace," he said charmingly.

"That you let me know the minute the Duke has agreed to the match, and of course, that the lady has said yes."

Bending over the gloved hand, he whispered, "I promise after the family you will be the first to know. I will dispatch a messenger to you myself. Now if I can impose on Exmouth to escort you back to the house I will attempt to complete my mission before we are missed."

Turning to Exmouth, he called, "You will escort the Duchess inside, will you not, sir?"

Left with no escape, Exmouth agreed and walked towards the elderly Duchess, with a forced smile on his face. As he passed Carlisle a hand on his arm momentarily delayed him.

"Say one word to anyone about tonight and I will seek you out," threatened Richard.

Nodding his head briefly, he took his leave and escorted Lady Brentwood back through the gardens. Finally left alone, Richard turned to Isobella and even in the dusk the paleness of her face could be seen.

"Bella, I am so sorry that I could not reach you before Exmouth."

She turned sharply away from him. "I do not know why you would want to reach me, my lord."

Her words and the coolness of voice made him wince. He knew he had been absent for some time after the passion of their last meeting, and it was clear she was angry with him. Moving forward, he placed his hands on her delicate shoulders and turned her to face him. *She is more beautiful than I remember.*

Richard waited for her to look at him but it soon became clear she would not. Placing a long finger beneath her chin, a chin he found most delectable, he raised her head until he could gaze into her eyes.

"You can inspect my shoulder and my tailor's handiwork as long as you wish, Isobella, but you will eventually have to look at me." His voice was tinged with amusement as he spoke.

Isobella, shaken by the encounters with Exmouth and Lady Brentwood, was completely overwhelmed by Richard's sudden appearance. She hated to speak harshly to him for having deserted her for days with no further communication. But this was why she had sought solace in the garden, and that brought Exmouth back to taunt her. It were his fault that she found herself in this predicament. But what was said to Lady Brentwood, she needed to ask the question of him. But now he had touched her and, if she looked at him, she would be lost.

She had kept her eyes on the delicate stitching on the dark blue coat he wore, but at his words she took a deep breath, raised her eyes, and looked into his. She could feel her heartbeats quicken, and tears prickled at the back of her eyes. But she would not let them fall and would not let him see how upset she was at his behaviour. So asked the question that was hovering on her lips.

"How did you deal with Lady Brentwood? What did you say to her?"

"I informed the Duchess that Exmouth was congratulating you, and that I was standing nearby all the time."

Frowning, she looked at him. "Why would Exmouth be congratulating me?"

"On your betrothal."

"Betrothal!!" she almost shrieked the words.

"Hush, Isobella, or the world will hear."

"To whom am I supposed to be betrothed?" she enquired, lowering her voice.

"Why to me, of course, my love. Sadly though, Exmouth came upon us and heard my offer before you could respond. But not realising this, embraced you and offered his congratulations."

Isobella could do nothing but stare at him as if his mind were lost. "And pray, when am I supposed to respond to this offer?"

"Once the question has been asked properly, my love."

"I am not your love. Not now and not ever," she said, glaring at him.

"Ah, Bella, you are angry with me for being absent for so long. You have missed our meetings by the lake as much as I have. And have longed for the embraces that we shared."

"No I have not," she almost threw the words at him and stamped her foot.

Dangerous Entrapment

He took no notice and slid his hands from her shoulders to the small waist and linked his fingers behind her back, holding her in a loose embrace. She wriggled but was held firm.

"Isobella," he said softly. "I know you are angry with me but if you will hear me out I will explain why I have been absent, and when I have done that we will deal with the matter of the Duchess."

Leading her to the stone seat, he sat alongside and explained about his brother's involvement with Ashton's wife, the events that transpired, and that this was the reason he was obliged to return to London. It was not his wish to disclose his brother's philandering, but needed to be completely honest or he could lose her, and that was something he was not prepared to do. Continuing, he then told how his mother had been made aware of the liaison and the distress this caused her.

"So you see, my love, I was required to tend to my poor mother and persuade her to come back to London. Sadly, the persuasion took longer than I had hoped and I have only just arrived back tonight. I might be tired and weary after the journey but I could not wait a moment longer to see you, so trusting you would be attending, I hastened here only to see you disappear into the garden. I was intending to capture you and kiss you into surrender, but then I saw Exmouth on the path in front of me. Fortunately, I know the gardens here well and was able to circle around and approach from the side. When I saw him put his hands on you I could have killed him. I was about to intervene when the Duchess spoke and knew I needed to think of a reason for the embrace that would satisfy her."

"So you told her you had offered for me, that was the first thought that came to you?"

"No, my darling. It was the only thought that came to me, for that is exactly what I was intending to do. Exmouth simply complicated the matter."

He waited but there was nothing but silence. "What, have you no more questions, Bella?"

She shook her head.

"Well then, the one thing that is left to be done is for me to make the story I told the Duchess true." With that, he slipped off the seat and onto one knee.

"Isobella. My darling Bella, will you please do me the honour of marrying me and becoming the Duchess of Carlisle?"

He waited expectantly as she stared at him, the delectable mouth partly open in seeming shock.

"Bella, please give me an answer before I age and have to account to my tailor for the state of my breeches, which are not meant to be in contact with gravel."

His jesting words broke the silence, and she laughed softly. "Do you really mean it, Richard? Do you really wish to marry me?"

"Of course I do, you silly goose. I have wanted to marry you since I first rescued you from Exmouth's hands. So, do I get the answer I desire or do I have to depart and join a monastery?"

This time she laughed out loud. "Yes," she replied.

"What, yes I have to join a monastery?"

"No. Yes, I will marry you."

He was on his feet the moment the words left her mouth and she was pulled up to him. At last he was able to claim the lips that had been teasing him since first coming upon her. Deepening the kiss, he prized the soft lips apart and tasted the delights of her mouth with his tongue.

She gasped between kisses. "Richard, someone will see us."

"I do not care, my darling. I want the world to know that you are mine. But you are right, my love," he said with a deep sigh. "We need to do this correctly. So I will escort you back to the terrace and you will return into the house alone. I will enter through one of the other doors shortly afterwards. I will stay only long enough to arrange to call upon your cousin tomorrow to seek his agreement to the marriage."

As he spoke the words, he pulled the edges of his coat around himself and held out his arm to her. Together they walked slowly back to the house. He watched as she slipped inside and waited a moment before entering through one of the other open doors.

Isobella longed to turn back and see him. Pausing to speak to Juliette and James, she cast her eyes around and saw Richard in conversation with cousin Charles. Then, without a backward glance, she saw him take his leave of the party. She could scarce believe she had just agreed to become Richard's wife. This was all she had ever hoped for since their meetings at the lake.

Once Richard had left, the evening paled even further for her. She espied Exmouth skulking in the corner with a glass of wine in his hand. Seeing her it was raised in a brief acknowledgement that would not have looked amiss except for the sneering look on his face that made Isobella shiver.

She was glad when they left the party and returned home. Bidding her aunt and cousin goodnight she started to ascend the stairs with Juliette when Charles called out requesting she remain a moment. Telling Juliette that she would see her in the morning she returned to the hallway.

"Carlisle has requested permission to call on me tomorrow at noon. Do you have any knowledge as to the meaning of his call?"

Isobella felt her cheeks flush as she looked at her cousin. "I may have, Charles."

"Thought you might. Carlisle has somewhat of a reputation, Izzie. Has he spoken to you already?"

She nodded, suddenly afraid to speak.

"I know what is said of him, but I have never seen that side to him. He has always been a gentleman when with me." *Well, almost always.*

"Hmm. So what am I to do tomorrow when his lordship calls, Izzie?"

"That choice is yours, cousin."
"Have you said yes to him?" Isobella lowered her eyes.

"I see. So I will have to think very carefully whether Carlisle is the kind of gentleman whom I can entrust your future to. I will have a lot of thinking to do this night."

As he spoke the words, Isobella raised her eyes and looked at him trying to decide if her cousin was jesting, but he looked so serious that she felt tears prickle the back of her eyes. *Was he intending to refuse?*

Watching, Charles offered a small smile, but then saw the brightening of her eyes and knew that he had jested too far. "Go to bed, Isobella."

As she turned to leave, he called softly after her, "Sleep well, cousin, there is no cause to endure a sleepless night."

She turned back, saw the smile on his face and ran to him, and hugged him. "Thank you, Charles."

"Go to bed, cousin, or you will not look your best in the morning."

She ran up the staircase and could not keep the smile from her face as Anna helped her to undress.

Chapter Ten

At exactly noon, Richard Duke of Carlisle knocked on the door of Rothbury house to ask the most important question of his life. That he was actually shaking came as something of a shock to him. Having been shown into the library, he found Charles, Duke of Rothbury, sitting behind a large oak desk. Standing when his visitor entered he rounded the desk and held out his hand in greeting.

"Carlisle," he said. "Do have a seat."

"Rothbury," replied Richard, taking refuge in the indicated chair, hoping his discomfort was not noticeable. *How can one question cause me to be so nervous?* But he already knew the answer. This was the most important question he was ever likely to ask, well apart from the one he had put to Bella last evening. His whole life and their future depended upon the reply.

Charles seated himself in a chair facing his visitor.

Pulling himself together, Richard looked squarely at Charles. "I have a matter of importance that I wish to discuss with you."

"I am intrigued," replied Charles "I cannot think what we would have to discuss."

Richard eyed him with suspicion and suddenly realised from the slightly amused look on his face that Rothbury knew well what he had called to see him about. His nerves disappeared in an instant and he was certain his relief must have showed clearly on his face.

"I suspect, Rothbury, that you already know the matter I wish to discuss with you. But to keep matters on a proper level I will speak the words. I wish to offer for the hand of your cousin Isobella."

"Thought you might. I gather you have already spoken to Isobella and that she is agreeable to the match."

"Yes. I spoke to her last evening before approaching you and arranging to call."

"Well, I suspect that my approval to the match is somewhat un-required but I must speak of certain matters. Isobella is charming as you already know, but she does not have a large dowry."

Richard interrupted. "I do not seek a dowry, Rothbury. I would have her if she were destitute. All I seek is Isobella's hand in marriage. I will make her happy and she will want for nothing. I give you my word on that."

Charles remained quiet before rising and holding out his hand.

"I have no objections to the match, Richard. You have my permission to wed. Before I take you through to Isobella, whom I am sure is waiting with forced patience in the small sitting room, I think you would benefit from a strong drink."

Taking the outstretched hand the two men shook and Charles walked to the small table and poured them both a brandy. Handing one to Richard, he ventured to say, "I think this will settle your nerves."

Taking the glass from him, Richard noted that his hand shook slightly. "Well noticed, Charles. Entering matrimony is not to be taken lightly." He used the same informal address as his host now that they were about to be connected by marriage.

"You will stay to lunch, will you not? My mother and sister will be back shortly and I have no doubt will be eager to hear all. I packed them off to the dressmaker when I knew you were coming, otherwise I would have had to suffer an interrogation all morning. Now we can present them with a completed matter that will no doubt send mama into a spin."

Finishing off his brandy, he stood and Richard did the same, placing the empty glass on the side table.

"Come, I will take you through to an impatient Isobella."

Pacing the floor in the small sitting room, Isobella was almost beside herself. Charles as good as said last night that there would be no opposition to the match but she fretted that he may have had a change of heart. It seemed so long since Richard arrived, and although she had ventured to the door, she did not have the nerve to open it. Now, as she stood by the window, she heard the very same door open and swung round to see her cousin standing in the doorway. She held her breath, and then Charles smiled, and stepped aside to allow Richard to enter the room.

"I will leave you alone for a short while. But mother will be back shortly with Juliette and I cannot promise to keep them away." With that he left the room, closing the door behind him.

Suddenly, Isobella felt shy as she looked at Richard. He was so handsome in his cream breeches topped with black polished boots. The white shirt and grey cravat were neatly worn under a black tailed coat, and her heart skipped a beat at the thought that this was to be her husband, or she hoped he would be.

He waited until Charles closed the door before walking slowly towards her.

"Well, betrothed, have you nothing to say?"

"Charles has agreed?" she asked the question she already knew the answer to.

"Yes. I do believe he took pity on this poor nervous soul."

That made her laugh, and she ran across the room to be caught in his arms and held onto his shoulders as she was swung around. Setting her back down in front of him he caught her lips with his, possessing her and her mouth until she thought she would faint. Wrapping her arms around his waist when she was eventually released she rested her head on his chest.

"I am so happy, Richard."

"And so am I, my love. I cannot wait to make you my wife and show you all the delights that you have been missing. What we shared at the lake was only a taste of what we will share. In the interim I am to face your family at lunch and after that I would ask that you accompany me to Carlisle House so that we can inform my mother of our betrothal."

They were wrapped in each other's arms on the sofa when they heard the shriek from outside, and then the door burst open and Juliette flew into the room, followed closely by her mother.

"Izzie, Izzie is it true. Are you and Carlisle really to wed?"

Richard and Isobella had jumped apart at the noise from the hall. And now she found herself wrapped in her cousin's arms and then her aunt's, and given little time to reply to their questions. It was Richard who spoke.

"Lady Rothbury," he said, bowing low over her hand, "I do hope that our news is welcome to you and you are not distressed by my stealing your niece away from you?"

"Oh, Lord Carlisle, not in the least. I could not imagine a finer match for my niece. Oh what am I to do, two weddings to arrange. When do you plan to wed, Isobella?"

"I do not know, aunt. We have not yet discussed a date." She looked at Richard as she spoke.

"I do not want to unduly pressure you, Lady Rothbury, but I would prefer the marriage to take place as soon as decently possible. I have waited long enough to find someone I wish to spend my days with, and now I want nothing more than Isobella by my side without delay."

Words spoke softly but to Isobella's ears they conveyed his love for her clearly. She could not wait to be his wife but was conscious of the pressure this would place upon her aunt. Juliette's wedding was less than nine weeks away and it would be hard indeed to arrange a further wedding before then.

As they ate lunch the talk was of how soon Isobella's wedding could take place. The formal announcement was to be placed in the London Gazette the following day and it was finally agreed that the wedding would take place four weeks before Juliette's. Realising that the Rothburys were going to be exceedingly busy Richard spoke to Isobella's aunt.

"I recognise that this will place a large burden upon your shoulders, Lady Rothbury, and perhaps I could offer my mother's assistance in the organisation. Having been blessed with only sons she has always longed for a daughter. Isobella will more than fulfil that dream, but if she could assist in the arrangements for the wedding in any small way, I am certain she would be deeply honoured."

"That sounds an excellent idea, Richard. If I may call you that, now that you are almost family. Your mother's assistance would be of considerable help and perhaps I could call upon her shortly to discuss matters?"

"I am certain my mother would be delighted to receive you. At the moment, however, she is in total ignorance of what has happened, so I must beg you to allow me steal Isobella away after lunch so we may appraise her of the good news."

As they drove away from Rothbury House, Isobella's heart was thumping. She was about to meet her future mother-in-law who, at present, was unaware of her existence, or that her son was about to be wed.

"What if she does not like me, Richard?"

"Then we shall pack her off to the country."

"Richard, you cannot do that," she said in horror. Then looking at his face realised he was jesting.

"Oh, Bella, my mother will love you. She has always desired a daughter and you will be a perfect daughter for her."

"Oh, so you are marrying me to be a daughter for your mother, sir"

She did not get the chance to say anything further as he moved quickly forward, pressing his lips to hers. As he did, he picked up her hand and placed it against the front of his breeches. He heard the gasp when she felt the hardness of him.

"Does that feel like I am marrying to provide my mother with a daughter, my love?"

"No..." she gasped, "I was but jesting with you as you were with me."

"I know, my love, but I need little opportunity to let you see how you affect me, or how much I love you. So for the rest of the journey I will remain seated opposite to you and compose myself."

Lady Carlisle appeared surprised when the footman announced her son and Lady Isobella Rothbury into the sitting room. Turning from her needlework, she watched as Isobella walked into the room followed closely by Richard. She was about to rise when her son stopped her.

"Mama, I think it would be best if you remain seated. I have some news for you and have brought someone to meet you...someone very special to me. Could I present Lady Isobella Rothbury who has done me the greatest honour of agreeing to become my wife." He took hold of Isobella's hand as he spoke.

Isobella thought her future mother-in-law was going to faint as she sank back in the seat seemingly at a loss for words. Turning to Richard, she looked at him with some concern as he continued to look at his mother with a glimpse of humour on his face.

"Mother, have you nothing to say?"

Recovering her composure and speech, Lady Carlisle rose and walked towards the couple.

"Richard, you should know better than to spring such delightful news on me without warning," she said as she reached the couple.

She hugged her son and then turned to Isobella who dropped into a deep curtsey.

"Come, child, no need for formalities." She reached out and kissed Isobella on both cheeks as she rose.

Having managed to present a reasonable curtsey without falling on her face due to her shaking legs, the spoken words were a relief. The Duchess's silence had concerned her but the greeting when it came was most welcome.

Seated on the sofa alongside Richard, she was thankful of his hand holding hers. While his mother rang the bell for refreshments, he turned and placed a swift kiss on her lips.

"Told you mother would love you."

They spent the rest of the afternoon discussing the assistance the Duchess could bring to the marriage preparations. That she was delighted to be asked to assist was evident, as she told Isobella that she always envied those mothers preparing for their daughters weddings knowing that she would never have that experience.

"Oh I have two fine sons, both of whom have managed to avoid marriage, so I was beginning to believe that I would die without seeing either of my sons married, and Richard with an heir."

Her words brought a blush to Isobella's cheeks as she remembered the way she aroused her betrothed. She had no doubt if it were left to him his mother would be seeing a first grandchild before the year was out. The thought of having his child made her breathing unsteady, and she took a deep breath to take control. Turning, she saw his eyes watching, and there was a wicked smile on his face that made her blush even more.

His voice teased as he whispered, "You will make a wonderful mother, Bella. And I shall take the greatest delight in helping to create our child."

Dangerous Entrapment

Isobella slapped his hand and flashed green eyes in warning to him. Looking across at his mother she was relieved to see she was engrossed in one of the latest Ladies Brochures looking for an article relative to the wedding preparations. He laughed softly and raised her hand to his lips.

Travelling back home in the Carlisle coach, her head was spinning with ideas put forward by her future mother-in-law. She hoped that there would not be a clash of ideas when the Duchess and Aunt Eleanor came together. Pulling up outside the house Richard helped her out of the carriage and, as befitting of his new status in her life, kissed her gently on the cheek, trailing his lips across hers as he withdrew.

"Until tomorrow, my love. I will call shortly before noon and we can go shopping together."

"Shopping?"

"Why yes. We are to be formally announced tomorrow and in the evening we are both to attend the Granton's Ball, and I have no intention of facing our peers without my ring upon your finger. So we shall visit the jewellery store and see if anything catches your eye. I could give you one of the Carlisle rings but I would much prefer for you to have something of your own choosing."

"Oh, I had not thought about a ring."

"Well think upon it this night, my darling, and decide what you want, sapphires diamonds rubies or emeralds. They are all there for your choosing." He escorted her to the door, and with a sweeping bow left as the door swung open and she went inside.

Entering the carriage, he instructed the driver to proceed to Brentwood House. There was a promise to keep and was certain that his personal deliverance of the news would be more than enough to ensure the Duchess's silence on what she had seen.

Chapter Eleven

The following morning, the Carlisle coach pulled up shortly before noon. Isobella was ready and waiting. If truth be known she had been up shortly after dawn, throwing open the closet doors and trying to decide what to wear. Finally deciding, with the help of Anna, to wear a dark green velvet day dress with a matching jacket. Her hair was pinned loosely up in soft curls and held in place with small green combs, and a small bonnet finished her attire. Pulling on dark green silk gloves, she took Richards hand as he assisted her inside the carriage.

Once the carriage pulled away, she was swept into his arms. She sighed as his lips caressed hers whilst his tongue teased until her lips opened, allowing him to invade the warmth of her mouth. Isobella felt as though the very soul was being pulled from her body. She clung to his shoulders and was thankful that the curtains were drawn across the windows. What those outside would make of such a passionate display she could only imagine?

As he teased the inside of her mouth, she longed to be back at the lake and with his body atop of her own. She wanted to feel the hardness of him but she did not dare touch him, not here, not in the middle of the day. But the thought was there alongside the thought of his child within her. All of these things would shortly be hers, she told herself, and the next few weeks would probably be the longest time she had ever known. His lips and hands only left her as the carriage came to a stop. Moving back in his seat he tucked a stray curl back from her face.

"My darling Bella, you look as if you have just tumbled out of bed with your lover, and as long as that lover is me I am not complaining."

She put both hands up to her cheeks, "Oh I do not, do I?"

He pulled the hands away and kissed her fingertips. "No, my sweet. Only I know that is what you have been doing. You look as enchanting as always."

Rapping on the roof, he waited while the footman opened the door and climbed out. Turning, he held out his hand and watched as she put one dainty foot on the step and then on the pavement. *Such perfect ankles*, was his thought, *and legs to match*. He knew what was hidden beneath the skirts and how wonderful they looked in breeches.

The smile was still on his face as they entered the most fashionable and expensive jewellery store in London. Richard, having already sent a message ahead to request a private consultation, and Isobella were led directly into one of the back rooms, and served refreshments while the owner brought out a selection of his finest rings.

"What gem do you wish, Isobella. Rubies seem too harsh for you, but the choice is yours and I will abide by your decision."

Looking at the rows of rings, he noticed the confusion in her face, but as time passed he could not fail to see her eyes being drawn to a sapphire, so blue it reminded him of the sea on a summer day. It was a large square cut stone surrounded by two rows of small diamonds. She indicated to the ring and waited, removing her glove while the owner selected it from the tray.

Picking up her choice, Richard looked at it through the owner's glass, and nodded his approval. Taking her left hand, he slipped on the ring and then held it up to take in the full effect.

"Do you like it, Isobella? Is it the ring of your choice or do you wish to see some more?"

She shook her head. "No, this is perfect. But it is too large."

Even before she finished speaking, the shop owner was assuring them that the size could be altered and could be made ready that day if they so wished.

Richard confirmed this was what they wanted. After the required measurements were taken, they left the shop. Walking along the street they encountered many inquisitive looks from acquaintances who either spoke or touched their hats. Isobella wanted to giggle. The news of their betrothal was not yet announced but she knew it would be within the hour when the newssheets were made public.

Escorting his now betrothed back to Rothbury House, she was gently informed that he would present himself at nine that evening to escort her to the Burlington Ball. "Where, my darling, I have no doubt we will be the talk of the town." His words filled her with panic and she told him so, but he simply laughed.

"You will have to get used to it, my love. You have taken an eligible man out of the wedding stakes and I am eternally grateful to you for doing so. But if I could ask one favour of you."

"What is that?"

"That you wear the blue gown tonight." With that, she was kissed on the cheek, and he climbed back into the carriage without waiting for an answer.

At two minutes to nine, the footman opened the door to the Duke of Carlisle and showed him into the small library where Charles Rothbury was waiting. After the formal greeting they enjoyed a small brandy before Richard begged for a moment alone with Isobella before the party left.

Entering into the library, Isobella smiled as Richard walked towards her, took her face in his hands, and embraced her with a long, passionate kiss. She parted her lips in anticipation of his exploration, and was not disappointed. Her new status gave her the bravado to tease his tongue. And if that were not enough she was becoming increasingly aware of his need. She opened her eyes and found him looking at her, but more than that, she saw the flare of passion in his eyes.

Pulling himself together he forced himself to withdraw from the tempting lips and to maintain his hold at arm's length.

"My love, if we continue like this we will never make the ball."

"Perhaps I do not care if we do."

"Oh no. We are going to this ball tonight. This is our first outing together as a couple and nothing is going to ruin this night. And to make everything perfect, my darling, you need this."

He pulled the chosen ring out of his waistcoat pocket, picked up a slightly trembling left hand and slid this onto her ring finger. She sighed. She now knew the reason for the request to wear the blue gown; it set off the ring so perfectly. Once in place, he kissed the ring then placing her hand on his arm walked her to the door.

She was shaking with excitement and nerves by the time they reached Burlington House. That news of their betrothal was common knowledge was clear the moment they stepped through the doors. Isobella had never received so many compliments or congratulations and she was quite worn out by the time they reached the main ballroom.

Richard appeared to take it all in his stride, giving her a conspiratorial wink as they slowly made their way through the crowd. Having reached the edge of the room he picked up her dance card and promptly crossed off every dance.

"Now I can have you all to myself tonight, and delight in the feel of your body in my arms," he added softly.

She tapped him on the arm with her folded fan. "Behave, Richard, or I will free up some of your claimed dances."

He grinned and bowed low over her hand, before sweeping them out onto the dance floor. This was exactly where she wanted to be, held by him in a world far removed from those around, where she could let her thoughts run freely. That she was to be married within a month was something she was still finding hard to believe. So wrapped up in her own thoughts she failed to notice the odd whispered comment about a hastily arranged marriage.

Having delivered his betrothed back to her family home, he sat silently in the coach as it made its way through the streets. The whispered comments had not gone unheeded by him. He had been so intent on making Bella his wife as soon as decently possible, he had not considered the gossip this might arouse. That there should be any stigma attached to Isobella or their marriage was something he would not tolerate, but in this case the matter was within his control. It would mean just having to wait a few required months before planting his seed and his heir inside her. Until then, he would have to remain in control and come outside of her or use a French letter. Something that did not entirely please him as he wished for there to be nothing between them.

At the allotted time, the Carlisle coach pulled up and Richard jumped out, and waited to be admitted to Rothbury House. Tonight he was to escort Isobella to a musical evening. His concerns of the previous night were gone since the means to prevent the gossips had been decided in time. Now all he wanted was Isobella and was hardly able to contain his eagerness as he was shown into the small lounge.

She turned as he entered and gave him a smile that took his breath away. How he had survived all these years, without her by his side, was a question to which there was no answer. Walking quickly across the room he swept her to him and kissed her deeply.

It was only when his tongue teased its way inside her mouth that she found the strength to put her hands up and hold him away. "Richard!! You will undo me if you do not stop," she said, gasping for breath.

Breathing heavily, he stepped back. "Perhaps I would prefer to stay indoors and undo you, than attend tonight's musical."

"Oh!" She was at a loss for words, but then saw the twinkle in his eyes. "You wicked man, how could you say such a thing to me."

"Easily, my love, because it is true, as you will find out on our wedding night." "Enough," said Isobella, blushing.

"Come, my darling, let us leave, while you still can," he said, walking to the door. He held it open as she passed through, taking in the gentle smell of gardenias from her perfume. The remaining weeks to their wedding were going to be the longest he would ever know.

The musical evening was somewhat boring, and an elderly Earl had cornered Richard, and it was clear he was not going to make an early escape. Selecting a glass of wine from the refreshments room, she wandered back out into the main room and then through the open doors onto the terrace. Going carefully down the steps, she walked a short way along the path until she found a bench. Sitting down, she sipped the wine and breathed in the warm scented night air. A crunching on the path warned of someone approaching. She rose to leave but found her way blocked by Exmouth.

"So, my lady, you have ensnared Carlisle. Would you wish me to congratulate you on your betrothal? No, thought not. Well do not get too excited about your forthcoming nuptials."

"What do you mean?" said Isobella, as a cold hand gripped her heart.

"A lot can happen in the next few weeks, things go wrong, people get hurt."

"You would not dare attack the Duke," she said. "He is more than a match for you."

"Who said anything about the Duke, my lady?"

"So you would harm me?" said Isobella, finding some strength in her voice.

"Ah, no, I would not harm you. But I will bed you before your intended can, and I doubt Carlisle will want soiled goods. I will have your virginity, Isobella. It belongs to me and should have been mine. You were to be mine until that evening when I set my eyes upon the woman who turned out to be false. No virgin bride, but a fallen woman who wantonly succumbed to the charms of her music tutor and carried his child. A child that was lost before it was born. So all I ended up with, Isobella, was tarnished goods, not a pure innocent like you.

I will take the greatest pleasure in breaking you in, my lady."

His words were spoken softly and chillingly. Isobella started to tremble. She was alone with him, and needed to return inside. "Let me pass," she said.

"As you wish, my lady...for now."

He stood to one side and Isobella swept by him as quickly as she could, but he trailed his hand down her arm as she did so. A shudder of revulsion went through her, and tears prickled the back of her eyes. Reaching the terrace, she halted and took several deep breaths and a good mouthful of wine. She was about to go back through the doors when Richard came out.

"Here you are, I have been looking everywhere for you, my love."

She put the glass down on a nearby table and turned, pressing her face into his chest.

"Bella, what is wrong? You are shaking, my darling."

She heard the concern in his voice, but knew she could not tell him what had happened. He would call Exmouth out and she did not wish anything to spoil this evening. "I wandered along the path and then I heard a noise that startled me and I took fright." She gave a half laugh as she spoke. She hated the lie, but she hated more the thought of him calling out Exmouth and perhaps being injured, or worse.

"Oh, you silly goose. You should not be out here alone. Come, let us go back inside."

Later that night as she lay in bed, Isobella went over Exmouth's words. That he meant what was said was clear to her. The thought of him capturing her again and forcing himself upon her was enough to make her ill. There was only one thing that she must do, and she knew exactly what that was. All that were needed was to decide when it would be done.

Chapter Twelve

The visit to Carlisle Hall took place three days after the encounter with Exmouth. Richard had persuaded Aunt Eleanor to allow him to take her to the hall so they could discuss any alterations she wished to make before the wedding. As chaperone for each other, cousin Juliette and James were to accompany them.

They arrived shortly before noon and sat in the large drawing room, enjoying the picnic her aunt had provided for them. The house was empty as the servants were in London, and this is exactly what Isobella dared to hope. The only person to greet them was the caretaker, and Richard promptly dismissed him for the day as soon as they arrived.

Pulling her cousin to one side she suggested that, since she and Richard would be some considerable time looking through the rooms, perhaps Juliette and James would wish to enjoy some private time together. She smiled knowingly at her cousin as she made the suggestion.

Ever since the incident in Juliette's bedchamber Isobella was aware of the sexual tension between her cousin and her betrothed and thought perhaps an interlude of uninterrupted time together might resolve the situation. Even though this suggestion was more to benefit herself than her cousin.

"I will keep Richard occupied and no one will bother you, Juliette. Just enjoy some time together, free of chaperones."

The look on her cousin's face was one of amazement, and Isobella was obliged to suppress a smile.

"Do you really mean it, Izzie?"

"Of course I do. I am a betrothed woman as well you know. I may also wish some time alone with my betrothed, and not just to discuss furnishings," she said, with a mischievous smile.

Climbing the staircase to the upstairs rooms, she saw her cousin and James disappear into the small library below. She felt pleased with the progress of the plan so far and was in no doubt that her cousin would enjoy the fruits of her planning. Isobella had long since decided that virginity was a millstone around a woman's neck and something that needed to be disposed of as quickly as possible. The experience with Exmouth had taught her that. His words at their last encounter, that he thought her a prize to be broken in like a filly had filled her equally with fury and fear, and she made a vow then to be rid of it.

Following Richard into what he was describing as the master bedchamber, she immediately noted the stunning view from the windows out across the park. This would be a beautiful room once the décor had been changed. But at this moment any thoughts were not on changing décor, but on changing her own status. Taking a deep breath she turned and closed the door softly behind them, turning the key in the lock as she did, and placed this in the pocket of her dress. Then she walked towards the centre of the room to join her betrothed.

"Well, Bella, do you think this will make a suitable bed chamber for you."

The word "you" struck an unwelcome chord. "I do not require a bedchamber of my own. I have every intention of sharing a bedchamber with my husband," she threw back at him.

He turned from the window and looked at her. She was standing with both hands on her hips and the green eyes were flashing in what...anger, temper, passion...he could not decide. This was another side of her.

Teasing, he replied, "But what if your husband requires a bedchamber of his own."

"Then perhaps my husband had better look for another wife." She was simmering beneath the surface, but was not quite sure with what. Perhaps it was a fear that she would not be able to persuade him to accede to the request she was about to make.

He laughed then and walked towards her. "Oh, Bella, my darling Bella, what am I going to do with you? You know I have the greatest difficulty in keeping my hands off you and the thought of endless nights in the same bed is more than I can bear to think about. But what is worse is the thought of not having you in my bed. So I am more than willing to share your bed every night, but I will keep the small dressing room adjoining for those nights you do not wish to be disturbed."

Taking her courage in both hands, she replied, "I doubt there will be any night when I do not want to be disturbed. I look forward to sharing my bed with you, in fact, since we have a bed available now, we could put this to use and you could seduce me, as we are on our own. I have no doubt that is what James is doing with my cousin." Her words brought him to a halt and she heard him catch his breath, almost making him choke.

He looked at her, but could not tell if she was jesting. "Bella, you do not know what you are saying. I know I have jested before about you being undone, but I was only jesting. I am content, no content is the wrong word for I am not content, but I am willing to wait until we are wed before taking the greatest pleasure in undoing you."

"Yes I know you were jesting, but I am not, and I do know what I am saying. I want rid of this stupid virginity before it causes any more problems. Since we are to be married in three weeks I cannot see any reason to wait," she said, lowering her voice. Looking at him from beneath lowered lashes she allowed her lips to curve into a smile.

"Isobella, you cannot expect a man to perform to order." Even as the words were spoken he knew them to be untrue. He was ready now and this conversation was increasing his readiness. It would take little persuasion on her part for him to take what she was offering. His words were said to gain time and to allow her to retract the offer.

"By perform I presume you mean seduce?"

He sighed. "Yes, I do."

"So you have no wish to seduce me now. You would rather wait a further three weeks and hope Exmouth does not beat you to it?"

"What the devil has Exmouth got to do with it?" he demanded.

"He is intent on denying you a virgin bride, or indeed, a bride at all."

"Bella, you are not making any sense. Has something else happened with Exmouth?" Although his voice was soft there was an undercurrent in his tone.

"Perhaps, but I will not speak of it just yet as it will spoil my mood."

She had been planning this for days, ever since she knew they were coming here. She was well aware of Richard's state of arousal when he was near her, something that both excited and scared her. But, after their last encounter, she was even more scared by the thought that Exmouth was again going to try again to capture her. It was time for her to take matters into her own hands.

Richard stared at her. Had she taken leave of her senses, he wondered, or had she just regained them. He had wanted this for months and had been very unrestrained at times in his attentions to her. But he was of the belief that she would wish to wait.

Did he want to seduce her? Of course he did, but had talked himself into waiting until their wedding night. Now she seemed hell bent on that event taking place now, here in the bedroom they would eventually share as husband and wife.

Even as he watched, she took off her jacket and began to undo the buttons on her outer gown, slowly exposing a swell of bosom. He felt the movement in his breeches and knew that there were two choices, to either stop her now or do as she wished. That Exmouth had something to do with the request was clear, but she was not prepared to speak of it now, and he had no wish to distress her, particularly as she was removing her clothing. To stop her now she would take as a sign of rejection.

He knew she was waiting to see what reaction she got to the undoing of her buttons and clearly was annoyed when he made no move or comment. Opening the last button she lowered the gown and stepped out, standing before him in her petticoat. Before he could say anything she quickly disposed of the petticoat, sending it to the ground alongside the gown.

"Well, are we going to get this over with or not?" she put the question to him direct.

He moved at the words. "Bella, my love, this is not what you want."

"Oh but it is, Richard. I am so sick of my virginity being bandied about like a prize to be won or lost. I want to decide where and when I change from being a maiden to being a woman...and with whom," she added coyly, looking at him from beneath her lashes.

He ran a hand through his hair. This was the last thing he expected today. Oh, he expected kissing and more than a little touching, but full seduction had not been in his plans. He was standing a few feet away from her and still arguing with himself as to whether to concede defeat and give her what she wanted. No, what they both wanted. His body was telling him to do as she wished whilst his shaft was straining against his breeches.

He watched, mesmerised as she nervously undid the ties of her corset, dropping this at her feet. She was now standing before him brazenly in stockings and chemise. And he had never seen anything more delightful. But this was too much for him, and he covered the remaining distance, pulling her into his arms. His lips took hers and he felt her soft mouth open as his tongue sought hers.

"Bella, Bella, you are driving me insane," he whispered against her mouth.

She made no reply but felt a hand move between them, and then she touched him, feeling his hardness. He gasped loudly at the action and pulled back, looking at her as if for the first time. Her eyes were glistening, and there was a wildness in them he had only glimpsed before. Her breath was coming in short gasps. He was finally seeing the passion he knew was beneath surface and knew he was lost, and about to give her what she desired.

"I need to lock the door," he said, his breathing becoming heavier.

"'Tis already done. The key is in my pocket," she said, staying his move to the door.

"So, my lady, you appear to have this well planned, and I am simply a pawn in your game?"

"It is no game, and you are certainly no pawn."

"I know it is not a game, Bella. What is about to happen is serious and hopefully will be exceedingly enjoyable for both of us."

Pulling her after him, they moved to the four-poster bed that dominated the room. Throwing back the cotton sheet covering, he then pulled down the covers, exposing the clean linen beneath. Turning, he took her face in his hands.

"Are you sure this is what you wish.

"More than anything," she answered, placing her hands over his.

He did not need to be told again. Turning her, the chemise was quickly undone and lifted over her head, allowing her breasts to fall free from the confines of the garment. Still with her back to him, he rolled down the stockings and then lifted the delicate feet one at a time as the shoes were removed, then her stockings. Finally, he removed the pins from her hair and let it run through his fingers as it fell about her naked shoulders.

His hands were now doing what his eyes had been doing these past weeks. He did not dare to turn her around until he was ready. Pulling off his jacket and shirt they were thrown onto the floor. His boots and breaches followed, together with the rest of his clothes.

Richard stood at the side of the bed and put his arms around her, gently removing the trembling hands from her chest. Moving his fingers down to where he knew the perfectly formed breasts were, he felt the quiver as they reached the nipples, and began gently rolling them between his fingers. As they hardened so did he, but this was a journey to be taken slowly and gently. He had seduced women before but this was different, this was his future wife, his duchess, and if this deed were to be done then he needed to make the transition as painless as possible for her.

Moving his head forward, he buried his face in the loosened tresses, smelling the gentle scent of roses on her skin. His senses were drugged by the smell and feel of her. Drawing the soft body back against his, he felt the quiver as she came into contact with his hard shaft. He bent his head and started to kiss and nibble gently at the creamy shoulders and neck. Moving his lips, his tongue flicked around the outer edge of one delicate ear, hearing her moan softly at his touch.

Holding one arm across her breasts, the other moved down below her stomach, to the place where his future heir would one day be carried. Down through the soft hair to the spot between her legs that he knew would bring the greatest pleasure. She cried out when his fingers touched and her body arched. Moving his hand from her breasts to beneath soft thighs he lifted her, then turned and placed her on the bed.

Her cheeks were flushed a deep pink and her breath was coming in short gasps. Lying alongside her, his eyes swept over her naked body. *God, she is adorable and she is mine,* he thought, enjoying a moment of pure indulgence. Leaning across, he put his lips to one perfectly formed breast and gently teased the nipple as she groaned in pleasure. His left hand moved and once again found the sweet spot of desire between her legs. This time he saw her bite down on the cry that threatened to escape but the green eyes flared with the passion he knew she had.

"Can you do it now, Richard?" she asked between gasps of air.

"No, my darling. Not yet. I need you to be ready so that it will not be so painful."

"What do you mean, ready?"

Her words caused him to question his own actions. She was naive...how could he do this to her? But looking down at the expectant face, he wondered how he could deny her.

"I need you to be wet. Very wet inside so I do not hurt you when I enter."

"How will that happen?"

He smiled at her innocence. "Leave me to worry about that. You just lay back, my love, and enjoy the experience. It is a few weeks earlier than planned but I will be as gentle as I can."

He moved his lips to hers, then to a breast, and trailed a path down across the flat stomach to her groin. He parted the slender legs, and sitting between them raised her derriere and kissed her in what he knew to be the most pleasurable spot.

Her body almost jerked out of his hands.

"Richard..." The word barely a gasp.

He smiled. Then suckled and stroked her with his tongue, long leisurely strokes that caused her to moan. When she was writhing under his hands he thrust his tongue inside, hearing the gasp of pleasure from her lips.

The waiting had been agony. Exposed by her nakedness, she had first covered herself with her hands. His clothing being thrown to the ground told her she had her wish. Not knowing how this was to proceed, she had allowed him to take the initiative. She shivered not from cold but from anticipation. All her life had been moving to this one moment.

The feel of his hands on her body was exquisite. When he touched her, the tightness in her breasts brought both pain and pleasure, and when she was moved against his body, the shock of his hard shaft against the small of her back almost caused a re-think of this daring plan. But then he teased her, found the spot between her legs, the one she had herself discovered whilst in the bath, and she was again lost in the sheer pleasure of his hands and lips.

Isobella thought she was going to faint as feelings she had never known before raged through her body. That she was naked in bed with a man who was not yet her husband was something she thought she would never do. But the feelings that were being aroused were breathtaking. Just when she thought she could take no more his tongue entered her and she was swept into another world. Her body went into convulsions and she felt as though a volcano was erupting inside her. It was as if she were falling from a great height and then she fell back down to earth with a shattering cry and lay gasping for breath.

"That did not hurt," she managed to get out between breaths.

"That is because you are still a virgin, my love."

He saw the flash of anger in her eyes and quickly moved his body to lay aside of her. Leaning across, he placed a kiss on the now pouting lips, and as he withdrew, looked into the sparking eyes. "I needed you to come."

He saw the look of puzzlement on her face. "Needed you to come to fulfilment so you would moisten yourself from inside. Now I will take what you have so beautifully offered to me, my love.

Unless you have changed your mind?" She shook her head and smiled at him. All signs of anger gone.

He eased himself up, and running a hand down her body, poised at her entrance, feeling the wetness. He looked deep into her eyes.

"I love you, Bella, and I pray that I will not hurt you too much."

As he said the words he pushed a finger gently into her, feeling the untried body stiffen as he did. He smiled, placed his lips to hers and slowly and seductively teased her tongue with his, while all the while his finger pushed slowly inside her, and then withdrew to allow her body time to accept the intruder. He felt the cover of her virginity and knew he needed to push through this.

Withdrawing slightly, a second finger were eased inside and, at the same time, he moved his head and took one small perfect breast in his mouth, gently suckling the nipple. She gasped with pleasure and lifted her body to him. At that moment, he thrust quickly forward, spreading his fingers as he did, breaking through the veil of her maidenhood and making her his own. There was a short cry of pain that he took from her lips with his own.

He felt the tears, and moving from the soft lips, kissed her eyes and licked away the wetness. For once he did not know what to do.

He raised himself up on his elbow and looked down at the tear-filled eyes.

"Oh, my darling, I am sorry it hurt. I did all that I could to make it easier but the veil needed to be broken. I knew it would be painful but I promise it will never hurt again and all you will feel from now on is pleasure."

He was not used to making speeches after making love to a woman. Often there was little to say, but then he had never made love to his future wife before.

"I need to withdraw my hand, my darling, and it may hurt."

"Why do you have to withdraw?"

"Because I have taken what you wanted me to take," he said, easing out as gently as he could.

"Ah yes. But have you seduced me like you would seduce other women? You have not been inside me with your body."

He gave a wry smile. "No. I have not seduced you properly. I thought your wish was to dispose of your virginity."

"Yes, but I also said I wanted you to seduce me. You say it will not hurt the next time so prove it to me."

"Bella, you do not know what you are asking of me."

"I do. I am asking you to sed...no, to make love to me." As she spoke she turned her body to him and slowly moved a leg across his.

Her breasts pressing into his chest, legs wrapped around his bare skin was doing little to soften his desire. He was so hard and longed to be buried inside her. It would take very little to bring her back to the point of desire. But could he... should he. She was tormenting him and even as that thought went through his mind she moved against him, pressing herself into him and it was his turn to gasp.

Her lips came against his own and it was enough to send him back into the arms of seduction. If this were what she wanted then how could he deny her? Teasing her breasts with his tongue and his teeth, she was soon brought back to the height of passion. He laid her back on the bed. Covering her with his body, he moved his hand down between them and placed the tip of his shaft at her entrance.

"This may hurt a bit, my love, for I am bigger than my fingers." Then he started to push slowly inside her, taking care to restrain his need. With the barrier gone, he was able to explore the depths of her body.

He took the journey slowly, feeling her body resist at the large intrusion. "Relax, my love, let your body accustom itself to me." As he spoke, his weight was taken on one side as a hand slipped between them to cup her. His thumb teased over the small nub that would give her pleasure, caressing it as his lips moved to her breast. He felt her body opening to him, and a fraction at a time allowed him to edge nearer and nearer to his goal. He wanted to be fully encased inside before starting the rhythmic courtship that would bring her to him again. Finally, he reached his desired objective, and moving above her, supported himself on his hands and started the journey that would bind them together as one.

He felt her body tremble, gripping him eagerly, seeking more of him, and knew that she was building for fulfilment. He pushed deep into her keeping up the rhythm until she came flowing around him seconds before he quickly withdrew and turned, spurting his seed into the cotton cover at the foot of the bed.

He turned quickly back and gathered her into his arms, holding her until she lay still. The joy he felt at being joined with her had almost swept him away giving barely enough time to withdraw. To put her with child before they were wed was not intended.

"You were right," Isobella said. "It did not hurt that time, well perhaps a bit at first, but I am glad that the first time is now gone."

Still puzzled at the insistence for this seduction to take place, he ventured to ask the question.

"Why today, my love. Why could this not wait? Not that I am protesting. I cannot think of a more wonderful way to spend the afternoon than in bed with you, and once we are married we shall do so often."

As he spoke, his fingers gently pushed the stray curls back from her forehead, and could not fail to see the still faint mark from where her head was struck. He clenched his lips together at the thought of what could have happened had he not arrived in time. Exmouth would have taken her, not gently as had just taken place, but he would have ripped into the tender body and ruined her forever. Bending his head, he placed his lips on the mark and waited for her reply.

She giggled and then bit her lips together. Curled up in his arms, and wrapped in a cover, she told him of the encounter with Exmouth at the musical some three nights past.

"He scared me, Richard. Really scared me and I knew that he would stop at nothing to get what he wanted. I dared not tell you for fear you would call him out."

"What was said that frightened you so much that you could not tell me?" He asked the question quietly not wanting to betray his anger that

Exmouth had dared to approach her again, and at a time when she was betrothed to another.

"He said he would have me. Would take the virgin that he had expected when he were married."

"What! You mean that sweet little innocent he wed was not so innocent after all?"

She shook her head. "It would seem not. It would appear the young lady was involved in a liaison with a music tutor and ended up with child. But the child were lost, and that is why they were delayed in Italy. To give her time to recover and regain her strength."

"And of course Exmouth did not know this until they were married." He could have felt sorry for the chap in other circumstances, but his previous behaviour was inexcusable, and now it would appear he was again threatening Bella.

"No. He said he found out on their wedding night. He told me all his life he had waited for his virgin wife and when he got her she was tarnished. So said he was going to take the virgin that he should have had. The one he should not have let go. Me."

Her voice broke as she said the last words. Richard held her close and waited until she were able to continue, but inside he was seething with rage.

"He said there was no way you were going to have what was his. That there were some weeks to our wedding and anything could happen. Then when taking his leave his words were quite menacing, told me that he would have me. That having captured me once, could do so again, but this time would make certain there was nothing you could do to stop him.

"He was different that night and it was frightening. That was when I decided that I wanted to get rid of my virginity as soon as I could, and certainly before our wedding night. I could not stand the thought of spending the next weeks worrying as to whether he was waiting around the next corner. I want to enjoy the time before our wedding and not be worrying as to whether I will actually get there."

Richard pondered on what she had just told him. He was furious but as long as she was in his arms she was safe. His gut instinct was to call Exmouth out but that would need an explanation, something that would be difficult to give without disclosing what had happened previously.

Kissing Bella's hair, he asked, "So how is he going to know that what he so desperately wants is no longer available?"

"I shall tell him," she announced clearly. "I will tell him that the prize is gone and he can go and find another virgin for his game."

Richard could not help but laugh at the determination in her voice. "Oh, my love, I do not know whether to hate Exmouth, feel sorry for him, or thank him. One thing I do know is that I am angry, very angry that he frightened you so much that you felt the need to give yourself before you wanted to."

"I have wanted to give myself to you for a long time, my love. I thought you might have realised that during our meetings at the lake. I was certainly aware of your desires."

"Yes, my darling, I do have desires, and if we do not arise from this bed I may just show you again how much I desire you."

Isobella caught her breath at his words. "Perhaps I do not wish to rise; perhaps I wish to experience again the delights you bring to me." She trailed a finger down his chest as she spoke, teasing the dark hair and, moving forward, placed a kiss where her finger had been.

He caught the hand in his. "No, Bella. We have guests downstairs."

"Who are most likely doing exactly the same as us, except they do not have the luxury of a bed."

"And what makes you believe your cousin would allow that, or indeed that

Preston would take such a liberty?"

She laughed and proceeded to tell him of what she saw in the bedchamber. He listened with growing admiration for Preston, whom he previously thought a bit slow in that department.

"Well, it would appear that you are probably right about what is taking place downstairs. And in that case I would hate to disturb the lovers, particularly when I have such a wonderful bed companion."

He could not stop the smile on his face from widening as he lowered the cover and let himself enjoy the pleasure she gave to him. This time, he was ready to withdraw, and watched as his seed poured onto the cotton sheet and waited for the convulsions in his own body to cease.

Held in his arms he delighted in telling her that he would be counting the days to their wedding.

"You have given me a taste of heaven, my darling, and I cannot wait to be with you again. Soon I will not withdraw. I will stay inside you as we come together and, god willing, you will be carrying our child before the year is out. But now I fear we need to rise and go back to your cousin, looking as though all we have been doing is discussing décor."

As they rose from the bed, she asked, "Did I please you? Were you satisfied with my body?"

He smiled at the words and took the small hands in his own, his eyes roving over her still naked body. "How could you not please me, my love? The glimpse I had many weeks ago was a tantalising memory that has now been fully awakened."

She gasped. "What do you mean the glimpse you saw?"

Immediately he realised his mouth had run away with his thoughts and was now going to have to confess seeing her uncovered at Exmouth's.

"I did not venture to say anything before, and I would not have done so until after we were wed, had my memory not escaped through my lips without thought. The night you were kidnapped, Exmouth had undone your gown and you were exposed. Oh, he did not see anything. I pulled him off and struck him before he could. But it was I who covered you and fastened your gown before carrying you out."

"But I thought Juliette was with you, and that she attended to me."

"I know you did, my love. But you were so distressed by what had taken place

I did not wish to add to it, so let you believe it was your cousin."

Isobella looked at him. "So you have seen my breasts before today?"

He nodded, a smile creeping across his face. "Delightful they were. Even in the dreadful circumstances under which I saw them I felt a strong desire to kiss them. Had Exmouth not been there, I may have given in to that desire, but my need to protect you was stronger."

Isobella tapped a naked foot on the floor. "So it was my breasts that made you offer for me?"

Richard could see where this conversation was going and had no intention of having this delightful encounter tarnished in any way. "No, it was not your breasts, Isobella. It was you, all of you. Your laugh, your smile, the way you speak and walk. Your hair, the way it falls onto your shoulders, I have a need to bury myself in it. But above all, the way you make me feel, and now, the way you make love with me. Your breasts, my love, are only part of you, but a quite delightful part," he said, bending and kissing each pink tip.

Isobella shivered at his touch and her body swayed into his until she was pressed against him. "I think I could stay here forever," she said.

"I wish we could, Bella, but we would get exceedingly cold since there is no fire, and our guests would eventually come looking for us. What they would think of finding us coupled together in bed does not warrant thinking about. So we must return to our position as hosts and leave the further delights of the bedroom for our wedding night."

They talked quite loudly as they walked back down the staircase, discussing the various rooms they had hastily looked into before coming down.

Juliette and James appeared from the small library, and Isobella bit back a smile as she saw her cousin's flushed face. Not that she imagined her own would look much paler.

Once delivered safely back at Rothbury Place, the cousins escaped upstairs and sat on Isobella's bed discussing the day's events. "Oh, Izzie, thank you for today."

"What do you mean? Thank you for what?" asked Isobella innocently, knowing full well what her cousin meant.

"You know. The time you let James and I spend together. It was...well, let us say exciting."

"Juliette, I hope you are not suggesting that I allowed anything improper to take place."

Her cousin laughed. "Oh come now, Izzie, you and Richard were a very long while upstairs and you looked somewhat flushed when you came back down."

"I looked no more flushed than you, cousin."

"So I can take it that we both got what we wanted today. You are lucky, Izzie, to be getting married in three weeks. James and I have to wait a further four weeks after that and it just seems so far away."

"It will soon be here, and by then I will be an old married woman."

And spending every night in my husband's arms, she thought as feelings of desire spread through her body. Today she had discovered a passion that had long been kept confined. A passion that she would soon share each night with her husband. She sighed at the thought.

Chapter Thirteen

It was some three nights later that she saw Exmouth at the ball at Hartwell House. She had just finished dancing with Richard and he was escorting her to the refreshments when she saw him standing at the edge of the ballroom. Drawing Richard's attention to his presence, she informed him that she was intending to speak to him now and to allow a few minutes before following her. He was reluctant to allow her to approach him alone but she was insistent.

"No, I need to do this on my own, to let him know I am no longer afraid of his threats. But I would ask that you be nearby."

Securing his promise that he would follow very shortly she could not fail to see his fists clench as she left his side to walk towards her target.

Exmouth saw her coming and his smile was almost a leer when she approached. Having requested a moment to speak in private, she followed him into a nearby alcove.

"I knew you would see sense, Isobella, and that you would come to me. I can give you more than Carlisle."

"I have not come to you, as you mistakenly believe. I simply came to inform you that the prize you sought from me is no longer available. It is lost. Given freely to another."

As she spoke the words she saw his face turn almost purple with rage.

"You lie, madam. You would not do such a thing out of wedlock." He almost spat the words at her.

She was about to answer when a masculine voice came from behind.

"It seems you do not know her ladyship as well as you thought, Exmouth. I can assure you that she is not lying. The prize has been given, and if I may say the recipient certainly has no complaints."

At that, he lifted Isobella's hand and kissed it before placing his lips on hers, leaving Exmouth in no doubt that Isobella was speaking the truth.

"I will bid you good night, Exmouth. If I hear of any more threats to my betrothed I will call you out and I will not miss. Go home to your wife. If your wife cannot satisfy you then get yourself a mistress, but do not approach me, or any member of my family again. Do you understand?"

Isobella had never heard Richard speak so coldly, and she watched as Exmouth fairly crumpled under his glare. A nod of the head showed the words were heard before he hurried past them and disappeared.

Isobella slumped against Richard's chest. "Oh, I am so thankful that is over and that you were here."

"I will always be here. And talking about here, this is a very discreet area, my love. I might just taste a morsel of your soft skin before we go back." She laughed softly as his lips sought the swell of her bosom, and gasped as his fingers eased the material down, giving his mouth access to the tip of a breast.

"Richard, we cannot...not here. What if someone comes?" she gasped.

"The only person likely to come, my darling, is me, and for that reason alone I will forego any more pleasure and escort you back to the refreshment room."

As he spoke, the material was lifted back into place, and she did not miss his gesture as he pulled his coat straight to cover the evidence of his own arousal. Holding out his arm to her, they walked discreetly back into the crowd nodding to acquaintances as they walked by.

Enjoying the attention lavished on them for the rest of the evening, Isobella went to bed happier than she had been in a long time. The only thing that would have made her even more happy was if Richard were sharing the bed with her.

Since their encounter at Carlisle Hall she had been having such wanton thoughts and could not wait for their wedding day, or more precisely, their wedding night.

As Isobella prepared for bed, Richard was at his Club. He did not intend allowing Exmouth to escape his punishment for kidnapping Isobella; nor his words to her tonight, or earlier. He had been pushed to his limits hearing what were said to her, his anger had been festering for days. He knew it were not possible to call Exmouth out without reasonable cause, and even then, the fact that he had once shown an interest in Isobella may make his actions suspect. The last thing he wanted was any hint of scandal attaching to either of them. So he needed an accomplice, someone who would be willing to help and to whom he needed to give no explanation.

Walking into the inner room the object of his quest was quickly espied and, after ordering a glass of wine, he sat down opposite Preston.

"Carlisle," said James, surprised at his sudden appearance.

"Preston," he replied, inclining his head. "I have need of your assistance in a delicate matter."

"I am intrigued," said James leaning forward. "If I can assist, I will. After all, we are soon to be related by marriage."

"Quite, and it is in relation to Isobella that I need your help." Pausing as a glass of wine was put in front on him, he waited. Once the servant left, he lowered his voice and continued. "Exmouth believes he has got away with kidnapping Isobella, and despite our betrothal, has tried to proposition her again this night. I need to call him out, but I cannot do it for fear of causing gossip because of his previous connection with Isobella."

"How can I be of help?" asked James.

"I need you to call him out." He saw him pale at the suggestion, and quickly continued, "Oh, do not worry, you will not have to face him. You will have an unfortunate accident and, as your second, I will step in and take your place."

James stared at Richard. "You cannot be serious?"

"Oh, I most certainly am. A quick shot to the shoulder will keep him out of the way for a few weeks."

"How do you know he will choose pistols?"

"He is useless with the sword so will choose pistols."

Nodding his head, he said, "I will do as you ask. If it had been Juliette, I would have done the same thing. When do you wish this plot to begin?"

"As soon as possible, in fact now would be a good time as Exmouth is in the bar, and we can get this done with before noon tomorrow."

"How am I supposed to call him out?"

"I am considering that," replied Richard, with a frown. Then, seeing the object of his thoughts starting to walk towards the inner room, jumped up quickly saying, "Follow me and take your opportunity."

Moving quickly towards the doorway, Richard confronted Exmouth as he was about to enter. Smiling, he murmured, "We meet again, sir, and as before, I am here before you."

He watched as Exmouth turned red and then moved back to allow him to pass.

As he did, turned and whispered, "Watch your back, sir."

Exmouth paled at the words and then turned sharply to pass through the doorway, but crashed straight into James, who was exiting behind Richard.

"Good god, sir," he exclaimed, looking at the wine stain quickly spreading across his coat. "Are you in your cups or simply bad mannered." Blustering, Exmouth replied, "I am neither, sir, the fault was yours."

"Are you calling me a liar, sir?" he responded.

"Well the fault was not mine," replied Exmouth, aware of the heads that were now turned in their direction.

"So you are calling me a liar, sir. Well, I will see you with your second and we can settle this like gentlemen," said James, lifting up his glove and slapping him across the face with it.

Listening to the exchange, Richard quickly stepped back and offered himself as James's second. One of Exmouth's companions rushed forward and offered as his second, and before he knew what was happening Exmouth found himself meeting the young Earl at an hour after dawn the following morning at a specified field on the outskirts of the city. There was a murmur going around the room about the duel and before matters could be undone Richard caught James by the arm and suggested they leave.

Once outside, James began to appreciate exactly what had been agreed to. "Hell, Carlisle, I hope you know where you are going with this. And exactly how am I supposed to be injured? I cannot sustain a serious injury, and neither can you. We are both to be wed soon. If the ladies find out about this we will both be in hot water."

"I am aware of that, but do not fear, I have it all worked out. I would suggest that you spend the night at Carlisle House so as to avoid any callers at your residence. If you are so minded to take up the offer of a bed."

"Yes, I think that would be an excellent idea. My family are at home and I would wish to avoid any awkward questions, or indeed any necessary lies."

"Good, then that is agreed. I will get one of my servants to call at your home and collect any items you require. In the meantime, we shall enjoy a good stiff brandy and then a restful sleep."

Waking the following morning, it took James a few minutes to realise where he was and the reason why. He groaned at the thought of what was to come. Rising from the bed, he moved to the washstand, then quickly dressed in the clothes sent by his manservant. Black breeches and black riding boots, with a white shirt and grey waistcoat, to finish off his attire. Picking up the dark grey fitted coat he pulled this on and glanced at his reflection in the long mirror. Was this the look of a man about to take part in a duel? He did not know, had never fought a duel before, and hopefully was not about to do so now.

Proceeding downstairs, he found Richard in the dining room. "Morning, James," said Richard cheerfully. "Hope you slept well?"

"Eventually," he replied. "Are you sure this is going to work, Richard?" He followed his host's choice of Christian name.

"Better, or you and I will be in trouble, and not only with the ladies if it does not," he answered with a grin.

"How can you be so calm?" asked the younger man.

"Only way to be. If I start worrying about it no purpose will be served, and I intend to make Exmouth pay for what he has done to Isobella."

Riding out together it took an hour to reach their destination. It was just showing light when they dismounted. There was no sign of Exmouth.

"What if Exmouth does not show?" enquired James.

"He will. He will not dare fail to show."

Richard had just finished speaking when they heard the approaching horses. "Told you he would show."

"Fine, so he is here, but how am I supposed to get out of this duel?"

"Leave that to me," said Richard, striding towards Exmouth and his second.

Reaching the pair, he nodded briefly to Exmouth. "Since Exmouth is the challenged party the choice of weapon is his," he said calmly. As expected Exmouth's second indicated that pistols were the choice. "One shot each then reload and fire again until there is first blood to the victor." He could have laughed at the fear in Exmouth's eyes but kept his lips firmly closed. Now all that were needed was to extricate James.

Waiting while Exmouth's second inspected the pistols to ensure they were both the same they were then carefully loaded. As this were being done James could be seen pacing up and down close to their horses.

"My lord is impatient to get this over with, so could I suggest that we proceed with all haste."

"Agreed, Carlisle," said Exmouth's second. "The pistols are in order."

Waiting until Exmouth had taken his choice of pistol, Richard took the remaining one of the matching pair out of the box, turned and walked back towards James. Reaching him he suggested that his coat were placed over his saddle and walked with him towards the horses. As James took off his coat and tossed this across the saddle, Richard came up behind him and, taking hold of the reins, swung the horse around and, at the same time, caught James a quick uppercut to the chin, knocking him senseless. "Sorry, old chap, but it is the only thing I can think of." As he spoke the Earl's body crumpled to the ground and Richard proceeded to make a great show of trying to restrain the horse.

Bending over the unconscious Earl, he looked across at the waiting men. Standing up he walked quickly towards them and was met half way.

"It would appear that his Lordship's horse has rendered him unconscious, and therefore unable to fulfil his obligation. I am sure that you would not wish to delay this and therefore as his second I will take his place. I would simply ask that we do this now so I can take his Lordship to his physician without delay."

Exmouth's second looked at his friend. "It is not uncommon for a second to take the place of the opponent, and I would suggest that we accept Carlisle's offer and get this matter over with post haste."

Richard watched Exmouth intently as they awaited his response. It was the merest nod of the head that indicated his agreement, and Richard smiled to himself.

"Perhaps you would like to take up your pistol, sir, and we can proceed."

Exmouth did as suggested and then stood back to back against Carlisle.

"Twenty paces, gentlemen, then turn and you will both fire when you are ready."

Just before they started to walk, Richard whispered to Exmouth, "Told you to watch your back, sir," leaving him in no doubt that this was the intended outcome of the duel.

Counting out twenty paces, Richard turned and faced Exmouth. The Duke's arm was raised and from the way it was being held the ball was to go to Richard's left. He waited for the sound of the shot and then turned his left shoulder slightly and felt the ball pass wide. Smiling, he raised his pistol and took aim, pointing at the Duke's right shoulder. Oh yes, he knew a gentleman should probably aim wide and declare that satisfaction were served, but that was not his intention, and Exmouth knew it. A vision of Isobella unconscious in the lodge came to mind, and his eyes narrowed as he pulled the trigger. The sound resounded across the field followed closely by Exmouth's scream as the ball lodged in his shoulder.

Walking towards the wounded man, he could not help but smile at his discomfort. "Sorry, old chap, wind must have caught the barrel at the last minute. Best get off and have it seen to. I think Lord Preston's honour has been upheld."

Bending down, Richard put his mouth to Exmouth's ear. "Do not think this was anything to do with Preston. This duel was mine as well you know, and you know why. Take yourself to the country, sir, and attend to your wife, as I will shortly tend to mine."

With that, he rose and nodded at the second. Collecting the other pistol, he walked back towards James who was attempting to sit up. "Sorry about that, James. It was the best I could come up with at the time."

"You hit me?" James rubbed his aching jaw.

"Yes, sorry, needed to be done, unless you wished to face a duel?"

"No, I did not. How did you explain it to Exmouth?"

"Easy, swung the horse round and said your mount had struck you, and they accepted it."

"And what of Exmouth?"

"Gone to have a ball removed from his shoulder."

"I take it that you are unharmed?"

"Naturally. Exmouth is a poor shot at the best of times, but he needed to be taught a lesson. And that has now been done."

Richard and James told no one of the duel and anyone who heard it being arranged must have presumed it were called off, or apologies made. Neither gentleman had any wish to inform their betrothed as to what had taken place.

Chapter Fourteen

The last three and bit weeks were a private hell for Richard. Every time he looked at Bella all his mind could see was her naked in his arms, and it took all of his will power not to take her again. She made it quite clear that he were not the only one to enjoy the experience since she teased him, in a way no lady should, in the weeks leading up to today.

Now he was standing nervously at the front of the church, waiting for the organist to start playing. *What if she does not come,* the thought teased him. *She was late,* all the waiting was too much?

"She is late," he hissed to his brother.

Flicking open his watch, Edward replied, "No, 'tis not yet eleven, she still has three minutes before she is late."

Just as Richard was about to ask the time again, there was a flurry at the back of the church, and then the organ began to play. Offering up a prayer of thanks, Richard stepped out into the centre of the aisle and turned to look at his bride. He felt the breath being sucked out of his body as his gaze took in the demure figure walking slowly towards him on the arm of her cousin. Dressed in white silk, trimmed with lace and carrying a posy of pink and white roses, she looked every inch the future Duchess of Carlisle.

She had been a bundle of nerves from the moment she had arisen. Juliette had been in her bedchamber shortly after dawn and had not helped with her whispered suggestions of what would happen that night. She did not need her cousin to tell her, she already knew what would happen, indeed, it had *already* taken place.

The ride to the church had seemed to take forever, and there had been little conversation between Charles and her. Now, as she walked down the aisle, Isobella only had eyes for her future husband. She knew she looked beautiful, oh, she was not vain, but even she could see her own reflection in the mirror, and the look on his face told her she was not wrong.

Their vows were said in front of a selected number of invited friends and family, and after the lunchtime feast, the new Duchess of Carlisle rode away in a be-ribboned carriage with her new husband, to an unknown destination.

Suddenly feeling shy, Isobella looked at Richard from beneath the rim of her hat. She had believed him engrossed in thought, but his eyes meet hers.

"Well, your ladyship, I trust you have enjoyed your wedding day...up to now?" he added with a smile.

Isobella nodded. "Where are we going?"

"It is supposed to be a surprise."

"Oh," she said. *What is wrong with me? This is Richard, the man I love and who has already bedded me, so why do I feel so shy and awkward?*

"What is wrong, Bella, have you no words to whisper to me now that we are alone?"

She shook her head wondering how he managed to read her thoughts. "I do not know what is wrong with me. I feel, well, not quite like myself."

"Are you scared, Bella, is that what it is? Scared that now there is just you and I, and you are now the mistress of your own household? Or are you just afraid of being alone with me? For you have no need to be afraid." he said teasingly.

Seeing him smile, she began to relax. "I am sorry, Richard. It is most likely all the excitement of the day."

"Do not worry, Bella. We will shortly be at the Inn where we are to stay for the night. I trust you will be able to manage without Anna for one night. I can always offer my services as deputy ladies maid," he said with a soft laugh.

That was too much for Isobella. She laughed out loud. "Oh, Richard, the thought of you as a ladies maid is quite something."

Arriving at the Inn, she waited in the carriage while her husband made sure their rooms were ready. Just thinking of him as her husband made her heart race. Returning shortly, he instructed the driver where to take the carriage and then assisted Isobella, while a young boy saw to their luggage. Their rooms were clean and neat, and the large bed in the bedchamber brought back memories of their afternoon at Carlisle Hall. She felt her face heat as Richard walked into the bedchamber and saw her gazing upon the bed.

Coming up to her she was pulled close as he whispered softly, "Do not worry about the bed, my love. It has been a testing day for us both, and I have no intention of seeking my marital rights tonight, much as I would wish to do so. I would much rather have you refreshed for tomorrow, and tomorrow night," he said, dropping a light kiss on her head. "I will assist you to undress though, since you do not have your maid, and I will promise to keep my hands under control."

Isobella laughed and her body shook in his embrace.

Joining in the laughter, he held her at arms' length. "Come, wife, take off your bonnet and cloak and let us rest before our refreshments arrive."

His words sounded serious but Isobella could see the twinkle in his eye, and keeping with his mood, bobbed a curtsey. "As you wish, my lord."

His laughter was still ringing in her ears when she walked back into the sitting area. Taking off her bonnet and cloak, she kicked off the silk covered shoes and walked in stockinged feet across the carpeted floor to the window. She could not see anything of note to keep her attention so turned back into the room and curled up in a large chair near to the roaring fire.

As she sat quietly thinking back over the day's events, she could hear Richard moving about in the adjoining room. Eventually curiosity got the better of her and she walked to the open doorway. Her husband was standing at the side table washing. He had shed his jacket and shirt, and she felt the quickening of her pulse at the sight of his exposed chest.

As if sensing another presence he turned and she was caught discreetly staring at him. Turning fully to face her, the towel was put aside on the top while he rested his hands on his hips.

"Well, wife? Is there something amiss?" The words were said with a smile and a hint of mischief.

She shook her head, embarrassed at being caught. "No, I was just wondering what you were doing."

"I am making myself comfortable so that I can enjoy a pleasant dinner, when it arrives, with my new duchess. I only hope that she will not expect me to dress formally for dinner, for I have a liking to adopt a casual attire, and I would like to think that she will too."

"How casual?"

"As casual as you like, my love. But I still intend to keep my promise," he said, referring to his promise not to seek his marital rights.

She nodded. "That sounds like an excellent idea. I am quite exhausted by the day. I will follow your example for dressing."

They did not have to wait long for dinner. There was a knock on the outer door and Richard moved to open it. The landlord and two serving girls entered carrying an array of dishes that they set down on the small dining table. Closing the door as they left, Richard poured two glasses of red wine, and carried one through to the bedchamber.

"Dinner has arrived, my darling, if you are ready to eat."

Isobella rose from the seat in front of the small dresser.

"I thought you were intending to dress informally?" he asked noting she was still wearing her gown.

"I have no informal dress, only my travelling attire."

"You have your night rail and a robe, have you not?"

"Yes, but I cannot sit with you wearing only those."

"Of course you can. I have on only breeches and a loose shirt. But if you would feel underdressed, I could always take off my breeches and leave just my shirt," he said with a grin.

Isobella blushed but could not stop the memory of his unclothed body entering her thoughts.

"There is no need for you to remove any clothing. If you will allow me a moment I will divest myself of my gown and undergarments and will join you shortly."

He turned to walk away but then turned back. "Do you need any help with removing anything, since you do not have Anna?"

"No thank you," she said primly, and turned her back to him.

She could hear his soft laughter as she pulled off her gown and then the petticoats. She did not have any hoops but the corset was tied tightly at the back, and she was unable to undo the fastening. Although she struggled there was naught she could do, she would have to seek his help. Marching through the door, she found him sprawled in one of the chairs with a half empty glass in his hand.

He looked up as she came in and she saw him bite back the smile that threatened. He knew she would have to seek his help and had simply been waiting for her. She felt like stamping her foot in annoyance, but she would not give him the satisfaction.

"Problem, my love?" he enquired, keeping his face straight.

"It would appear that I do need assistance. I cannot unfasten the ribbon on my corset. If you would be so good as to untie this for me, I will be but a moment longer before I join you."

It was a long speech for Isobella to make, especially flustered as she was. She could see he was amused by the situation. His face gave nothing away but she could not miss the sparkle in his eyes that told how much he was enjoying this moment.

Placing his glass on the small table, he rose slowly from the chair. "Of course I will help you, Isobella, you only have to ask. Now what is it you wish me to untie?"

She turned her back to him, and twisting a hand around pointed to the tight bow that fastened the lacing on the corset. She shivered as his hands brushed against her arm, and then felt him tug gently at the bow, easing the lacings apart. She wore only a chemise underneath and could feel the warmth of his hands as he pulled at the ribbons. She felt her breasts free of the confinement of the corset and put her hands up to hold this in place.

"Thank you," she said.

"It was my pleasure, Bella," he replied, dropping a kiss on one bare shoulder.

She shuddered violently at the contact and cast a quick glance at him over her shoulder before hurrying back into the bedchamber. Once inside, she dropped the corset on the chair and then removed her chemise. Picking up the pale pink night rail she slipped this over her head before pulling on the dark pink silk robe. Collecting her wine from the table, she walked barefoot back into the sitting room.

If she thought it would be awkward eating dinner in such casual attire, she was mistaken. Richard was most attentive and the wine helped to relax her. He kept them both amused with stories from his childhood until noting her eyes beginning to close.

"Either I am boring you, my love, or you are in need of sleep."

"I am not bored but I am tired."

"Then you must retire." He rose as she stood, picked up one hand and placed a kiss on the inside of the wrist. "I will be in shortly."

Having finished her toilette, she climbed into the large bed and pulled the covers up to her neck. She was nervous, despite him having said that he would not take her that night. She had longed for this night for weeks, ever since the time at the hall but now it was here, she was...well; she was not sure what she was. She looked up as the door opened and her husband walked in.

Striding across the room, he went behind the small screen and removed his shirt and breeches. Washing quickly in the cold water, he pulled on a nightshirt, came from behind the screen and walked to the bed, turning down the lamps as he did. It was difficult to avoid eye contact with Bella. He could see her sitting primly in the bed, but he had promised, and was not about to break that promise. Climbing into the bed alongside the small figure he could just make out her face in the dim light.

"Come, Bella, it has been a long day and we both need to rest."

She slid down the bed before turning to look at him. "Good-night, Richard," she said softly.

He was on his back and staring at the underside of the canopy. His head turned as she spoke. She looked adorable and knew he would not sleep until he had stolen at least one kiss from her.

"Good-night, Isobella," he said, turning towards her.

Stretching out a hand, his fingers wound through the loosened locks, and gently pulled her towards him. The feel of the soft lips on his had him cursing his promise. His body was kept apart from hers, he would be lost if they touched, but her lips, these he could take and enjoy the pleasure they gave him. He resisted the urge to tease the welcoming lips apart and seek the softness of her mouth with his tongue. If he did they would both be lost.

"Sleep well, my duchess." With a sigh, he turned away from her and closed his eyes, begging sleep to take him quickly.

She awoke suddenly, wondering for a moment where she was. Then she remembered her wedding day, and all that had taken place, and felt the heat from another body close to her. She did not know whether to be sad or pleased that he kept his promise. His kiss had awakened her body to him and she had wanted more than just a goodnight kiss. When he turned away she had closed her eyes and had soon fallen asleep, her thoughts full of what tomorrow would bring. But it was now tomorrow and her husband was laid alongside her.

Turning, she saw he was faced away from her, seemingly asleep, and she edged towards him carefully, wanting to feel the heat from his body against her own. She put a hand cautiously across his hip and nestled into his back pressing her body against his. Moving slowly, she pressed further into him but then suddenly her hand was grasped. She gasped; not only at the realisation that he was awake, but also at the place she now found her hand. Held firmly in his grip she could feel the heat from his arousal and, even as he spoke to her, it moved, growing larger.

* * * *

Richard had been awake since dawn and fully aware of his wife sleeping next to him. He remained turned away from her, scared of what may occur if he did not. He felt her stir, and then the most delicate of hands crept around his waist to his front. It was all he could do to keep still when she pressed into his back. Nothing could disguise the feel of her breasts through the thin cotton night rail, and it was wreaking havoc with his sanity. A certain part of his anatomy was hardening by the second and he had no wish to go back on his word, although it was now no longer last night, so his promise would not be broken. Even so, there was still travelling to be done and he did not wish to delay their departure, no matter how delightful the cause would be. Tonight he would make love to her slowly and gently, and it would be all the better for the wait.

He had just talked himself into rising when she moved and pressed further into him. He would have to put an end to this before it got out of hand. Turning quickly and taking hold of the errant hand at the same time, he placed this on his hardening shaft.

"If you continue as you are, madam, you will not be leaving this bed for many hours, and I will have broken my first promise to you as your husband." The passion in her eyes told him everything he wished to know. "Tonight, Bella, you will not escape me tonight."

"I will not want to escape."

He groaned at the reply, and freeing her from his hold pulled her to him, kissing her until she was breathless. Then before she could say anything he threw back the covers and walked to the washstand and proceeded to wash his overheated body.

After a hearty breakfast, they departed the Inn. It was mid-afternoon when they drove into Brighton and then pulled up at a charming white villa fronting the promenade.

"Oh, Richard, it is delightful," she said, taking his hand and alighting from the carriage.

"I am pleased you like it, my love. It is ours for the next two weeks, complete with Anna and my manservant and, I am assured, a very good cook and housemaid."

Having rested after their journey he enquired if she would wish to go out to dine and then to a musical. He watched the small frown and knew what she was thinking. Did she wish to spend time in a busy dining room and then a noisy theatre, or would she prefer to spend time alone with her husband in the quiet of this charming villa. He waited a few moments longer, hoping she chose the latter.

"Come, Isobella, surely it is not that hard a decision to make?"

"No, it is not and going out does have some appeal, but I think to stay at home, just the two of us, will have more appeal."

Richard could have kissed her for the reply. The thought of mixing with society when all he desired was to be on his own with his wife, would have been too great a strain.

"If you are sure that is what you want."

"Oh yes, more than anything," she said, smiling demurely at him.

Damn her, he thought, seeing a hint of mischief in her eyes. *She is reading my thoughts and quite clearly has seduction in mind as well.* "Very well, I will give instructions for us to dine at home. Would you wish to go out before dinner?"

"Yes, I believe I would like to take a walk along the promenade and watch the sea. If that is agreeable to you?"

"That is very agreeable to me, Bella," he said, picking up her hand and kissing the back before turning it and placing a kiss on the inner wrist.

The walk lasted but thirty minutes before they returned windswept and laughing. Sitting down to dinner he did not think Isobella had looked more beautiful. His thoughts ran away with him as he pictured her carrying his child, giving him an heir. Not that he desired only one child. He could imagine three or four, two of each, the girls being a replica of their mother. If she knew his thoughts he doubted if she would let him near her. Well, not until he had persuaded her, and looking at her glowing face and the way her eyes looked into his, he doubted that much persuasion would be needed.

After dinner they retired to the upper rooms. There was a sitting room adjoining their bedchamber that looked out across to the sea. The fire was burning and the lamps were lit. Richard was lounging on one of the chairs near to the fire, while Isobella was sat on a window seat looking across at the waves as she sipped a cup of tea. He dismissed the servants once they had dined, saying they would see to themselves later, so they now had the privacy they had waited for, but he was in no rush to start his seduction. He was content to wait awhile.

Leaving the warmth of the fire, he walked across to his wife and stood watching with her as the waves crashed onto the beach. Taking the empty cup from her hands he placed it on a nearby table. Then drawing her to her feet, led her toward the bedchamber. There was a second fire burning and, on a table near to the fire, was a bottle of port and two glasses. Pouring a glass each, he sat down in a nearby chair and, taking hold of one hand, pulled her gently down onto his knee. Handing one glass to her, he toasted their future and downed the port in one go. Isobella followed his actions and ended up choking as he wiped the tears from her eyes. Finally composed, she settled back in his arms and they watched the flames in the fire.

"Do not go to sleep, Bella, or I will be sorely disappointed," he whispered in one small ear.

"I would not dream of disappointing you, husband, but if you do not make a move soon I shall be asleep."

"Minx," he said, laughing. "So you think your husband is slow to move. Well, madam, let us see how slowly you think he moves after this."

Before she had time to guess what was intended he swept her up in his arms and carried her to the side of the bed. "Turn, wife," was all that were said as he set her on her feet.

She did as bid and turned her back to him. Then with a quick turn of hand the buttons on her gown were undone and she was lifted out of it. Next went the petticoat and corset. The stockings proved no difficulty to him and she was then left with just her chemise. "Do not move," he said.

* * * *

She could sense movement behind and waited, almost holding her breath until the ends of the chemise were raised and lifted over her head. She stood naked before her husband. Well, with her back to him, but naked, very naked. She shivered in anticipation, all earlier nerves and worries gone. This was what she was wanting for weeks, and now she was going to enjoy again the lovemaking they had already shared.

She waited for his touch, wondering where it would come. When it came it was his lips on her shoulder, and then the side of the neck, just below her ear. He did not touch with anything other than his lips. She could not feel his body, just his lips as they now worked slowly down her back, placing small kisses along her spine. Then he reached her derriere and a kiss were placed on each rounded mound. She sensed him rise up and then his hands crept around her waist and up to her breasts, pulling and rolling the nipples between his fingers. She arched her body, thrusting her breasts into his hands.

She did not know where the feelings she was experiencing were coming from, all she knew was that she did not want them to stop. Then his body touched hers and they both shuddered at the contact. His hand moved from her breast and trailed down across the flat stomach and through the soft downy hair until he reached her core.

Rubbing gently on the small nub, the part that gave the most pleasure. She groaned and wilted in his arms. His hand in that special place was making her weak and she had to force trembling legs to hold her upright. He was teasing, but she wanted him inside, and arched her body, trying to push him closer.

"Patience, Bella. It will all happen in time. Enjoy what is happening now."

His whispered words did nothing to dampen the feelings, and she was becoming quite moist between her legs. Moaning softly, she put her hand up behind her and around his neck. The movement stretched her body, curving it upwards and he groaned into her hair. She could feel his shaft pressing into her lower back as his hand moved further slipping a finger inside her. She gasped, and her heart raced as he pushed further in. She arched her body, the need for more overwhelming her.

"We need to adjourn to the bed, Bella, so I can have greater access to you."

She nodded; unable to speak, as his hand was removed and she was swept off her feet and held close. His lips sought hers, forcing them apart before his tongue burrowed within her mouth. She found his tongue with her own and they teased and twisted around each other as he carried her across the room.

This slow seduction of his wife was something he had been anticipating for weeks. She was no longer a maiden, and now they could enjoy the delights of the marital bed without the fear of pain. Although, if he became any harder she could be stretched too far, so slow and gentle was his intention. Feeling the trembling body arching up into his waiting hands he could almost feel his resolve slipping. *God, how I want to be inside her.* The thought did nought to cool his desire. He wished to cover her with his body but needed to move his hands to a sweeter place and that required being closer to her. And for that she needed to be on the bed.

Lowering his gaze, he looked at his new wife. The eyes had a dreamy look and her cheeks were flushed pink.

"So, do you still think your husband is slow, madam?"

Biting back a smile, she replied, "No, just not quick enough, your lordship."

The words had barely left her lips when she was dropped onto the bed and he was alongside her. Pulling her up the covers he proceeded to kiss every part of her face and then moved down her body, until he lay with his face in her groin.

"Open your legs, Bella," he said softly, and she did so without hesitation.

He moved further down until he was laid between the parted legs, and placing his hands beneath the tantalising derriere raised her and placed his lips on her core. She screamed softly and quivered in his hands, and he took a deep breath before starting a journey of exploration that ended with his tongue teasing the entrance to her before embedding a finger deep inside.

Moving slowly at first, he eased his finger in and then almost out, pushing deeper each time. He watched as her hands gripped the covers, and the tempting body arched up from the bed. He swallowed hard. This slow seduction was becoming most painful for him. Adding a second finger, he stretched her wider and proceeded to push deeper and deeper, moving slowly at first and then increasing the speed until she began to fall apart in his hands.

A sob was wrenched from her lips and she cried out his name. He could not hold back any longer. Removing his fingers, he poised at her entrance and then eased gently forward, feeling the wetness of her coming assisting his passage. Further and further he pushed and then withdrew to his tip, before pushing slowly forward again. He knew what this was doing to her, knew how the feel of him gliding over her inner core would arouse and excite before bringing her again to fulfilment. Hands left the covers and gripped his shoulders as she pushed her hips at him, straining for that further contact.

"Deeper, Richard. More, more..." she moaned, and his world was turned upside down hearing those words from her.

"I do not want to hurt you."

"You will not, but I need you more of you," she panted.

Sitting backwards, he lifted and tilted her, giving him better access to her core, and then thrust deep. "Is that enough, my love?"

"Oh, yes...yes..." The rest of the words were lost in a soft scream as she fell about him again.

Longing to spend himself inside her, it took all his resolve to withdraw and spurt his seed, not onto the covers, but onto the soft rounded belly. Needing her to feel his liquid; his desire for her. He remained kneeling between her legs until every last drop of his seed were exorcised from his pulsating shaft. Then he gasped in air to his lungs and watched as his liquid pooled and then slowly trickled across her belly. Looking up, his gaze was caught by her green eyes, as she lay part lifted on her elbows, watching him.

Grinning at the dishevelled appearance, he said, "I trust that was quick enough for you, Bella, or do you have another complaint?"

"I am not complaining, Richard. And, yes it was quick enough, this time. But pray why did you not stay inside me?"

"I wish to keep you to myself for a while, but I have marked you as mine. My seed rests on your skin. Here, feel," and he reached up, taking hold of her hand, and placed it in the wet, then held his own hand on top. He could feel her fingers moving and spreading the liquid. Then he lifted the hand and kissed it.

"I will go and collect a cloth to clean you and then we can formally retire to the inside of the bed."

His words made her giggle. "Does that mean we have to do this again on the inside of the bed?"

He was part way across the room when she spoke and halted before turning around to look at her, but any reply froze on his lips. She had sat upright and was kneeling on the bed, her whole body exposed to him and with the sweetest of smiles on lips still swollen from their love making. The sweetness only betrayed by the passion and heat that could be seen in her eyes.

"Bella," he managed to splutter, "behave or I will wonder what I have unleashed."

Watching his face as he spoke she tilted her head to one side and waited while he returned with a wet cloth.

"Lie down, wife," he said with a grin, and was somewhat surprised when she did without further remark. Carefully, he placed the cloth on her body and gently wiped the product of his desire from the damp skin. That she did not flinch at the coldness told him her body was well heated. *Well, my teasing wife,* he thought, *I too can tease,* and slowly moved the cloth wiping between the slender legs and over her core, taking his time until he could hear her breathing becoming laboured. Then with a flick of the cloth on her groin, declared she was clean, and stood up, moved behind the screen and proceeded to wash himself.

Returning to the bed, he noted that she was once again wearing her night rail and wondered if this were a sign that the night's escapades were at an end. He would see. Climbing in alongside his wife, he placed an arm around her shoulders and gently pulled her towards him. As she rested her head on his shoulder, he heard the sigh.

"Are you happy, Bella?"

"Exceedingly so," she replied.

"And I did not hurt you?"

She shook her head. "Not at all."

"Good, but if I had it would not have all been my fault. I have never heard of a new bride crying for more and deeper," he said laughingly.

"Do not say that," she said playfully, slapping him on the arm. "You make me sound like a wanton woman."

His laughter echoed round the bedchamber. "Bella, you could never be described as wanton, but I would take great pleasure in bedding you if you were wanton. So take heed, my love, I will expect nothing and hope for everything from you."

Having stated his intentions, he eased down the bed pulling her with him. Resting in his arms with her head on his chest, he watched as the eyes began to close and before long the steady breathing told him she was sleeping soundly. Holding his most treasured possession in his arms it took quite a time for him to succumb to sleep. With every breath he could see the rise and fall of tantalising breasts through the thin material, and his hardening shaft was letting him know that it was aware of his thoughts.

He awoke suddenly and was instantly alert, but then realised it was the sea birds calling that could be heard. It was barely daylight. Relaxing he turned and looked at his wife who lay curled up and faced away from him. Moving across the bed, his arm slid tenderly across her body so she was moulded to him. He could feel the warmth of her body through the material of the thin night rail. Moving his hand and trailing down, he was delighted to find the night rail had moved up in the night, exposing a perfect round derriere for his pleasure. Gently caressing the soft skin and daring to push the material further up, she was soon exposed to the waist. *Ah, this is more to my liking.* His hand drifted around to the soft belly before finding the silky hair between her legs.

She moved, turning part way onto her back, his hand stilled, but she did not awake. His mind was running away with his thoughts as he ventured a finger between the silky legs. It were almost impossible to stop himself from groaning as he slipped easily through the damp opening. Pushing inside, he pressed his forehead to her shoulder and bit down on his lips. She was so wet and this allowed him to move so easily inside her, he were certain she could be brought to satisfaction before she awoke.

So intent on his mission, he jumped when a soft voice whispered, "If you keep doing that, sir, I fear we will spend the morning abed."

The body in his arms quivered with laughter as she waited for his reply.

"So, my darling wife, you are awake and simply enjoying the pleasure I am giving to you, and repaying me for my words of yesterday."

"I think I will always enjoy the pleasure you give me."

"Do you, my little minx. Well, I think it is time that your husband took his pleasure, for I cannot wait to be inside you, my love."

Even before the words were spoken, she was pulled fully onto her back, the night rail lifted over her head and thrown onto the floor. His own nightshirt followed as kisses were rained on her hair and face, and finally his lips sought hers. Thrusting his leg between hers, she was spread wide and he then poised above her, supporting himself on his hands. "Guide me, Bella, or I may thrust too hard."

She looked at him and stayed the hand that was part way to do his bidding. "I think you can find your own way, my darling, and I would welcome your thrust."

"Agh, minx," was all he uttered as his hips pushed forward and his shaft came to rest at her entrance. Giving himself no time to think he thrust and sank deep into the soft wet opening of her body. Once embedded there was no intention of relenting, since she had wanted it deep last time, he was prepared to give the same again. Raising himself fully on his hands his head was thrown back as his hips pushed forward with a sudden force that jolted her body.

He glanced down and found she was gazing up at him with a wildness in her eyes that only served to heighten his desire. Thrusting forward again he found she met him with equal force, and it were not possible to prevent the smile that curved his lips. Isobella's complete response to him pushed him to push her further. He drove forward again, need, desire, love, driving him on. The soft moans and gasps were the only sounds that were registering with him. His only wish was to give her everything and more.

She was writhing on the bed beneath him, hips pushing into him as he thrust at her over and over again. She fell about him in a coming so overwhelming that for a moment he thought she had fainted. Then he heard the soft groan and his arms slid beneath the limp shoulders lifting her to him, giving him better angle and greater access to her.

Sitting back on his heels, Richard held her firmly lodged on his shaft and pushed deeper and deeper. Legs were spread at either side of his body as she was gently lowered down onto the bed. He was about to blow but had no desire to withdraw, but knew this must be done. But not yet as he could feel her start to shake as she began to come to him a second time. Watching the enchanting body quivering on the bed he waited until she was still and then, with his seed already leaking, pulled out and spent himself over her groin.

Even before he finished, she was pulled up into his arms and kisses were showered on her, as she whispered words of love in his ear. Words that told him of her complete satisfaction within their marriage. Sometime later, as they lay wrapped in each other's arms, he delighted that he had found in his wife a match for his own passion.

As she bathed in the warm water a short time later, Isobella wondered again if she was turning into a wanton hussy. She could still feel the throbbing between her legs and squirmed in the water as she remembered the feel of him inside her. Oh, she enjoyed their union at Carlisle Hall, when she had disposed of her virginity, but last night, and again this morning, it was so different. She felt different, brave, almost daring. That night at the Inn she had felt an awkwardness but here, with just the two of them, she felt embolden to do things, and ask for things, that a lady should not.

She thought back to when she had espied Juliette in her bedchamber with James and wondered if her cousin's feelings at the time were the same. They always shared things but Juliette had made no mention of that encounter, and Bella did not have the courage to confess to what she had seen. Perhaps when Juliette was married they would be able to speak of such things. Her thoughts were interrupted by the appearance of Anna as she entered carrying warm towels.

The next two weeks were spent in days of exploring and nights of passion. By the end of the honeymoon, Isobella knew what her husband desired of her and what she wished in the bedchamber. The Journals she and Juliette had shared, never gave any suggestion that the coupling of a man and woman was so exciting. Aunt Eleanor taught them both what was expected of a wife, when the time came, but gave no hint of the pleasure that it could bring. A pleasure that she hoped would continue to be explored.

Chapter Fifteen

Returning to Carlisle House, they found Richard's mother had taken herself to the country for a few days, to give the newlyweds some time to adjust to their changed status. Of Edward there was no sign and on enquiring Richard found his brother had left for Chester. Further enquires disclosed this was in pursuit of a certain lady who was minded to take a new lover. Richard sighed at the news and only hoped that his brother would not encounter more trouble in this latest quest, but the fact that the lady in question was a widow at least meant that no husband would come calling at the door.

If Isobella thought that their return to London would bring a change in the bedchamber she was pleasantly surprised. Richard sought her bed every night and, on the one night when he returned late, and slept in his own dressing room, she sought his bed. Slipping between the covers she curved her body around his and slept until his lips and hands awoke her in the early hours, before his body possessed hers in a haste that was almost indecent.

Juliette and James's wedding was the talk of the town. Everyone of note was in attendance.

Richard and Isobella caused a stir when they arrived at the church, and comments were made on the change in the new duchess since her marriage. Looking at his wife, Richard could not deny the changes. She had blossomed; she looked more like strawberries and cream to him than ever before. And only he knew she tasted even more delicious than the fruit itself. Her complexion was flawless and the silken hair was a mass of soft waves, held up with pins and allowed to fall in soft curls about her shoulders. The deep green bonnet she wore matched the green velvet gown, and the panniers made her waist look smaller than it was. But Richard would rather see his wife in a simple muslin or silk day dress with only a petticoat underneath. He delighted in the sight of her and that did not go unnoticed by the other members of the congregation, as they watched his eyes follow his wife as they slipped into their pew.

Taking hold of her hand once they were seated, it was raised to his lips and a small kiss placed on the inside of the wrist. This simple gesture melted the serious look on her face and she turned and smiled, her love for him clear for all to see.

As the organist began to play they rose to their feet, and Bella saw for the first time her cousin as she walked down the aisle on the arm of her brother. Juliette looked perfection and James's pleasure shone on his face as he watched her approach. With the words said and the couple officially wed everyone returned to Rothbury House for the wedding feast. After an afternoon of entertaining their guests the newlyweds began to make preparations to leave.

Isobella managed to secure a few minutes alone with her cousin, before she left with her new husband, when they were able to exchange girlish chatter amidst a great deal of excitement.

"I can hardly believe that I will be lying in James's arms tonight. What was it like, Izzie, did it hurt when you lost your maidenhood?"

"I thought you already knew what it was like, cousin?"

"What do you mean?" she asked surprised.

Biting her lip, Isobella knew she was going to have to disclose to Juliette about seeing her and James in the bedchamber. Taking a deep breath she confessed to what she had seen only to watch the flush creep up Juliette's face.

"Oh, I did not know that we had been seen, but I am still intact, we did nothing more than...well, let us say, go further than we should have done. What made you think I would let James seduce me before we were wed?"

Isobella made no answer. What could she say? She could not tell her cousin she thought that because she herself were seduced before her own wedding. Shaking her head, she simply replied, "I do not know, cousin. I suppose I just thought it might have happened."

Juliette was about to speak when the door was flung open and Aunt Eleanor came bursting into the room in a flurry of deep rose pink petticoats and feathers. "Come, Juliette, your husband awaits you and the carriage is at the door. And you, Lady Carlisle," she said, addressing her niece, "need to return to your husband who is seeking you out as we speak."

"Yes, aunt, I will return at once," she said, turning and hugging her cousin. "I will see you when you return, Juliette," and then whispered in her ear, "Perhaps we can compare notes on your return." The cousins looked at each other and burst out laughing much to the bewilderment of the duchess.

Walking down the staircase, Isobella saw Richard making his way towards her through the crowd. She paused for a moment and took in his looks. The dark hair was swept back and touched on the tall collar of his dark green coat, a coat that matched her gown. A white shirt and dark green cravat were worn beneath the coat. His white breeches and buckled shoes completed his attire, and to Isobella he had never looked more handsome. *And he is mine,* she thought, *and tonight I will lie in his arms and feel his love.* It was all she could do not to convey the wayward thoughts by a look, so she lowered her eyes and concentrated on descending the remaining stairs. His hand was held out waiting as she alighted from the last stair, and placing a hand on top of his, allowed him to lead them back to the revelry.

As she lay beneath her husband that night, feeling his shaft caressing her inner body she thought of Juliette and hoped that her cousin was experiencing the same pleasure that she was.

The extended honeymoon of Juliette and her new husband meant that Isobella missed her cousin. The next two months passed in days and evenings of socialising but the nights were spent in sharing the passion she was growing to love and expect from her husband. He pushed the boundaries with her and she with him. Testing him more each time they came together. If her aunt knew of the way she ravished her husband she would collapse with the vapours, but for Isobella this was a journey of discovery that she was eager to follow.

There were mornings when she was stiff from their lovemaking but this did not prevent her from giving herself again that night. The only matter that was troubling was that Richard was still spending his seed outside her body, and she was at a loss as to why. She had asked the question once, and been given an answer. But they had been married now for some three months and she longed for him to remain within her to the end.

Tonight they were to attend a ball at the home of the Earl and Countess of Rochester. Bella temptingly tried to persuade Richard that they should stay at home, and preferably abed, but he reminded her that this was the first invite to be received from the couple since their marriage and it would be seen as an insult not to attend.

Duly chastised, she had pouted her lips and then found herself swept into his arms and kissed most profoundly. "Do not tempt me, madam, or you may get more than you crave for," he whispered teasingly, before setting her upright on her feet. "Now, go and let Anna work her magic on you and we shall take tonight by storm, and then, my little temptress, come home to the delights of the marital bed."

Now, as she looked around, she could see her husband dancing with their hostess. Having already declined several offers to dance, she now wished she could catch Richard's eye. She was tired but thought if they were able to partake of some refreshments together they could then share a dance or two before taking their leave.

Realising the dance would not finish for some time she sought the quiet of the ladies powder room and slipped into one of the cubicles to attend to her needs. About to leave the cubicle she heard voices coming into the powder room. Recognising the voice of Lady Ashton and her confidant Lady Somerset she hesitated. She had no wish to encounter either of the ladies in question so took the coward's way and waited hidden from view, hoping they would not be long.

"Well of course I knew it would never last. He has such a voracious sexual appetite it was clear that the dainty lady that were chosen would not satisfy him for long. That he has waited three months since the wedding before taking a mistress is a wonder," the poisonous voice of Lady Ashton stated.

"I know what you mean. But I have heard that the lady in question being pursued is one of the ton. Not an actress or the like, and that will prove extremely difficult to keep hidden."

"What makes you think she is one of us?" asked Lady Ashton.

"He was seen coming out of the Arlington house some two days since, while his new wife was still in the country, and the Arlington's were otherwise engaged. Word has it they were alone in the house apart from the servants, and one can only imagine what misdeeds were taking place."

"Indeed, and knowing Carlisle they would be all consuming for the lady in question."

Isobella thought she was going to faint. They were talking about Richard. Her husband, and saying he had taken a mistress. She felt the bile rise in her throat at the thought of him with another woman. The first instinct she had was to throw the door open and tell them it was all lies. But her mind was working fast, and remembering that Richard had been out when she and his mother returned home from the country, and he had not come to their bed that night. The thoughts running through her head were making her dizzy and all she wanted was to escape. She wished only to leave the ball and go home, but she could not expose herself now and was obliged to wait until the two spiteful, and she could think of no other word for them, ladies left. The time seemed interminable before the powder room was empty. Leaving the sanctuary of the closet she looked in the mirror at a face that was now as pale as flour and nipped her cheeks to put some colour back in.

Leaving the room cautiously and without being seen, she made her way to the refreshments and picked up a glass of wine. She was still there when Richard found her.

Slipping an arm around her waist he gently kissed her hair and was surprised when he felt her stiffen.

"Isobella, are you all right?"

"I have a headache and think it would be best if I return home."

"Of course, my love. I will make our excuses and have the carriage brought round."

"No. There is no need for you to leave. I am sure you have plenty to keep you here and I would not wish to ruin your evening."

She saw the way he looked at her and knew he was sensing that something was amiss but he said nothing of his suspicions, for which she was thankful. She did not wish to have this conversation with him. And certainly not here in full view of society.

"I would not wish to stay if you are not here, my love, so we will leave together." The tone of his voice brooked no argument.

Not wishing to argue since the headache was by now a reality, she simply tilted her head in acquiescence.

"As you wish."

The ride home was completed in silence and she knew he would be a fool not to realise that all was not well. And he was no fool.

Once inside the house, Isobella excused herself and retired to her bedchamber.

Anna helped her undress and put on the silk night rail before she dismissed her, saying she did not wish to be disturbed. Once alone, she ran to the connecting door, leading to the adjoining small bedroom, and turned the key. She did not wish

Richard in her bed this night. She needed to consider all that had been overheard.

She would have to speak to her husband; she at least deserved an answer to the rumours that were abounding. But she knew Richard; she could not believe that he would do this to her. *Was she wrong in her assumption? Was Lady Ashton mistaken,* she so wished that she were. She did not wish to be cast aside for a mistress. She could not bear the thought of her husband in another woman's arms.

The mention of the Arlington house could mean only one person, the Duke's goddaughter, Lady Sophia. She remembered how Richard had been with the young lady in the country and how she had been jealous. But he explained later how he had been obliged to escort her and entertained no romantic feelings for the young lady. She had believed him. She still wished to believe him. She could not accept that Richard would betray her, and so soon into their marriage. But why would he have been at the Arlington's when they were not at home, and why say nothing of this visit to her.

With these thoughts running through her head she climbed into the large bed and curled into a ball telling herself not to shed tears over something she was not yet sure of. But wanting to do one thing, and being able to do it, she found impossible and the tears were soon running down her cheeks. Turning into the pillow to stifle any sobs, she soon fell into an uneasy sleep.

Richard spent the journey home and the next hour or more pacing the library floor wondering what the devil was amiss. When they left for the ball together they were both in fine spirits but something had clearly occurred, and something serious. Having downed a second brandy he decided to face the problem. Isobella, by now, would have been made ready for bed and if her surrender could not be brought about in his arms, then he was in real trouble.

Going into the adjoining bedchamber, he undressed, and donning a silk robe went to the connecting door. Turning the handle it was somewhat of a surprise when it did not yield, and it took a moment for him to realise that it was locked. Whatever had taken place that night would appear to be serious. And at this moment he was at a loss as to understand what.

Walking back across the room he proceeded out onto the landing and entered the master bedchamber by the main door. He smiled to himself. She had locked him out but forgotten to lock the main entry door. Approaching the bed, it were evident she was asleep but the trace of tears on her face could not be missed. He was torn apart at the sight and at not having the means of undoing whatever was amiss. He was tempted to lie alongside her but quickly dispelled the thought. Clearly tonight was not the time so, reluctantly and quietly, left the room and spent a thoroughly miserable and uncomfortable night on his own.

The following morning, he entered the main bedchamber by the main door, resolving to make no mention of the locked door. She was already up and dressed and Anna was attending to her hair.

"Good morning, Isobella. I thought we could breakfast together?"

"I am sorry, I have already eaten."

"Well perhaps we could spend the morning together. Perchance take a ride through Hyde Park?"

"I have an appointment with my dressmaker this morning and will be out for most of the day."

Richard watched through the mirror. She did not look at him as she spoke and he heard the distance in her voice. She was angry with him. But for what? He did not know and this was clearly not the time to find out.

"Very well, my love. My day without you will be dull but I will see you at dinner."

He moved forward and set his hands on her shoulders, placing a kiss on the side of her neck. She flinched, the movement made him feel ill, but he made no comment to her. Taking his leave, and after eating a solitary breakfast, then took himself off to his club.

It was late afternoon when Isobella came home. She was tired and sick of the worries that had plagued her all day. She stayed out as late as she dared but knew that she needed to return home eventually. Finding Richard was still out was a blessing and a worry. *Was he with her? Had she pushed him into her arms?* Oh, the frustration of it all were too much, so she escaped to her rooms requesting a tray to be sent up later, as she would not be down for dinner. Deciding that she needed to calm herself she called for Anna to prepare her bath, and then sat by the dresser waiting for the water to cool.

By the time Richard left his club he was as miserable as never before. And had no knowledge of what awaited his return home. He had spent the worst day of his entire life trying to appear as though nothing were wrong. Now, apart from being miserable, he was beginning to become angry. He never thought his anger would be directed to Isobella but it was crucial that he find out what was wrong. He felt as though he were being condemned for something of which he had no knowledge. Again the question plagued him. *What had occurred last night to turn his wife away from him?*

Arriving home, he enquired if her ladyship were home and was informed she was, but was not intending to join the family for dinner, and requested a cold tray be sent up.

"Thank you, Johnson. Make that two cold trays to her ladyship's rooms and offer our apologies to my mother for missing dinner."

"Very good, my lord."

Taking the stairs two at a time he entered his dressing room and took off his jacket and waistcoat. Pulling the shirt out from his breeches he rolled up the sleeves and walked in stocking feet out into the corridor and into the master bedchamber. Opening the door without knocking, it was then firmly closed behind him.

Isobella was sitting at the dressing table wearing only a chemise and a flimsy robe. Turning, she glared at him.

"I did not hear you knock, sir?"

"No you did not, my lady, since I did not knock. I do not knock on the door of the marital bedchamber."

"Well perhaps it is time that you did. I am about to bathe and I do not wish an audience."

"Careful, Isobella, I am on a short temper at the moment. I am at a loss as to what has happened to turn you away from me. To lock me out of your room and refuse me your bed."

His words and voice were cold, but they did not stay Isobella's words.

"I have no doubt that you have another bed to go to, sir."

Richard's mouth fell open at the words and the harshness of her voice. He sank down into the chair and looked at her. *What the devil was she talking about?*

"I have no other bed to go to, Bella. The only bed I have is this one," he said, indicating to the four-poster across the room.

"If you wish to bed me, sir, I cannot stop you." She all but spat the words at him.

"Bed you. Bed you," he shouted, jumping up from the chair. "I have no wish to bed you, Isobella, but I would very much like to make love to my wife, and would hope that she would wish me to."

"I do not wish you to, sir."

Her words cut into him like a knife. "Why?"

"I will not share you with a mistress, be she a lady or not." Anger fuelled her reply.

Now Richard was beginning to work out what was happening.

Very quietly, he spoke, "You do not share me, my love...with anyone. And I would not desire anyone other than you. But before I go out of my mind, will you please tell me what you believe you know, or what you have been told."

Isobella looked at him. She was about to reply when there was a knock on the door, and Richard called for them to enter.

Johnson came into the room with one of the servants, both of them carrying trays. Putting them down on the table they made to leave.

"Thank you, Johnson. Her ladyship and I do not wish to be disturbed. Tell Anna she may retire."

"Yes, my lord."

As the door closed, Richard walked to the table and picked up the wine and poured two glasses. Walking to Isobella he handed one to her.

"Now, my love, you are going to tell me what transpired last evening to upset you and to leave me so out of favour."

Richard rested against the dresser and watched as she took a sip of the wine. Then she raised her eyes to his and started to speak. He listened intently as Isobella related the conversation she overheard.

"Whatever made you consider they were telling the truth, my love?"

"I do not know. I did not wish to believe it. But then I recalled you came back to London Early, from our stay at Rothbury Hall, when we journeyed to escort your mother home. And then were not at home when your mother and I arrived. You then stayed out late and did not seek my bed that first night. I am aware you have taken mistresses before we were wed, and I was suddenly afraid that I was not enough for you, and you had felt obliged to find another way to relieve your feelings." She paused briefly and took a sip of wine before continuing. "And as well as hearing that gossip, some of the ladies were looking at me most strangely, as if seeking something. Confirmation of your infidelity perhaps? I do not know." She shook her head.

"Oh, Bella." He put his wine down and took the glass from her hand before kneeling down in front of her. "I do not want or need anyone else but you. What you overheard was not true. You satisfy all of my needs. I have not yet taught you everything that will please you, nor all that will please me. That is a journey we will make together, you and I, without the need for anyone else. As for people looking at you, in what way do you mean?"

"It were as if they could not look me in the face. Their eyes were cast down. If they were a man, I would have thought they were looking at my bosom."

Richard smiled; having some idea of what the ladies were seeking. Evidence of a growing child, to confirm their suspicions of a hasty marriage.

Pulling her into his arms she was held close, but then he felt the tender body start to shake as she began to sob quietly into his shoulder.

"I thought I had lost you," she cried.

"Never, my love," he whispered into her hair before lifting her head and taking the trembling lips with his own. Kissing was not enough, not after the worries of the past hours, and his hands began to roam under the robe pulling at the ties on the chemise.

"Did you say you were about to bathe?"

"Yes. The water was brought up shortly before you entered."

"Good. Then I think we will bathe together, Bella, before we enjoy supper."

"Bathe, together?"

"Yes. I did say that I had not yet taught you all that will please you, and bathing together will be a most enjoyable experience. And while we do that I will explain all to you. Or at least all that I can without breaking my word to keep the matter a secret."

With that she was pulled to her feet and led across the room to the adjoining bathing closet. The steam was rising from the bath and the smell of jasmine filled the room. He would probably smell like a dandy after this, but nothing was going to prevent him from sharing this experience with his wife. Turning, he slowly undid the robe and then removed the rest of her clothes until she was naked before him. He was hard and quickly pulled off his shirt and shed his breeches and stockings until he was as naked as she was. Holding out his hand he assisted as she stepped into the bath, and then slid in behind.

Small kisses were trailed across the creamy back before she was wrapped in his arms and drawn back against his chest.

"Now, my love, I will explain what I am able. I was not here when you arrived home since I was at a pre-arranged meeting of my peers. Nothing of note, just banking and government matters. After that, I was persuaded to partake of dinner with the Earl of Belmont, and the Earl is not a man to be turned down. When I arrived home you were abed. I came in but you were asleep and I did not have the heart to wake you, despite the longing I felt to make love to you. So I behaved like a gentleman and slept in the adjoining room. And a long night it was too, Bella," he said with a sigh, and nuzzled into the back of her hair.

She settled back against him. "And what about you being observed coming out from the Arlington's?"

"That is the part I cannot fully disclose to you and must ask you to trust me, my sweet. I do confess to being with Arlington's goddaughter."

She stiffened at his words and his hands moved swiftly from the small waist up to the rounded breasts, and he rolled the nipples between his fingers, as his lips softly teased and kissed the back of her neck. Her body arched as he continued to arouse her.

"Stop. Stop, Richard. You cannot tell me you were with another woman and then do this to me."

"Oh I can, my love, and I intend to. I was not with Lady Sophia because I wished to be. I was there as a go between for someone else, someone who is greatly taken with the young lady."

He felt her relax against his body and ceased playing with her breasts and allowed his hands to rest on the smooth rounded stomach.

"Why cannot this other person approach the lady himself?" she asked.

"Because the gentleman in question is wary of being refused and made to look a fool. You remember when we were in the country, before we were wed and Arlington was there with his family and Lady Sophia. There was a fine to do because she wished to marry another and her father refused the offer. She was heartbroken and even asked me to persuade her godfather to intervene but I was obliged to decline. I believe her father made the right choice but I could not be cruel enough to say that. Anyway, it would seem that the young man in question soon turned his attentions to another and that made a delicate situation even worse.

So this friend of mine..."

"Oh, so the gentleman is a friend, this person on whose behalf you are acting?" she interrupted.

"Of course he is a friend, I would not entertain such a task for a stranger. As I was saying before I was so rudely interrupted," he said, moving one hand and pulling a nipple gently in reproach. "This friend of mine wishes to pay his respects to the lady and asked me if I would approach on his behalf to see if she would receive him."

"And will she?" asked Isobella.

"Apparently yes. So I have informed my friend of her decision and the rest is now up to him."

"So this is why you were alone with her?"

"Yes, it was unfortunate the family were out, but I wished to deal with the matter as quickly as possible to put my friend out of his misery. Sadly, it would appear I was seen leaving. But what was clearly not seen was the partly open door as I spoke with Lady Sophia, and the servant standing discreetly nearby."

"And you do not intend to take a mistress?"

He laughed. "No, I do not. Unless of course you would care to consider the role of mistress as well as wife?"

She slapped his hands playfully at his words.

"I would not know how to play the part of a mistress. I am only just learning the role of being a wife."

"Oh the roles are similar. To please and pleasure the man in your bed...or bath," he ended with a smile as his hands roamed down to find the soft downy area of her groin. He knew where this was going and needed to be back in the bedchamber post haste.

"Come, wife," he said, easing forward and removing his hands. "Much as I would love to pleasure you in the bath, I much prefer the bed."

Climbing out, he took one of the large towels and held out his hand to steady her as she stepped out from the bath. Wrapping the towel around her, he collected a smaller one and quickly dried his own body while she watched. Having dried himself sufficient for his needs his attention turned to his wife.

Chapter Sixteen

Holding the towel beneath her chin, she quietly watched her husband as the small towel moved quickly over his body. She never tired of looking at him. The muscles in his arms moved as he worked, and her eyes were drawn to his groin, the part of him that she desired to see the most.

She had thought of coupling as being something to be endured. Not the wild exciting encounter she found it to be. Looking at him now she felt nothing but desire but reminded herself that she was the Duchess of Carlisle and thus required to act with some decorum. A thought that was enough to dampen some of her ardour; until she chided herself that she was also the Duke's wife and could please him as and when he desired. And clearly her husband wished to be pleased now, especially as she had refused him last night.

She stood silently while he finished, not daring to let her thoughts run wild. When he was done, the towel was thrown onto the chair and she was swept up into his arms and carried through to the bedchamber. She was set gently on the bed before he followed, and the glint in his eye told her that he was intending to take the one thing she had denied him yesterday eve.

Isobella shuddered in anticipation as his hands started to roam over her body. He teased her breasts, first with his fingers and then with his tongue and teeth until the tips were tight. She was panting, her breath coming in short gasps. Then he moved between her legs and she was lost as he teased with his tongue. She wanted him more than anything and wondered what it would be like to be a mistress in this situation and not a wife. *Dare she?* was the wanton thought. She was lying meekly, allowing him to take his pleasure, but what would a mistress do? *Would she seduce him?* Not allowing herself time to consider she thrust her groin up and opened her legs wider. He lifted his head and raised an eyebrow. She smiled seductively at him. Or at least she hoped it was seductively. But she must have got it right from the look on his face.

"Bella?"

She made no answer, just smiled again and raised herself up on her elbows. He lifted his head from her groin and moved back up the outstretched body until his face was in front of her. Moving slightly forward, she placed her lips on his and teased until he opened, and then tentatively touched his tongue with her own. He moved, his tongue stroking over hers and then halted. Their eyes held, but he did not move. This was her game and he was allowing it to proceed as she wished, and the thought was thrilling.

Her tongue began a slow dance with his own. His sharp intake of breath made her smile. She liked being in control, and lowered herself back onto the bed taking him with her. Then raising her hands up to his face, kissed him as passionately as she could, wrapping her legs around his, feeling the hardness of him against her.

His hands were pushing beneath her body and then he turned, taking her with him, so he was beneath her. Her lips withdrew from his and began to kiss his face and then his neck before moving down to his chest. He would tease her nipples with his teeth so she proceeded to do the same to him, revelling in his apparent pleasure at her touch.

Moving down to his waist and then his stomach she paused for a moment. *Dare she go further?* She caught her bottom lip between her teeth and glanced up at his face and saw him watching intently, before an eyebrow were raised. Taking a deep breath, she moved down his body placing small kisses as she did, until she came to his shaft. Running a hand along its length she delighted in the soft feel of his skin.

The groans coming from his lips offered further encouragement. Lowering her head she ran her tongue around the tip. His body jerked in response, and she heard his gasp. Smiling to herself, she went further and placed him between her lips and gently sucked.

He gasped, his voice barely a whisper. "Bella."

She liked this game. It felt so different, and she was being allowed to have control of the situation. She sucked him again feeling him harden in her mouth. His shaft was so big she wondered how he managed to breach inside her.

Glancing up at him she delighted in seeing his head thrown back and his eyes closed. *So this is what a mistress does for her master, but what would she do next*? Moving so she sat upon his thighs, she lowered again and teased him with her tongue and then her mouth. She was feeling very...well, she was not quite sure what she was feeling except she was becoming very excited and moist between her legs and there was a desire to do more. She halted the seduction momentarily as she thought what to do next.

"What is wrong, my love?" his husky voice broke into her thoughts.

"I want to do more for you, but I do not know what to do."

"Move forward and sit on my shaft."

She did as requested and immediately succumbed to the urge to press into his groin, feeling his hardness against her. She moved her hips as she ground herself into him, and heard him groan. She felt exceedingly hot and decidedly wet between the legs, and knew it was time to forego this adventure and allow her husband take control.

"I am ready for you," she whispered the words.

"I know, but you are in control of this, my love, so go with what you want to do."

"I do not know. Teach me, Richard?"

"You can ride astride, can you not? I know you are a good rider and you will ride me well. So mount me, my darling, and take what you want."

She looked at him in partial shock. This was the wife coming to the fore, she thought, so she pushed the wife away and embraced the mistress. Ride him was what he said. Well she was astride him so she lifted up intending to take hold of him, but his hand was already there and holding his shaft upright.

"Lower yourself, Bella, slowly," he rasped.

She did as instructed, supporting herself with her hands on his stomach as she felt him at her entrance. Her eyes held his as she lowered onto him, feeling the velvety warmth as he gently pushed inside, then she opened, took him in and closed around him.

She took the outstretched hands as he told her to ride. This was most brazen. But also exciting and thrilling and so much more than anything read in her journals. His words to ride encouraged her to move up and down as though on horseback, and when she did the feeling was exquisite.

Dangerous Entrapment

She needed more so increased the movements. This was her game. The more he gave the more she wanted, and there was now a need to gallop, so thrust herself up and down on him supporting herself with his hands, wanting more each time. He was caressing the inside of her but she wanted firmness, not a caress, so the speed of movements increased until she felt the hard length of him pressing and expanding against every side of her. As the thrusts became ever more demanding she was moving within reach of the end and then felt herself falling from a great height as the creamy wetness burst from her body. She fell onto his chest crying out his name.

He held her for a short time and then turned them both, careful to remain inside, and proceeded to take his own gratification. His vow not to remain inside her, for fear of feeding any gossip about a hasty marriage, had been kept. But he did not intend denying himself that pleasure any longer. He took her lips with his, as he pushed deeper and deeper inside until he came undone and sowed his seed deep into the depths of her body. Holding her in his arms he was completely sated and overwhelmed with what had just taken place. A trembling hand stroked the dishevelled tresses, as he kissed the top of her head.

"Bella, my love, are you all right?"

It was a moment before she answered. "I think so. You stayed with me, came inside me. I made you do that and I do not know what to say."

"Say...about what?"

"Behaving like a ... well, you know."

"What...a mistress rather than a wife?"

"Yes."

"Well I am not complaining, my love. I love my wife but I also love my mistress and I can see no reason why the roles cannot be joined in the bedchamber."

"What, you mean you would like me to be like that again?"

"Only if you want to, Bella."

"I think I might like that."

"Good. I would hate to have to find another mistress who could please me so well."

She lifted her head and slapped him on the chest. "Do not even think of doing that for this mistress would be sorely displeased. But I believe at the end you made love to your wife as you did not withdraw from me, and I would trust that you would not do that with a mistress."

He laughed. "No, I did not withdraw, my love, nor will I do so the next time. Even as we speak you could be with child, and I would certainly not put a mistress in that position. I have waited long enough for the gossips to be silenced but I have no intention of denying myself the pleasure of coming inside your adorable body any longer. As long as I have you I have no need for any other mistress."

"What do you mean silence the gossips?" He could hear the puzzlement in her voice.

"Oh, Bella, sometimes, my darling, you are so innocent. Our marriage was a somewhat hastily arranged affair, and you yourself said the ladies looked at you in a strange way. They were most likely trying to see if you were with child. This is why I have not spent inside you until now, so there would be no suggestion that you were with child when we were wed."

"Oh," gasped Bella. "How dare they think I would give myself before my wedding night."

Richard threw back his head and roared with laughter. "My darling, that is exactly what you did, not that I raised any objection. It was the most unexpected and delightful experience."

Bella blushed. "Well, they did not know that I had, and should not have presumed that I would."

Still laughing, he kissed a flushed cheek and climbed off the bed and, picking up the trays, carried them back to her. "As you wish, my love. But now I think we should have some of the supper that was brought up." He said, placing the trays on the covers.

He refilled the wine glasses and carried them back. She was rested back against the pillows and watching as he approached. She looked utterly delightful to him. Her flushed cheeks from their lovemaking and the redness on her body told of his caresses. "I trust you are enjoying the view, my lady." He could not help but tease as she took the wine he held out to her, and was rewarded by a deeper blush to the cheeks.

"I need to fetch my robe," she said, sounding somewhat flustered as he climbed on the bed next to her.

He shook his head. "Not yet. I have a longing to lie here and look at you as we eat."

She smiled at him seductively. "Naked. Is that what you would do with a mistress?"

"Most definitely, and then I would do this..."

As he spoke he poured some of his wine between her breasts and proceeded to lick it up with his tongue.

"Richard," she gasped.

"Next, I would do this." A small piece of cold meat was popped inside her mouth.

Following his lead, she sat upright and began to feed him and they sat completely, naked until the plates were empty.

Pouring more wine and watching as she drank, his eyes following the flow as she swallowed, before roaming down the delectable body to her breasts. Putting out his hand, he took the glass from her, placing it on the tray then setting it on the side table. Holding his glass in one hand she was drawn down to lay flat on the bed. Taking a mouthful of wine, he lowered his head to a pink nipple and placed it in his mouth, letting some of the wine trickle down the breast.

He intended to take her into another world. A world where what was being done was so seductive she would never want it to stop. When he was done teasing his tongue trailed along the path of the wine until she was gasping for breath. Then, when he believed she could imagine nothing more pleasurable, he moved between her legs, and gently pushed them apart.

Kneeling between the opened legs, he took another mouthful of wine and, bending forward, raised her with one hand, and placed his mouth upon her allowing the wine to run down over her core. Then his lips were placed over her tender spot and his tongue stroked over the wine stained area until she was shaking in his hands. Draining the glass, Richard tossed this across the bed and proceeded to move up her body, kissing every inch as he went.

Reaching her lips, he put his hand between them and guided himself into the soft flesh. As she closed around him, he deepened the kiss and started to move within her, drawing her further and further to the end of his sheath. Then when he was fully encased, he looked down at her and asked a simple question.

"Wife or mistress?"

"Oh, most definitely mistress," she replied.

"Are you sure? It may hurt."

"Does not matter. I wish to please you, and I would wish you to please me." She bit her lip nervously.

What was he doing, he thought. *What game were they playing? This was his wife and she was asking that he treat her as a mistress. Wives were meant to be loved and caressed. Mistresses were there to be fucked and then left.*

"Bella, I cannot. I cannot bed you again like a mistress. You will be sore."

"Please. Even if it is only this one more time, although I hope it will not be." To entice him, she moved and tightened around him.

"Aagh, Bella, do not, I am already too hard."

"Well you had better get on with it," she said with a flash of impatience.

Looking down, he saw the passion in the green eyes. *So, if that is what you desire, my lady, then let us do the deed, and I guarantee you will not wish it like this again.*

"All right, Bella, but do not forget that you asked for this."

Even before he was finished speaking, he pushed hard forward and felt her body jerk beneath him. She did not cry out for which he was pleased. He had no wish to cause pain. Closing his eyes, he gave himself up to her request. Thrusting into her over and over again she made no complaint, no cry, but rose to meet with him every time. The more he pushed at her the more she came back at him. When he was ready to blow, she shattered around him, like a chandelier breaking into a thousand pieces, and he remained within her until every one of his seed was swimming to its destiny.

They needed to move, he knew he would be heavy on her body, and they were both bathed in sweat. But felt almost ashamed to look at her after what had just occurred. Her fingers in his hair goaded him to action. Easing out he rolled to the side, keeping one arm draped across her body. Daring to look he found her staring up at the bed canopy.

Bella lay in a daze. She was not sure what she had just experienced but it was rougher, unlike anything they had done before, and she had liked it. But from the way Richard spoke, she should not have enjoyed it. What was she to do now? Pretend she hated it, but how could she? If playing the role of a mistress would keep a husband from straying then every wife should do it. Was she a hussy to have enjoyed it? She glanced at her husband laid atop of her with his head rested on her breasts. Raising a hand she ran her fingers through his hair. She felt him stir, and then he moved and was gone from her. His voice broke into her thoughts.

"Bella?"

She turned to him, and when she saw the concern in his face she smiled the sweetest smile she could muster. *Well,* she thought, *I cannot let him worry himself to an early grave, so honesty has to be the answer.*

"Thank you. I quite enjoyed that," she said primly with a sparkle in her eyes.

She had not known what he would say, but he surprised her by bursting into laughter.

"Oh, Bella, what am I going to do with you?"

"Well I hope you will treat me like a mistress again, but I also like being treated as a wife."

"If you wish, my love, you can have the position of wife and mistress, but the mistress stays strictly in the marital bed. Are you sure that I did not hurt you?"

"I would be lying if I said it did not hurt a little at first but after that it was, well, quite wonderful."

"Well wonderful or not we are both in need of another bath, but I fear the water will be cold, and that will be sufficient to dampen any further romps you may have in mind, my love."

She was carried into the next room and then stood down as he proceeded to wash her from the now very cool bathing tub, ignoring her shrieks and giggles at the cold cloth. Having attended to her needs, he proceeded to wash himself but she was not intending that this be over. Pulling the cloth from his hand she took over the task, and very carefully began to wash his body, taking more time than was necessary on a certain part of his anatomy.

"Bella, do not play with fire, or you may get burned."

"Maybe I wish to be burned, sir," she said, tilting her head to one side and smiling seductively at him.

"What have I awoken in you, wife? You are indeed playing the part of a mistress to perfection. But the mistress and the wife must wait until tomorrow."

Bella pouted. "But why?"

"Because, if I take you again, and if you continue to look at me like that I will, you will be sore, and will not be able to enjoy the seduction I have planned for tomorrow."

Bella blushed at his forthright words. "So you intend to seduce me again tomorrow?"

"Most certainly, tomorrow and every day after that," he said, taking the cloth from her hands. Then she was turned and smacked lightly on the derriere. "Go and put on your robe, temptress," he said softly.

Bella giggled as she went back into the bedchamber. Picking up the night rail she was about to put this on when it was whipped out of her hands.

"I said robe, not this," he said, tossing the offending article onto the chair and holding the silk robe open for her. Slipping her arms into the sleeves, she tied the sash around her. Turning, she found him similarly attired. Pouring a glass of wine each, he sat in the chair next to the fire and she was drawn down onto his knee. They stayed there for some time until the embers started to die, and then he carried her to the bed.

She waited at the side of the bed as he placed the trays outside the door, unsure as to what to do since her night rail had been taken from her.

"Are you not getting into bed, my love?"

"In my robe?"

"No," he said, reaching forward and deftly pulling the sash undone.

She watched as the silk slid from her body to the floor.

"Now you may get into bed."

A shiver of excitement ran through her body, as she quickly climbed beneath the sheets. She had never gone to bed naked. Oh, he had taken off her night rail but then she had always put it back on. But this was different, it was as though what were done earlier had changed things, and she quite liked it. She watched as Richard disrobed and then climbed naked into bed alongside her. Turning, she was pulled into his arms and gently told to try and sleep.

"What, like this, naked and alongside you naked as well?"

"Yes, it will make tomorrow all the more enjoyable to resist temptation tonight."

Bella was sure she would not sleep. She was so aroused by this intimate embrace, but she had not taken account of the wine or the previous encounters and it was not long before she was in a deep sleep, held gently in her husband's arms.

Waking early next morning, Richard carefully eased out of the embrace in which he held Bella. Moving silently to his dressing room he called for Anna and requested she pack for her ladyship, enough for a week's stay at Carlisle Hall. Giving similar instructions for his own clothes, and then for a rider to be sent to the Hall to announce their arrival, he returned to the bedchamber.

Bella was still sleeping as he slipped back into the bed, and ran a hand along her spine, feeling the silkiness of the skin under his fingers. He was not intending to take this any further than to awaken her and ignored the hardening of his shaft. If he took her now it would delay the surprise that he had planned. Whispering into a delicate ear, he gently woke her, watching through gritted teeth as she turned and stretched, displaying naked breasts to his eager eyes. The eyes were heavy with sleep as she opened them and smiled. Dropping a kiss on her lips, he could not resist trailing his lips across the exposed breasts, before reluctantly turning away and throwing the covers back and climbing out of the bed.

"Come, my love, we have an exciting day ahead of us."

"Oh, and pray what form does this excitement take?" she asked, sitting upright and giving him full view of her upper body.

He inhaled sharply. "Not the kind of excitement you are tempting me with by your display, my lady. Well, not yet anyway. We are leaving for Carlisle Hall after breakfast so you need to be bathed and ready to go within the hour."

"Hour, Richard, you jest. I cannot be ready within the hour. There is packing to be done and things to organise."

"All in hand. Anna is packing as we speak, and your water is waiting so you need to bathe as quickly as possible."

Sighing, Isobella swung her legs out of bed, but before her feet touched the ground she was picked up in his arms and carried through to the bathing chamber. Wrapping both arms around his neck, she nuzzled into him and gently nibbled his ear.

"Stop, minx, or you will delay us, and I am not in a mood to be delayed."

She laughed softly as she was deposited in the water, and then he dropped a kiss on the top of her head before walking through to his dressing room.

Having bathed and dressed there was one more stop that needed to be made while Isobella was being dressed. Walking to his mother's rooms he knocked gently on the door and entered.

"Good morning, mama," he said, smiling at the figure sat upright in the bed with a breakfast tray on her lap.

"Good morning, Richard, to what do I owe this early, but very pleasant visit?"

Picking up a small bunch of grapes from the plate as a kiss was dropped on her cheek, he sat in the chair alongside the bed. "I am taking Isobella away to Carlisle Hall for a few days." He popped a grape in his mouth as he waited for her reply.

"But it is the middle of the season. Will it not look strange you suddenly disappearing?"

Richard laughed. "I am taking my wife away, not vanishing from society. Anyway, it is society's fault that I feel the need to do this."

"Why, is Isobella out of favour, or is she ill?"

"Neither, mama, but something did happen two nights ago that greatly upset Isobella and put me sorely out of favour, for a reason I did not know until last night."

"Are you intending to disclose this happening to me, or do you intend to leave me wondering at what could have occurred?"

"Bella overheard two ladies, and I use the term ladies loosely, anyway... she heard them discussing that I had taken a mistress, and a mistress from the ranks of society. As you can imagine she was greatly distressed and we both spent a most miserable day apart yesterday, until I was able to obtain the reason for my disfavour from her last night."

"I trust the gossips were not right?"

Richard sat upright in the chair and looked shocked at his mother's suggestion. "Of course they were untrue. I will never take a mistress again, I am more than satisfied with my wife."

"I am pleased to hear it. You should not put yourself in such as position as to attract gossip. So am I to assume that Isobella has believed you since you are to go away."

"Yes, she believes me, and why would she not, it is the truth. So now I am carrying her off into the depths of the countryside so we can spend a few days alone together, before facing the gossips again. So I will bid you farewell for a few days, mama. I have spoken to Edward, who is only too willing to accompany you to wherever you wish to go."

His mother laughed. "I am sure that he was pleased with the instruction."

"I would not go so far as to say that, mama, but it will keep him out of mischief for a while." Rising from the chair, he leaned across the bed and kissed her before tossing the last of the grapes into his mouth and making his way back to his rooms.

Walking into the bedchamber, he found Anna finishing the final touches to Bella's hair. "No need to fasten your hair up, my love, tie it with a ribbon to match your gown. I would be greatly pleased if you would," he added softly.

Tipping her head in acknowledgement, she opened a drawer, pulled out a selection of ribbons and handed them to Anna, and watched as she selected one that would match the pale blue dress. With her hair held back with a satin ribbon, she looked younger than her one and twenty years and Richard's heart skipped a beat as she stood up and turned to him.

He held out his hand. "Come, let us partake of breakfast, then we shall leave."

Visiting Richard's mother before they left she did not miss the reproachful glance passing between her husband and his mother, that told her she was aware of the reason for the sudden journey.

Now seated in the travelling coach, she settled back to enjoy the journey and view. The curtains were pulled across to prevent prying eyes from seeing in and Bella made to move them back, but his hand stayed hers.

"Leave them, my love."

"Oh, but it is such a shame to close out the sun."

"You will see plenty of the sun over the next few days, but for now the darkness of the carriage is more pleasurable."

"More pleasurable? In what way?"

"In lots of ways, my darling. In this way to start," he said as his hands pushed the skirts above her knees.

Isobella gasped, but made no move to stop him.

His hands rested upon her knees, while his eyes watched carefully, unable to prevent the smile as he saw the eagerness in her face. She knew what was planned. He intended to take his pleasure, but it would be more Isobella's pleasure. His hands travelled up to her thighs and carefully rolled down the silken stockings, and then her legs were gently spread.

She offered no resistance to him; indeed, he doubted if the thought of stopping him even entered Bella's head. The look on her face told him she was lost in a daze of sensual arousal. That he was able to do this to her in a moving coach with people just outside was overwhelming, but oh so thoroughly enjoyable. She rested back against the cushions and tilted her head to look at him from beneath lowered lashes as he pushed up the petticoats and released the cotton pantaloons. Then, he heard the gasped cry, "Oh," as his finger ran gently over her most pleasurable spot.

He kept his eyes on his wife's face. She had teased him with her body this morning and believed she would be safe until they reached their destination. Well, he was about to prove that she would never be safe with him. Rubbing his thumb over her centre, he smiled as she gasped again.

"Like that, Bella?"

"Yes," she said, her voice barely a whisper. Her breathing becoming more unsteady.

"Good," he replied, not taking his eyes from her. Pushing gently forward, he moved through the soft folds of flesh until he found the entrance he sought. Then moving two fingers forward, eased slowly inside her, feeling the welcoming touch of her wetness.

"Richard, we cannot, you cannot."

"Oh, my love, I think you will find that we can. Or rather you can. Relax, Bella, let yourself go. Feel me inside you, take me in and hold me while I please you."

Even as the words were spoken she clenched around him. Pushing forward with more force brought forth a further gasp of pleasure as her body rose and opened to take him further. Sliding off his seat, he knelt on the floor placing one arm around the slender waist and held her firm, while his other hand thrust into her, taking her to another world, until she fell about him with soft moans, and the milky fluid flowed around his hand.

She opened her eyes and met her husband's gaze, certain the outside world must know what had just happened. But she could not have stopped what had taken place. "You will ruin your breeches down there," she said, with a giggle.

"What a wifely thing to say, Bella. But would you have me rise or would you have me clean you?"

She caught her bottom lip between her teeth. "I think I would like you to clean me first," and then she moaned as he gently wiped between her legs with his handkerchief.

When he was done, he fastened the pantaloons then pulled her petticoats and gown down before sitting back on the squab opposite and smiling roguishly. "I told you I have much to teach you, Bella, and this time on our own is going to be most instructive."

"Then I can hardly wait, husband, for you have fairly taken my breath away already. But what of you, are you totally untouched by what has just happened?"

He gave a wry laugh. "What do you think, my love?"

"I am not sure, that is why I asked," she said teasingly, leaning forward and boldly placing her hand on the front of his breeches, feeling the hardness of him straining against the material.

"Ah, I thought not." Before he could reply, she slipped off the seat and started to undo the buttons on his breeches. Once undone, his shaft sprang free, hard and looking very enticing. She had done this before as his mistress, but now she would do it as his wife. Taking hold of his length she angled him towards her and placed moistened lips around the tip. As her tongue teased him she gently drew him further into her mouth until she was sucking him, as a child would have sucked its thumb.

If Richard had any thought of stopping her, that thought was long gone. He was beyond all coherent thought. She was drinking him dry and it were all he could do not to push further and further into the warm soft mouth.

"Bella, I am about to blow. Let me free or I will stain your gown."

Lost in another world she could feel the salty liquid starting to leak from him. It was only his words and his hands on her shoulders that caused her eyes to open and look at him.

"Please, Bella, I have no wish to spray you. Let me see to myself?"

She shook her head and felt so heated and excited; all she desired was Richard inside her. Rising, she lifted her gown and petticoats, trying to balance in the swaying coach as she undid the ties of her pantaloons and straddled him.

"Do not waste it," she urged; then felt his hands guiding his leaking shaft into her welcoming flesh.

"Oh God, Bella," he groaned as his seed flowed within her.

When they arrived at Carlisle Hall, Bella was the picture of the demure duchess and played the part to perfection. But once in her rooms, she was left with her rioting thoughts as he left her for a short while to tend to business matters. She had thought the journey would have been tedious and long but her husband had just pleased her in the most wanton and wonderful way.

She loved being married and she loved her husband, and loved that it was her purpose in life to please him, to bear his children. That thought excited her and she vowed to keep her husband satisfied and in her bed alone. She knew how certain members of the ton strayed after the first flush of marriage dimmed but this would not happen with them. She could not bear the thought of Richard with another. So she would seduce her husband, become mistress to him on those occasions when he, or she desired, and thus keep him at her side.

Chapter Seventeen

Richard awoke Early the next morning to find himself wrapped securely in his wife's arms. Turning to free an arm, he then tenderly pushed back the curls from Bella's forehead. Running his hand beneath the covers he came upon soft, warm flesh and could not help but remember the way she had come to him last night. He would never have thought to enjoy the marital bed the way one would usually enjoy the charms of a mistress. But Bella fitted both roles and he could not wait to further her education, although she was perhaps learning some matters somewhat too quickly, their journey from London brought a smile to his face.

Moving so that his teeth were able to nibble at an exposed breast, she was soon awakening. "Come, Bella, I thought we could ride out before breakfast."

Without allowing time for a reply, he slipped out of the bed and pulled the covers back, leaving her naked body exposed.

Sitting upright, she rubbed her eyes, and pushed the hair from her face. "What time is it?"

He smiled lovingly at the sleepy face. "Just after dawn."

"Oh, come back to bed, Richard, it is too early."

"No, Bella, we are going to ride and your riding clothes are here ready for you," he said, indicating to the bundle being placed on the chair.

The sight of breeches and a white shirt had her out of bed and running across the room to him. He scooped her up in his arms and accepted her kisses.

"You have brought my riding outfit."

"No, my love, I have bought you a new riding outfit. One that befits a duchess, or perhaps a duke's servant."

A short time later, he was striding towards the stables, followed by what appeared to be a young servant, to where two horses were saddled and waiting. Dismissing the groom he led them out and assisted Bella to mount, allowing his hand rest on her knee longer than was necessary.

They rode out across the fields and then, when they were out of sight of the house she took off the hat she wore and shook her hair free. Laughing, she tucked the hat inside the jacket, and kicking the mare, sped across the field after Richard.

They galloped for some distance until they came to a small wooded area.

Richard led the way, while Bella still unfamiliar with the grounds followed.

Shortly he brought them into a small clearing edging a lake.

"Oh, you have a lake," she cried, clapping her hands in delight.

"My darling, if there had not been a lake, I would have commissioned one to be dug. How could I forget our trysts at Rothbury Hall and not wish them to continue."

Isobella smiled at him and moved alongside his mount, leaning across she pressed her lips to his. He waited but a moment then pulled her across, out of the saddle until she sat in front of him. Her horse shied but she held the reins and pulled the mare back.

"Look, you have unsettled my mount, sir. I think you should unhand me," she said, laughing.

"I intend to unhand you, wife, in fact, I have much more in mind for you, so I will dismount and assist you down."

He watched as her cheeks turned pink. She waited until he was on the ground before sliding down to him.

She was caught expertly in his hands, and he allowed her body to run down the full length of his own, all the while keeping a wicked grin on his face. Soon he would fulfil the dream that had tortured him for so long.

Tying the horses, he spread his cloak on the ground near to the lakeside, but still within cover of the bushes. Isobella's jacket had been cast aside and she stood looking out across the lake dressed only in breeches, a shirt and riding boots. Coming upon her from behind, his arms wrapped around the tantalising figure, drawing her back against his chest. "Do you like our lake, Bella?"

"Yes, it is almost as special as Rothbury's," she said, with a short giggle.

"Ah yes, that lake was special, but this one will be much more so."

"How?"

"Well, that, my darling, is something that I intend to show you," he said as he took her hand and drew her back to the cloak on the ground. "Ever since that first morning by the lake at Rothbury I have entertained a fantasy, and I am now about to make that fantasy a reality."

Sitting alongside, he let his hand trail from her shoulder to a breast, and saw the smile curve the pink lips. Turning, he faced her, putting his hands to the opening of the shirt. This had been especially commissioned with small buttons all the way down. Starting at the top, he slowly and carefully unfastened every button until the shirt was undone and resting temptingly against her body. Sitting back, he removed her boots and then returned his attention back to her body.

As she was eased back onto the ground, he took hold of the shirt edges and slowly opened these, exposing the creamy breasts to the morning air. He had watched her dress, knew there was nothing beneath. He swallowed hard, watching as the breasts moved ever quicker as her breathing increased. Leaving the shirt open, he moved to the front of the breeches and slowly unfastened the buttons before pulling them off until she lay almost naked. Disposing, with some urgency of his own boots and breeches, his gentle assault on her body began, until she was brought quivering to fulfilment. Then he sank deep into the soft flesh, taking her gently at first, and then with an urgency that she encouraged until they were both fulfilled. As his seed flowed he could think of no finer setting in which to create their child.

Supporting himself on his elbows, he looked down at his wife as she lay gazing at him with a look of pure contentment. Smiling, he kissed her lips and then rolled to the side alongside her. Both of them were oblivious to their surroundings and it was only the gently movement of the horses nearby that broke the silence.

Isobella could find no words for what had just happened. Having always believed herself to be a proper lady. But what lady rolls naked in the grass and allows herself to be so wonderfully seduced. She could not prevent the giggle that escaped her lips.

"What is it, my love, what amuses you?"

"I was just thinking it is as well no one can see us, otherwise we would be cast out from our peers."

"Ahh, but would it have been worth it, Bella?"

Turning sideways, she looked mischievously at him. "Oh, most definitely worth it. Can we do it again?"

Richard laughed. "We can come back tomorrow, and the day after, and for as long as you wish."

"No, I did not mean tomorrow. I meant can we do it again now?"

To offer encouragement to him she leaned across and pushed up his shirt and started to kiss his chest, while one hand strayed down to where he lay limp on his belly. Stroking him gently, she moved so that she was laid partly across him. Her hand never left him, working on him and pumping him back to life. She pressed her bare breasts further into his body as she felt the hardness returning to him. Hearing him groan, she shifted and straddled his hips and lowered her mouth to his growing erection.

"What would a mistress call your...well, you know?" she asked between gentle licks.

There was a short intake of breath at the question. "Why do you ask that?"

"Well a lady would call it a shaft, but I am sure a mistress would call it something else, and I was curious as to what that would be."

"A cock. She would call it a cock, my love." He could hardly keep the laughter out of his voice as he replied.

Isobella thought for a while as she continued to gently suckle her husband. "I think I would quite like to call it that, but only when I am your mistress."

For Richard, the reply was too much. He quickly held her shoulders and moved them both upright. "Wife, you ask too many questions, and I fear you are perhaps becoming too adventurous in the bedroom, and in the field."

He watched the emotions passing over Bella's face and realised that she had taken his remark to heart and saw her face flush. She believed she was being chastened by him for being wanton, and this clearly did not sit well with her. As she pulled the shirt edges together covering her breasts, and made to get up, he gently pulled her back down. She did not look at him and kept her head lowered, allowing the hair to fall forward to cover her face.

Her actions took him by surprise. He had expected a rebuke from her but he had clearly misjudged his words. It was not his intention to chide her, it was simply his intention to take control of matters, but now it looked as though once again he was out of favour with her. *Well nothing to be done,* he thought, *control is what I intended and control is what will happen.*

Pulling her gently down and rolling so she was pinned beneath him, he put one hand beneath the small chin and forced her to look at him. He could not fail to see the water filled eyes. "Oh, Bella, my love." His words were soft as he brushed away a stray tear with his thumb. "I did not say I do not like you becoming too adventurous, but there are times when I would wish to take control and this is one of those occasions. I did not intend for you to think I was chastising you, for I was not. I would never do that. I have looked forward so long to having you by my side, and in my bed. I have much to teach you, but you are learning so quickly that I fear I will soon be the pupil and you the teacher." He saw her lips tremble and then curve into a weak smile. He placed a kiss on her nose. "You asked if we could do it again and the answer is yes. But I will take charge, so if you would grant me one wish and open your delightful legs, my darling wife, or is it mistress?"

He saw the smile broaden and the fire leap in her eyes as he pressed his lips to hers. Then he felt her do as he bid and spread her legs even wider with his own before settling between her thighs. Guiding himself, he entered slowly at first and then pushed until he was almost fully encased. All the while covering her face with small kisses.

"So, mistress, are you enjoying this," he asked firmly, as he pushed forward, feeling her body arch as he did. Then he withdrew, leaving only his tip resting inside her.

"Yes, oh yes," she gasped.

"What do you want, Bella?"

"You."

"Where do you want me?"

"Inside me."

"What do you want inside you, Bella?"

"Your..." she hesitated before adding, "shaft."

He shook his head. "Wrong answer, mistress."

Her eyes flew open and the look she gave told him she knew, knew what he was asking her to say. But he wondered if she had the courage to say it? Tired of waiting, he asked the question again and this time she answered.

"I want you inside me. I want your cock all the way inside me, as far as it will go. I want you, all of you, more than I have ever wanted anything before."

The blush spread across her cheeks as she spoke and he pressed a firm kiss to each.

"There, you see, Bella, it was not difficult to say, for a mistress. And since you asked so beautifully I shall give you what you seek." Even before he finished speaking, he thrust forward, pinning her body to the ground with his, and watched the flare of excitement in the green eyes as her body rose and opened up to take him. They made love fiercely and passionately, and he thought he would never stop pouring his seed into her as they both reached fulfilment. His body convulsed upon hers until every last drop of him was extinguished and making the journey to her womb.

He broke the silence, rolling over to lie alongside her. "I think you and I will have many exciting years in the bedroom, Bella. I will confess that on those occasions when I took a mistress I rode them hard. I avoided the subject of matrimony, since I did not believe that I could find that satisfaction in a marital bed. You, my love, have proved that belief wrong. I have found in my marital bed both a wife and a mistress, someone who is not afraid to experiment with her body and push it to its limits. I am indeed the most fortunate of men."

Laughing, she turned to face him. "You have a way with words, husband, but I quite like the idea of being pushed to my limits...but only by you," she added softly.

"Only ever by me, Bella. I can see in your eyes and feel in your body the passion that is waiting to be released, and I will take the greatest delight in releasing it. But I will not push you beyond those limits that you decide."

"You seem to know a lot about releasing passion, husband," she said trailing a hand over his chest.

"Yes, well, I discovered some time ago that a husband needs to understand his wife to fully appreciate her charms, and should never judge a wife by what is seen in public."

"That is a very profound statement, my love. One would almost think that you had personal knowledge of a wife in such a situation, or perhaps a husband?" she said questioningly.

"Sad to say I do have knowledge of such a situation."

"Will you not share this knowledge with me?"

Richard thought for a long moment while his hand strayed along his wife's spine. "If I do tell you I do not wish you to think badly of me, for this happened several years ago, and long before I had even heard your name, my love."

"How could I think badly of you, Richard, when you please me so much."

Dropping a kiss on her forehead, he continued. "I was once in a short liaison with a lady of very high breeding. Anyone who saw her would have thought she was the most proper of ladies, but in the bedchamber, she was a siren. She had married well within her own station but her husband saw only what the outside world saw. Being a wife she was expected to act in a certain way, and sadly her husband did not encourage any other way within the privacy of their marriage. Having an appetite for forceful and adventurous sex he sought this in the brothels and Inns in the town, seeing only to his wife's needs on an irregular basis. And then it was an act that brought neither of them pleasure." He paused, breaking off from his tale as he felt her shudder.

"Are you cold, Bella?"

"No, I was just thinking how sad it must have been to have no excitement in the marital bed. To have a marriage where your husband only serves you without any care for your needs makes me feel very sorry for the lady in question. Until we were married I had no knowledge of the delights that could be found within the marital bed and I thought it only a place where one did one's duty to your husband. But this is not so, and marriage is the beginning of an adventure, of which I wish to discover more."

"Quite, and you will, my love," said Richard before continuing. "Since the lady's husband sought and kept mistresses, eventually the lady in question did likewise. She enjoyed several lovers before me and I entered into the liaison with the lady knowing of her expertise in the bedchamber. As a younger man, I felt able to keep up with her, but even I was taken aback by her wantonness and insatiable sexual desires. It was at her hands that I learned the way to tease and bring a woman to fulfilment, and it was she who taught me what I needed and wanted to fulfil my own desires. The language she used was most unladylike, but from her lips it did not sound wrong. I experienced something with her that I have never found with anyone else since, until I met you, my darling."

"So I please you the way she pleased you?"

"Yes, my love, but in a more enjoyable way, and you will please me even more in time as you still have a lot to learn."

"Is that why you wished me to say the...the other word for your shaft?"

"Partly, I wished to hear a word from your lips that you would utter to no one else but me."

"And did it please you?"

"It did, but it will please me more when I hear it come freely from your lips as you are in the throes of abandonment and writhing underneath, or atop," he added with a laugh, "of my body. Then when you say that word, and tell me where you want it, it will truly be perfect."

"Then I will remember that, husband, when we are next in such a position," she said, a sensual smile playing on her lips.

"And I shall look forward to it, but much as I have enjoyed our interlude, my darling, I fear that we must rise and dress and return to the hall, otherwise they may send a search party for us. And delightful though your body is, it is for your husband's eyes only," he said, rising to his feet and pulling her upright.

Fastening the buttons on the shirt until she was covered, she then reached for her breeches, and he watched as she pulled them on, covering the part that he could not stop desiring. He quickly dressed, and then, taking her hand, they walked together back to their horses.

Riding side-by-side, Bella could not resist teasing. "I think, my lord, that you have perhaps taught me too well, for I am finding riding astride most enjoyable. It teases parts of me that only my husband touches."

Seeing the look of surprise on his face she laughed, and kicked her horse into a gallop and sped away from him, hearing his curse as he chased after her.

They were back in their rooms before she asked him the question that had been hovering on her lips. "What happened to her, Richard?" "Whom?" he asked, distractedly.

"The lady who taught you what you desired."

"Ah, well, her husband fell ill with a disease contracted from one of his other pleasures, drink, and did not recover. Being no heir to inherit, the title and lands passed to a cousin. As a widow she was free to marry again, and she did. Married one of her previous lovers and they now reside abroad. I have no doubt that they spend the better part of their marriage in bed since the last I heard she had borne him three children."

"I am glad that she found happiness. I would hate to be in a marriage that was not...well, as a lady would say, fulfilling."

"Very delicately put, your ladyship," said Richard, smiling as he fastened the buttons on his shirt. "I can assure you that your marriage will be very...as you put it, fulfilling."

The time spent at the Hall was, to Bella, like a second honeymoon. Every time she entered their bedchamber she was reminded of the day she gave herself to him, before they were wed. But once in bed, the experience of that day paled into memory as she were taught things that she never knew were possible.

On returning to London, they were quickly enwrapped in the rounds of the society balls. It was at such an event some three days following their return that Isobella saw cousin Charles dancing with Sophia Stansfield, and the look on her cousin's face was that of someone besotted. Suddenly Richard's involvement in Miss Stansfield's love life became clear. He had been helping dear cousin Charles find happiness.

Looking around the room for Richard, she espied him deep in discussion with the Earl of Wellford. Tapping the folded fan against her hand, she wished that Juliette were here so they could chatter about this liaison. She was suddenly tired of the company and wished nothing more than to be at home and discussing this new development with her husband, preferably between the bed sheets.

Tapping a foot gently on the floor she glanced again in the direction of her husband and found him disappeared. Seeking him out, she discovered him on the dance floor with Lady Wellford, and took a moment to watch him. The way he held the elderly countess, the way his body moved on the floor and his charming smile as he clearly listened to her conversation.

All of this imprinted in her mind and she felt a ripple of pleasure run through her body, then he looked across, as if sensing her watchful eyes, and gave a smile that were so seductive her legs almost buckled beneath her. Flashing him a warning look she saw the smile turn to a grin that told her he knew exactly what he had just done. Flicking the fan open, she fanned herself to cool her heated face and turned her eyes away from him.

When she next looked back, he was again with the Earl. She snapped the fan shut and started to walk towards them. Wellford saw her approaching and bowed.

"Lady Carlisle, you are more beautiful every time I see you. If I were thirty years younger I would give your husband a decent run."

Isobella sank into a curtsey. "You are most kind, sir, but I think you would sorely miss Lady Wellford."

"And I for one would hate to call you out," said Richard. "As I have no intention of relinquishing my wife to anyone." The words sounded stern but the humour in the voice belied this.

Bidding the Earl farewell, Richard turned to his wife. "So, my love, what is it that caused you to look at me so openly and has now brought you to my side?"

"I have a need, no, really a desire, sir."

Richard waited for her to continue. She snapped the fan open and lowered her eyes. He bent his head to hear the words.

"I have a desire, husband, to feel your cock moving inside me very, very slowly."

He had to strain to hear the words and only just managed to cover his gasp with a cough. Isobella smiled at him from beneath her lashes and waited for his reply.

"So where is this to take place, my love? Do I seek out a secluded room or do we return home?"

Isobella smiled to herself. She had not been sure that she could say those words, but she desperately needed to be close to him. "I believe we need to return home, sir, this deed could take some time to complete."

She heard the cough at the words and wondered if she had spoken too boldly. But he quickly took her elbow and steered them both through the crowd and towards the hallway. Calling for their cloaks and their carriage to be summoned he stood behind her as they bade farewell to their hosts, Isobella pleading a headache for their early departure.

When she saw his cloak being pulled around him she knew why she had been kept firmly in front. She felt the giggle rising and swallowed to cover it. The thought of their hosts seeing her husband's state of arousal was almost too much. When she was finally cloaked she took his arm and they proceeded outside and into their waiting carriage.

The journey home was short and completed in silence. Both kept their eyes firmly fixed on each other. Entering the house, Bella disposed of her cloak, and then lifting her skirts, started to run up the stairs, followed closely by Richard who called to the bemused servants that they could retire. Bursting into their rooms, she turned round and laughed as she was picked up and swung around.

Then she was brought down against his body and his lips claimed hers.

"Witch," he murmured against her mouth.

"Lover," she answered back.

"Mistress?" he queried.

"Most definitely, sir."

Their coming together that night was fast and furious, and Bella rode him as she would have ridden the fastest of stallions. He let her have free rein until she fell about him and then turned and he took his own ride to heaven.

Chapter Eighteen

It was two weeks after their return from Carlisle Hall when Juliette and James returned from their extended honeymoon.

Meeting at Preston House the cousins did indeed compare notes, but Isobella had enough forethought to leave out most of the more intimate details. In fact, she was somewhat concerned at her cousin's lack of forthcoming and sensed that something was amiss. Persuading Juliette to talk about the bedchamber side of her marriage was not easy as she appeared somewhat reluctant at first, but finally Bella persuaded her to speak.

"Oh, Izzie, I had no idea that a gentleman's, well you know what I mean, that it could grow so big."

"What, oh, you mean his nose, cousin?" said Bella, biting back laughter.

"No, Izzie, his shaft," said Juliette, lowering her voice.

They were sitting in the drawing room at Preston House, while their husbands had adjourned to their club for an hour.

"Oh that," said Bella, smiling. "Yes it does get somewhat large." Deciding to tease her cousin she added, "You know a mistress would call it a cock.

Some women suckle it. It gives a man great pleasure."

Juliette spluttered, splashing tea onto her day dress. "Izzie, where did you hear that?" she gasped.

"Richard told me," she said calmly as if they were discussing the latest fashion.

"You discussed it with him?" she said in astonishment.

"I suppose you could say that. I asked him and he told me. I think it is quite a strange word, but used in the right way it can be most seductive." Bella watched as her cousin's eyes grew larger at the words.

"You use that word with your husband?"

Bella nodded. "Sometimes. But surely James is passionate with you. You must enjoy the marital bed?"

Juliette hesitated for a moment. "Of course I do, well it hurt at first but after that it was quite pleasant, but I do not know how far to take matters. I do not want to seem to be too forthcoming and adventurous. I sometimes believe James finds me lacking, but mama says I have to act as befits my new station," she said sadly. "It is all so different to when we were betrothed. Then it was exciting but now I have a household to see to and I am a wife and a countess, and that brings more restraint than being single. I would hate it that he took a mistress to give him what I lack."

Bella was alarmed at her cousin's words. To be talking of James taking a mistress so soon after they were wed was a serious concern, and she could not help but remember the tale Richard told her while at the lake. She could not let her cousin share the same fate as the lady in question. She needed to help her cousin resolve this dilemma.

"Oh, Juliette, do not heed what your mama says. Be as adventurous as you need and do what you wish. If you wish to keep your husband from seeking a mistress, you must take on that role yourself. Do not act the lady because you feel it is what is expected of you. James is your husband and is young and virile and you must seek to keep him happy, especially in the bedchamber, then he will never have a desire to stray. I take it that you share a bedchamber?"

"Of course, although he does spend some nights in his own room. To allow me time to rest," she added somewhat sadly.

Isobella shook her head. "No, cousin, you need to keep him in your bed every night. God, I would not be one night without Richard, nor he without me. You need to tie James to you now, while you are just newlywed."

"You share your bed every night?"

"My bed and my body cousin," she answered with a whisper, and a quick wink of the eye.

"Oh I do not know whether I could entice James like that."

"Of course you can," said Isobella, and proceeded to give her cousin a few simple suggestions for the bedroom. By the time she finished, Juliette's cheeks were flushed red.

"I do not think I could do things like that, Izzie?"

"Well, if you wish to keep a rein on your husband, and keep him in your bed alone, you will need to and you may soon have the opportunity," said Isobella, hearing the front door open and the sound of her beloved husband's voice. All this talk of bedding was making her hot and she had an urge to return home.

Watching Isobella and her husband drive off in their carriage Juliette recalled Izzie's words. James was about to go into his study, but she stayed him with a hand on his arm. Smiling sweetly at him, she went up on tiptoe and kissed his lips.

"Jules," he said, using his pet name for her.

She kissed him again and pressed her body to his. "I think I would like to retire for an hour, if you would care to join me," she spoke the words softly and held her breath, praying that Izzie was not wrong in her advice.

Dangerous Entrapment

He did not need any more encouragement, and grabbed his wife's hand and rushed up the stairs, pulling her behind him.

Entering their bedchamber, James quickly turned the key and then assisted his wife as she undressed. He had begun to think that the excitement she felt in that department before they were married had disappeared, but this encouragement told him different. Naked, they climbed into the bed and began what was to be an afternoon of discovery.

Lying utterly spent with his wife wrapped in his arms, James pondered on what had taken place between his wife and her cousin but had a feeling he would be forever in Richard's debt.

Returning home, Bella enticed Richard, quite easily into the bedchamber and proceeded to seduce him the way she had instructed her cousin to seduce James.

"Whatever did you and your cousin talk about that has made you so aroused, my love," whispered Richard into her hair as she knelt naked on the floor in front of him with his shaft held firmly in her mouth.

She shook her head and bit lightly on her target. He pulled the curls in response, drawing her head back and pulled himself out of her mouth.

"Enough, Bella, bed I think, or do you wish me to take you on the floor?"

She lowered herself down on the carpet, and capturing his hands she drew his naked body down to hers. They had never been so base as to be on the floor, but it suddenly suited her wanton mood. A mood that had increased over the weeks and had her seek her husband sometimes more than once a day. Feeling him push inside she gave herself up to their urgent needs.

A gentle shaking of the shoulder awakened Isobella. Then a voice whispered in her ear, "My lady, my lady." Opening her eyes, she saw Anna crouched alongside the bed.

"What is it, what is amiss?" she whispered not wishing to awake her sleeping husband.

"My lady, your cousin is here, Lady Preston and wishes to speak to you most urgently. I have informed her you are still abed, but she insisted that I wake you. I have put her in the small lounge."

Sighing, Isobella went to rise, but remembered her lack of clothing. Feeling behind for the night rail she encountered the garment and pulled it gently towards her. But then it would move no further, and whilst she gave it a small tug, it still resisted. Turning, she saw her husband's eyes firmly closed, but thought she saw the merest of twitches to his mouth and knew he held a firm grip on it. Smiling to herself, she asked Anna to fetch a clean night rail.

"Tell Lady Preston that I will be with her shortly, and have them bring coffee to us."

Walking quickly to the dresser she picked up a brush and tidied her hair before fastening it back with a ribbon. Glancing at the bed she noted there was still no movement and wondered, for a moment, if she had mistaken the twitch. Shaking her head, she left the room, closing the door quietly behind her.

Entering the small lounge she was immediately grabbed by Juliette.

"Oh, Izzie, I can never thank you enough. I have spent the most wonderful of nights, well afternoon and night really," she added with a giggle.

"Oh, Juliette, do not tell me you have rushed here at this ungodly hour to tell me your husband has seduced you?"

"No, Izzie, but I have seduced my husband and then he seduced me. It was wonderful," she said, clasping her hands together.

Isobella looked at her cousin's face and could not be out of sorts with her. She looked so happy, and to come calling at such an early hour, in such a state, only told further that Juliette had indeed been overly worried about the previous marital problem. Which, from the look on her face, was now a problem no more.

A knock on the door halted any response and she waited until they were alone again. Picking up a cup of coffee, she handed this to Juliette and sat back in the chair sipping the warm drink while listening to her cousin's gratitude for enlightening her on the matters of the bedchamber.

It was some time before Juliette rose to leave. After hugging her cousin and bidding farewell, she instructed that she do the same again every night. As the outer door closed she walked back into the small lounge. The connecting door leading into the library was now partly open and she ventured inside. Richard was sitting in one of the high backed chairs in his robe with a knowing smile on his face, and dangling her night rail from his fingers.

"So you have been teaching your cousin how to tie a husband to the marital bedchamber?"

Bella felt the blush rush up her face. "I did not teach, I made but a few suggestions to her. She was worried she was lacking and that James would seek a mistress," she offered by way of explanation.

"I think perhaps you should come here, Bella, and tell me all that you have been up to. I have no wish for James to be out of sorts with me because of something my wife has done." Richard's words were said carefully.

Bella's hand flew to her lips. She had no wish to be chastened by Richard, and for him to do so now sorely displeased her.

"I have no wish to discuss my private conversation with my cousin, sir."

"Isobella," the name was spoken firmly and she felt her back stiffen. Was this to be a battle of wills?

He repeated her name and held out his hand. "Come, Bella, do not defy me, please," the latter word was said softly.

She took a hesitant step towards him, and then another until she was standing at the side of his chair. He put out a hand and grasped a slender wrist, and she was quickly turned and pulled down onto his knees.

"There, you see, that was not so difficult, was it, my love?"

She lay sprawled across his body looking into his eyes and trying to decide whether the glint was anger or humour.

"So, what information have you imparted to Lady Preston?"

Isobella lowered her eyes, "I would rather not say."

He moved his head and nuzzled into her neck, and whispered, "Perhaps you would care to show me then."

Bella's head snapped up and this time she did not mistake the glint of humour in his eyes. Slapping him on the chest with one hand, she said, "Husband, you almost put yourself out of favour with me."

"I will never do that, Bella. So come, show me what delights you shared with your cousin. Perhaps James and I should compare notes?"

That earned him another slap on the chest. "Do not even think of mentioning what we do to James."

He laughed. "My love, I would not share a fraction of a thought about us with any other person. What takes place between us is ours, and ours alone. Although it would appear the same cannot be said for your cousin."

"I will speak to her, but she is over excited at the moment and filled with relief."

"If she has learned from you, my love, she will be filled with child before long. I had a need for you before you left our bed so suddenly and I now wonder if you are willing to attend to your husband, or do I order breakfast?"

Bella slipped off his knee and kneeling before him pushed the edges of his robe apart before parting his thighs. She ran her tongue over her lips as she moved slowly toward the object of her desire. Glancing at his face she saw his eyes close as he settled back into the chair, ready to enjoy the delights she would shortly minister to him. But she knew that, before this encounter were over, he would not leave her wanting.

As she lay in the bath sometime later, Richard's comment about Juliette being filled with child made her consider their own situation. She could not recall having a flood for some time and Richard had spent inside her on too many occasions to remember.

Waking a few mornings later, she found herself spending the previous night's refreshments on the floor of the bathing chamber. Her need for sex had never been a concern but lately this need was becoming excessive. These matters put together were enough to send her poste-haste to the physician who confirmed that she was indeed with child.

Her husband's delight was only exceeded by his continuing pleasure in attending to her excessive needs, that showed no signs of abating as she grew heavy with child.

Chapter Nineteen

Exmouth's Redemption

Exmouth was in a foul mood. His shoulder still gave him pain even after four weeks. Having fled to his country estate a few days after the duel, he spend most of his time trying to avoid his wife. Now she was heavy with child and all he could think of was that she had been with child before, a child out of wedlock, and this made any thrill at a possible heir, feel somewhat tarnished.

He was on his way back to the Hall from the stables when he espied a young girl standing near to the kitchen door talking to one of the servants. She looked no more than ten and six years with golden hair that fell in ringlets almost to her waist. She was not one of the servants from the Hall and he approached with quick strides.

Maggie, the under cook, saw him coming and quickly told the child to be on her best behaviour. "You know what you need to do, Lottie?"

"Charlotte, mama," she said correcting her mother.

"Yes, of course, Charlotte."

Dangerous Entrapment

By this time Exmouth was upon them. "Good morning, ladies."

"Good morning, milord," said Maggie, bobbing a small curtsey. "I was just sending my daughter on a small errand for the cook."

"Your daughter, eh. Well turn round, young lady."

Charlotte turned slowly round and went into a deep curtsey. "My lord," she said, in a soft voice. Lifting her head she looked directly into his lordship's eyes. He was not ugly; in fact some would say he was handsome, and older than she by some ten and five years. Her mother had been plotting such a meeting as this for the past twelve months since she had turned ten and five.

Exmouth was, for once, lost for words. The creature was exquisite. A face that looked like a peach, and hair as golden as the corn in the field. That she was the daughter of one of his servants was a bonus. He had every intention of bedding the child and would use his authority and position to attain his desire. Tilting his head in acknowledgement of the greeting he turned to her mother. "You have a very desirable daughter, madam. How is it that she has not been seen before?"

Maggie slowly etched a grin "I keep a strict eye on the girl, milord. She aint never allowed out alone, but there was no one at home today so I 'ad to bring her with me."

Exmouth was almost salivating, not allowed out meant that she was most probably a virgin, and he could feel himself hardening at the thought. "She is quite charming, tell me is she educated?" There was something about the stature of the girl that made him ask the question.

"She can read and write, milord, and she can play the pianoforte," answered Maggie.

Beckoning Maggie to him, Exmouth asked quietly, "How is she so different from your other children. Your other daughters and sons are dark haired, are they not?"

"Yes, milord," she said, before lowering her voice. "Her father is different to my husband, although she has been brought up as his own."

"I see." He pondered for a moment and then asked, "Who, pray, is her father?"

"Would rather not say his name, milord, but he was a titled gentleman who stayed at the Hall, and who took a liking to me. She has good breeding on his side, sir. And I 'ave done me best, sir, to educate her as befits her birthright."

With his mind working quickly, he stepped back. "Have her present herself to me in the library tomorrow morning. I have need of someone to assist in the cataloguing of the books. If she can read and write then she can assist me."

Maggie bobbed a curtsey and watched as he walked away. Turning back to her daughter she relayed what the duke wanted. "You know what you have to do. You need to make him want you, but do not give in to him too quickly. If his lordship takes a liking to you he will give you gifts, and then you can sell these and get away from here and into the kind of life you should have."

The next morning Charlotte presented herself in the library as instructed. Exmouth was prepared to wait and behaved himself impeccably, asking that she read the book titles out to him while he wrote them down in a great book. Then he watched as she climbed the ladder to the top shelf. He could see the turn of her ankle under the pretty muslin dress she was wearing. The golden hair was tied back in a pale green ribbon, and she was like a breath of fresh air to him. He sprawled in the chair behind the desk and stroked the hardening of his cock with his hand. He would bide his time. There was no cause to rush, and he felt an unusual softness towards the young girl.

It was five days since Charlotte had first attended the library and each night, as she returned home, was interrogated by her mother as to the events of the day. She knew what her mother's hopes were. She wished the Duke to take her as his mistress so she could acquire some wealth from presents, but Charlotte was minded for something more than a mistress, something of longer term and that would give more than a few bits of jewellery. The Duke was tied into a marriage that gave him no pleasure and it was whispered that the Duchess was already undone by another before they were wed.

Her mother told her the tale, saying that the Duke behaved like a madman when the truth came out. "He wants a virgin, Lottie, and anyone who will give themselves willingly to him will be greatly rewarded, I am sure of it."

From that day her mother had ensured she be kept pure and intact for that sole purpose. She was to let the Duke seduce her, take her maidenhood and be greatly rewarded for it. But Charlotte craved more; she sought to be away from the small cottage where she shared a room with two other sisters, and spent her days cleaning and mending clothes.

It was the sixth day of attendance at the hall and she had again been forced to endure a lecture from her mother that morning. Dressed in her best muslin, with a lower neckline that gave a glimpse of her breasts, she dropped a curtsey as she entered the library.

Harry was already behind his desk and the sight of the slight figure entering the room sent the blood rushing through his veins. He had spent many a sleepless night since she had been helping him, unable to get her out of his thoughts. His initial plan of seduction was finding less favour with him. He wanted more; desired that she come to him, but was damned if he knew how to make that come about.

"Come, child, do not stand over there. Come and see how many books we have catalogued since we started." He gestured with his hand as he spoke, telling her to approach.

Charlotte stood to his side as he pointed out the rows of books and titles that had been written down. She was bending slightly over his shoulder, awed at the flow of his writing. She could write but not the way he did. Every word was a flourish.

"Your writing is most beautiful, my lord."

Harry paused in his speaking and turned his head to look at her and found himself staring into a pair of pale blue eyes, *the colour of cornflowers,* he thought, and felt his breeches getting tighter. He needed to move matters forward. "Bring me the large book on the second shelf over there," he said, indicating with his hand. "The red bound book." As she collected the book he rose and walked to the winged chair near to the fire.

Charlotte did as asked and then followed him to where he was sitting.

"Sit down, child." He indicated to a small footstool near his feet.

Charlotte did as instructed and held out the book to him, but he waved it away, requesting that she open it and read to him from the first page. She did as instructed, stumbling at first, as she was unused to the set of the writing.

The more she read the more she enjoyed it. It was a story, not one a lady should read, about a wealthy merchant who kept slave girls. Saying the name for certain parts of the ladies bodies made her blush at first, but she soon learned to overcome this.

His lordship sat in the chair with his hand resting on the arm and she knew that she should make some move. Her mother's instructions were to tease him, but not too much at first. She was wondering how to make such a move when his hand dropped onto her head and his fingers began to play with her curls. She turned and smiled up at him, surprised to see him resting back with his eyes closed.

She read on, the words at times making her feel quite overheated. He was planning to make a move, she knew this, otherwise why ask that she read from this book. It was strange but she liked the book even though it was very descriptive in what were taking place.

"Do you like the story, Charlotte?"

His voice suddenly penetrated her thoughts and she turned and found him looking down at her. She had been called by her birth name and that pleased her.

"It is very...enlightening, my lord."

He threw back his head and roared with laughter. "I have heard debauchery called some things, but never enlightening. Come, turn to me so I can see your face fully."

Charlotte turned and knelt on the footstool. She pulled her shoulders back knowing this would push her breasts forward. He was watching as she turned, and she knew he did not miss the straightening of her back, nor could he avoid the sight of her breasts as they strained against the muslin top. She saw him cover his groin and knew the gesture was to hide his arousal, she had brothers and had seen them rub themselves to hardness, and she knew this was the time to help him.

Setting the book down on the floor, she rested her hands on his knees, feeling him flinch as she did.

"Sir, you seem to have an affliction that requires some attention. My mama has versed me well in how to relieve such an ailment."

Harry stared at the beauty before him. His throat was dry and could not believe that she had just spoke those words to him. "Go, turn the key in the lock, Charlotte, so we are not disturbed." He lay back in the chair and parted his legs and watched as she rose and did his bidding.

Coming back, she knelt on the floor in front of him, between his parted thighs. Her hand trembled slightly as she reached for the front of his breaches and slowly undid the buttons. She could see him swelling as her fingers brushed lightly against him. When he was undone she pushed the material and his undergarment apart and exposed his cock that was partly held to one side. Taking him in her hands she eased him free and found herself holding the largest piece of a man's naked body that she had ever seen.

Oh, she had seen her brothers as they bathed but they were small, and even when they had rubbed themselves they were within their breeches. But she had never held or seen such an enlarged object before. But this was how her mother described it would be. She gazed at it in wonder before doing what her mother had taught her.

Lowering toward him, she put out her tongue and ran this over the very tip of him. She felt him jerk in response and raised her eyes to his. He was watching her, seemingly transfixed by what she was doing. Smiling to herself she lowered her mouth until she surrounded him with her lips and then began to gently suck, as she tempted him with her tongue. He was so big she feared she would not be able to take him all in, but as she progressed she found that she was not disliking the experience, and became more adventurous. She suckled and teased him with her mouth until she felt the first drops of wetness.

Even though she tasted the saltiness she did not break her working on him. It was not as harsh as her mother said it would be. Taking him further and moving her mouth up and down she felt the tremors starting through his body and she gripped him tighter. As he pushed further into her mouth his seed began shooting into the back of her throat, and she swallowed it away. His hands grabbed her shoulders and, with a roar, he pushed and pushed into her until she let him slide down the back of her throat. Eventually the convulsions eased and she felt him go limp in her mouth, then he sagged back into the chair, his grip on her shoulders loosening.

Harry could not believe what had just happened. It were his intention to seduce *her* not the other way round. But he had no wish to stop her. She was adorable and what she did was exquisite, and was quite content to allow her take the lead. Feeling the soft tongue rolling along the length of his shaft had his bollocks pulled almost into his backside. It was some time since he had enjoyed a woman and knowing he would blow before long, wondered what she would do then. He thought about bedding and blowing inside her, but did not wish that here, on the floor. He had a desire to take her in bed and with caution. He suddenly realised that he wished to make love, not ravage her. The thoughts were muddled in his head as the convulsions had sent the first of his juices leaking from his tip. Her mouth took him, took all he gave, without question.

Harry was spent, his seed was lost inside the tempting mouth and he had never felt so humbled. That she did that for him, without any asking. His eyes were closed as she lifted him from her mouth. The fingers on his cock felt like feathers as she gently stroked him. Forcing his eyes open, he looked down at her, at the heaving breasts as she lifted a small handkerchief and began to wipe him and then, before she could wipe her own mouth, his hand reached forward, taking the cloth and did this for her. When she was cleaned she smiled at him, and he pulled her up covering over his body and placed his lips on hers.

He could feel the swell of her bosom as she pressed against him. The lips were given freely to him and he teased until she opened them and his tongue sought the softness of her inner mouth. Harry was lost in a world of sensual desire that he had not known or felt for several years. Her voice broke into his thoughts.

"Do you wish to bed me now, sir?" The question was soft and low.

He shook his head. "No, not now. I will bed you, but it will be done, as it should, in a bedchamber and with time to attend to all matters. Now I would wish to repay what you have just done for me."

"What do you mean, my lord?"

"Stand up." She did as asked. He rose from the chair and, pointing to it, said, "Sit."

She sat in the large chair and gasped as he knelt in front of her, the way she had with him. Pushing the dress up above her thighs he then spread her legs and pulled her part way down. Selecting a cushion, this was placed behind her so she was comfortable. Having assured him that she was, she waited while he took off the pantaloons her mama had made her wear. She felt the heat from the room on her private parts, and then his mouth was over her core, licking her. She wriggled in his hands and he raised his head and smiled at her, and she saw how handsome he really was. There was none of the harsh scowling face that had been seen in the past, and she smiled back.

"Does it tickle?" he asked.

She nodded her head.

"Then I will try not to tickle and simply to give pleasure." Pushing out his tongue, his fingers peeled back the soft skin leading to her opening, and then very gently pushed his tongue inside.

Charlotte gasped as his tongue entered into her and moaned softly as feelings she had only heard of, swept over her. As her body started to push towards him his hands came up and held her hips, gripping her and helping her to move to him. She was panting for breath and her clothes were suddenly too much to bear.

"Can I undress?"

"Not this time, my little cherub, but when the time is right you will be completely naked in my bed."

Thoughts of being naked and in bed with him made her push at him quicker and sent her over the edge and into fulfilment. His lips closed over her core as she convulsed into him and he tasted the creamy milk of her fluid. Then, as she had with him, he wiped her and replaced the pantaloons, before pulling her dress back in place.

Before rising he could not resist placing his hands atop the soft breasts and gently kneading these with his fingers. "I cannot wait to see you unclothed."

"When will that be?" she asked not wanting to lose this connection made with him.

"Soon, very soon. Do not come tomorrow as I have arrangements to make but come the following day and tell your mother you may be late."

After she had left, Exmouth stared into the fire for a long time. She had raised feelings in him that he thought were dead. He had not wished to do anything more than arouse her to fulfilment. He would take her maidenhood another time, and intended to take his time over the experience. For once he was not interested in just rutting a woman for his own pleasure, he wished to seduce her and make love to her. For once he desired to please someone other than himself.

Rising from his seat, he went to the false bookcase in the corner of the room and flicked the catch and swung the door open. It was some time since he had last used this room but now it needed to be made ready. Ascending the steps he came onto the landing, then opening the door on the left, looked around at the starkness of the room. Oh, the drapes were fine as was the furniture but it smelled musty and that was something that could be changed, he thought as he closed the door and descended the stairs. Once back in the library he called for his personal manservant, and gave instructions for the upper room to be made ready with flowers, sweets and wine, and to tell no one.

Charlotte, on arriving home, was questioned most thoroughly by her mother. She watched as she smiled when she told her what had transpired.

"Good girl. Clearly his lordship likes you but did he not bed you?"

She shook her head. "He said we were to wait, so it could be done properly. I am not needed tomorrow but I am to go the following day and to tell you that I may be late."

"It would seem that he means to bed you that day then. You must wear a special dress and ribbon but when he does bed you, do not let him put his seed inside you. It is safe for it to be in your mouth but not inside your belly. He could put you with child and would then cast you aside."

Charlotte thought on her mother's words as she prepared herself the following day. What if he wished to seed inside her, could she stop him? Would she dare to stop him, or would she wish to tie him to her with children. Oh she knew her mother was playing him for money, but what of Charlotte, what did she wish? She liked him but she also liked the idea of what he could provide for her. So she needed to make him want her all the time, and want no other. A difficult task perhaps but one she hoped she could achieve.

Presenting herself at the hall on the second day she was soon shown into the library. He rose as she entered and moved quickly to the door, securing the lock.

Turning, his hands were set on her shoulders and she was lifted from her curtsey.

"Forget that, Charlotte, we are well past being proper with each other."

She rose and looked up at him. She wondered if she dared to kiss him and gave herself no time to think but rose and kissed him lightly on the lips.

She was crushed to him and the kiss was deepened, her lips parted for his tongue. It was some time before he were able to pull himself away from her arms, but when he did she was led across the room, and he opened a concealed door. She was pulled gently behind him as they ascended the stairs. He opened a door. Standing to one side he beckoned her to enter. Cautiously, she stepped inside the room and found herself in a bedchamber.

Charlotte gasped at the sight before her. The drapes were of gold and cream and the covers on the bed were the same colour. The bed she could not miss, she had never seen one so large before. The room was filled with the scent from vases of flowers, and there were sweets and fruit set out on plates together with wine.

"Do you like your bedchamber, Charlotte? I have had it especially prepared for you, and I trust it is to your liking?" he asked anxiously.

She spun round and flung her arms round his waist. "I love it, I love every wonderful part of it. Is it really mine?"

"Yes, for as long as you wish it to be."

She looked at him, and then lowered her eyes and whispered, "I believe I would like it to be forever."

She heard his sharp intake of breath and knew the words she had spoken were pleasing to him.

"There are some robes in the closets if you would wish to change," he said, haltingly.

Turning, she looked shyly at him. "I thought you may wish to undress me, sir. And then I could do the same for you."

Bloody hell! He did not think this entanglement could get any better, but it just had. Pushing the door shut he secured the lock and then took off his jacket. Walking to the table he poured two glasses of wine. Taking hold of one small delicate hand he pressed the glass to her palm and curled her fingers around the stem. Then he touched his glass to hers.

"To our union, my cherub."

She nodded her head, smiled, and took a large gulp of wine. Setting the glass down on the table she turned away from him, presenting a row of small buttons. "Would you care to unbutton me, my lord?"

Harry had never known his hands tremble so much when undressing a female. But by the time the plain chemise was reached he had himself somewhat under control. Well most all of him was, but there was a part that was as hard as a rock. He watched as she knelt down and undid his shoes and then rolled down his stockings. Moving upward, she undid his shirt and then his breeches. There were no under garments worn beneath his breeches so when the buttons were undone he sprang free. He stood before her completely naked with his erection straining towards his belly, while she remained still covered by her chemise.

She was as light as a feather as he gathered her in his arms and moved across to the bed. Sitting her on the edge, the one remaining item of clothing was lifted over her head and he then stood back and, quite openly and unashamedly, stared at the pale body. His eyes gazed from the delightful toes to the golden locks in a slow deliberate movement. The slender legs and narrow hips and the pale golden tufts of hair between her thighs had him breathing heavily. His eyes travelled up over the flat belly to the small rounded breasts. Breasts that would fit so perfectly into his hands. She was perfection and he desired nothing more than to please her.

Harry Exmouth had never taken more care or been more loving with a woman before. He aroused her; teased her and brought her to a coming before slowly entering the soft flesh using her own fluid to assist his forward passage. Then as she was brought to the edge again he finally took the virgin that he had spent his whole life dreaming of. As he broke through the veil of her maidenhood there was such a sense and feeling of belonging with her, that he did not believe he would wish to bed any other. The small spotting of blood on the sheet told him of her purity and that now, the virgin he so desperately had craved, was his, but at the same time, he was hers and destiny had found a woman he could love.

Lying in the small bed that night with its plain covers she could not stop herself from wishing to be back in the large bed with silken sheets. His care when bedding her had been surprising. She was given to believe that it would hurt but she hardly felt any pain as she gave her maidenhood to him in a moment of sheer wonderment. Oh, it had hurt for but a second but his caresses, and the teasing of those private parts with his finger brought pure pleasure.

That day was the start of many, and Harry instructed the other rooms in the private wing to be decorated, and it was not long before Charlotte was residing there on a permanent basis. Spending many hours in the Duke's company and in his bed pleasing him and being pleased.

If the young Duchess knew of the liaison she knew better than to say anything.

She married to gain a title and respectability; but her heart lay on the continent with her lover and their dead child. That her husband had taken a mistress was nothing new, there had been many others taken in the past. But this one was different, this mistress was residing in the hall, in rooms that were not available to her. She longed for the birth of the child she was carrying; a child that she did not desire, so she could gain back her figure. If her husband could take a mistress she could take a lover, and there was little distance between the continent and England, and there was a willing lover ready and waiting.

It was two months after Harry's commitment to Charlotte that he was given the one thing he needed, other than Charlotte, an heir. Having delivered the child, his wife passed him on to a wet nurse and left her husband with no doubt that he was no longer welcomed in the marital bed. Bowing, as he received the missive, great pleasure was taken by him when informing her that he did not desire her bed and had a far more pleasurable bed to enjoy. But it was made clear that she was expected to convey herself as befitted her position.

"In other words, madam, any hint of a lover and I will divorce you on the grounds of your pre-marital indiscretion and cast you back to your family. I will expect you to care for your son as befits a doting mother."

"And you, sir," she said angrily, "will you be the doting father?"

"Naturally, after all the child will inherit one day and I will do all that I can to prepare him for such a task."

After this there was little discussion between the Duke and Duchess and the parties lived separate lives.

Harry Exmouth was happy and content but wished for more. He desired somewhere away from the hall where he and Charlotte could live as a couple. A small country house, within a short ride of the hall and with lands that adjoined his own, proved to be the answer.

The lands were kept as part of his estate, but the house was put in Charlotte's name so she would have a home for the remainder of her life and a fund was set up for her, to cover any future costs, in the event that he was no longer there. Not that he had any intention of leaving her; he was content with his life for the first time in years.

Settling Charlotte into the house, they spent many hours together choosing furnishings that would please them both. On enquiring if she wished her mother to move to the house, he was not surprised when she declined.

"I need to forget that part of my life and concentrate only on the life we now have...together," she added.

"Are you happy, my love?" he asked.

"Exceedingly so, Harry. And I will be even more happy in a few months, when I deliver your child."

She had worried about his response but she was swept into his arms and kisses were showered upon her hair and face.

"Oh, my darling, you have made me the happiest of men." His voice broke and she could not miss the tears in his eyes.

She sighed in relief. She had so worried about allowing him seed into her; he had sought to do so many times since they had first come together, but she held him back. Now with a new life opening up before them she had felt a desire to carry his child and pushed her worries to one side. She had taken his seed for several months and now she could feel the soft swell of their child in her belly. But this was not a child conceived from a need to escape her old life. This was a child that would be born out of love. For she had found that she had come to love Harry and was more than content with their life together.

As Charlotte grew heavier with child Harry thought back to the dark time in his life, when he had not been a gentleman, and threatened to take someone else as his mistress and breed from her. The intention was put crudely to her, as she had no wish to entertain him. And what he had done later filled him with remorse.

Sitting by the open fire and now recalling that time, he felt ashamed for what had been done. Charlotte, seeing the frown on his face, asked what troubled him. Having always been honest with her he had no wish to be other now, so told her all that he had done and begged her not to think badly of him.

"I was another person then, someone who needed to lash out and hurt others, the way I was hurt by my so called marriage. What I did to the lady in question was unforgivable." Although he told Charlotte the tale he did not divulge the name of the lady in question. He would never disclose that to anyone. He still remembered the pain from Carlisle's ball.

"I do not understand why you did what you did to a lady, but if you are to forgive yourself, then you need to seek forgiveness from her."

"I was thinking the same, my love. But I do not know whether the lady in question would receive me."

"Then you must approach where she cannot do other than speak to you. But you must be sincere in your approach and in what you say, or you will make matters far worse."

"You are right, as always, my sweet," he said, caressing her swollen belly. "It will mean that I will be absent for a short while, but you will have your maid to see to you, and I will not be away for longer than I need."

Chapter Twenty

Bella was remembering back to their time at Carlisle Hall as she wandered out onto the terrace at the Burlington's town house. This was to be their last public attendance until after the birth of their first child. She gently stroked over her swollen stomach. Only one more month before she would hold their child in her arms and she could not wait. She had dispatched Richard to fetch some cordial from the refreshments and was enjoying the warm evening air. Walking carefully down the steps to the garden she ventured along the cinder path towards a small garden seat.

She had almost reached the seat when she heard footsteps behind her. Turning to greet her husband with a smile, she was shocked to find Exmouth walking purposefully towards her. She instinctively placed her hands on her stomach, as if to protect their child.

"Do not fear me, my lady. I mean you no harm."

His voice sounded conciliatory as he approached but she looked at him warily, and wished more than anything to see her husband striding up behind him, but the path was empty. "What do you wish, my lord?"

"I have delayed many months before approaching you but hearing of your pending confinement I could delay no longer." He paused and his feet shuffled on the gravel. "I wish to apologise, my lady, and to apologise most sincerely for my past behaviour towards you and your family."

What Isobella had expected, she did not know, but it was certainly not this. And Exmouth looked and sounded different. His appearance was more like the person he was when she first met him. She was aware he no longer frequented society and was rarely seen about town, and had kept himself out on his country estate. But there was something about him, an air of contrition and perhaps of contentment.

"Your apology is long overdue, sir, and I am not certain that my husband would welcome your approach to me."

"I am aware he would not, my lady. I have felt the sting of his ball in my shoulder and I have no wish to repeat the experience."

Isobella frowned at his remark. That Richard had taken a pistol to Exmouth was something she knew nothing of. This was a matter that she would need to explore later.

"If you wish to avoid my husband's wrath, then I suggest that you say what you wish to say, and then leave."

Exmouth swallowed hard before starting his apology.

"I was wrong, my lady, to kidnap you and try and ravage you. I was also wrong in the many matters that I spoke to you of, and the words that I used. They were not words that I should have used to any woman let alone a lady of quality. I have no excuse for what I did and I do not deserve your forgiveness, but I need to beg for it. I have learned over these past months what it is like to have something, or rather someone who needs and desires you. I believe I was taken with a madness upon learning of the deceit of my wife and her parents, and sought to lash out at those who did not deserve it."

Isobella listened in silence to his words. This, indeed, was more the man that she had first met and been charmed by, but she could not help but be grateful that he did not offer for her. If he had, she would not be as happy as she now was.

"So you have found happiness with someone?" It was curiosity that led her to ask the question.

"Yes. She is much younger than I and is not of our class of society. Well, she has the blood but not on the right side of the bed sheet. A visitor to Exmouth Park took a fancy to one of the housemaids, and apparently she to him. The child is the result of that liaison and has been brought up by the woman's husband as his own. Although I am sure the husband is aware she is not his, since there is stark difference between her and her siblings. To me, she is everything I have ever wanted or needed." He paused. "I am sorry, my lady, I am saying more than necessary in my need to seek your forgiveness."

Isobella ignored his final remark. "So I presume that she was the virgin you so badly desired?"

He nodded his head. "Yes, but I did not take her forcefully. I waited and she gave herself willingly when she was ready and I was all the more pleased by that."

"And what of your wife, sir?"

"She has given me an heir but will bear no more children. Not that she would wish to. I was simply someone to give the position she desired after her downfall abroad, and she takes no pleasure in our marriage. She cares for our son at the country estate and I visit."

"So you do not live with your wife, sir?"

He shook his head. "No, I spend my days on a small adjoining estate I have purchased with Charlotte. She is carrying our first child and I am at last happy, but that happiness has come at a cost to others. None more than yourself, and for that I most humbly and sincerely apologise."

Isobella was at a loss at his disclosure. "So you live openly with another woman who is not your wife?"

"Yes, terribly disgraceful, but I give not a damn." There was a hint of humour in his voice. "I have long since given up caring what the ton think. Tonight is a very rare outing for me and I made it with the specific intention of seeking you out. It has taken me some considerable time to be able to approach you, as your husband keeps you by his side so well."

"Yes," said Isobella, "and he will return shortly with refreshments, and it would not be in your interests to be still here when he arrives."

"No, and I will depart, but do you accept my apology?"

She paused before she answered. "Sadly I cannot accept your apology for what you did or said to me. But I will accept that you were not in your right mind at the time, and that caused you to do and act in a way that was out of character. I do, however, wish you well for the future and trust that your child is born healthy."

Bowing low over her hand, he spoke quietly. "I understand, your ladyship, but your words give me comfort. I will bid you farewell and trust that your confinement brings you much happiness."

"Goodbye, my lord," she replied firmly, drawing her hand back and bringing the encounter to an end.

Isobella watched as Exmouth walked off through the gardens and then realised that her hands were shaking as were her legs, and she sank gratefully onto the seat. Hearing footsteps she looked around and saw her husband approaching carrying two glasses. Waiting until he had seated himself next to her she accepted a glass from him and took a long drink of the cordial.

"So, husband, tell me, just when did you call Exmouth out?"

Having just taken a mouthful of wine when she asked the question, he almost choked. "What did you ask?"

"You heard me plainly, sir," she said, trying to appear stern. That a duel were fought on her behalf gave her a thrill, but it was also frightening that he could have been hurt.

"What makes you ask the question, my love?"

"Exmouth has just told me."

Richard was on his feet in an instant looking around. "What, he is here, and he has dared approach you?"

"Oh, Richard, do sit down. Yes, he has been here but has now gone. He wished to apologise. I confess that I was afraid when he first approached but he was not the same person, was more the person I knew when I first met him."

"You did not accept his apology?" He almost barked the question at her.

"No, I did not, and there is no need to shout, my love. I will tell you all that passed between us before we return inside."

Richard listened to his wife but could not dispel the anger that Exmouth had dared to approach her, and in her condition. However, he was made to agree that the matter would not be taken any further, and that the whole incident was at an end. If not, his wife had threatened, he would be banned from the marital bed for three months.

As they walked back inside she asked the question again about calling out Exmouth.

"I did not actually call him out, it was James who did that," he confessed.

"What, James had a dispute with Exmouth and called him out?"

"Not quite, my love. I asked James to call him out, but it was never intended that James fight the duel, it was always my intention to do that."

"I think you had better tell me the whole tale, sir, before we reach home, otherwise you will miss out on the delights of your wife's body tonight."

"Bella, you are but a month away from giving birth. How can you think of that now?"

"Yes, well a woman's body is fickle and sometimes, when it should not, it craves things it desires."

Placing an arm around his wife's waist she was pulled against his body as they walked. "And you have such a craving, my darling?"

Reaching up, she whispered softly in his ear, "I have a craving to feel your cock deep inside me." His gasp was enough to tell her that she would receive what she desired.

Epilogue

Richard was pacing the floor in the small lounge at Carlisle House. It was almost noon and the physician had been with Isobella for several hours. His mother sat in one of the chairs and tried to calm him. He had heard the cries coming from the bedchamber as he had gone upstairs to change and dared to venture into their bedchamber. Watching Bella bathed in perspiration and hearing the cries told him she was clearly in pain, and it were enough to tear him apart. Seeing him in the doorway he had been quickly shooed away and now, some two hours later, they were still waiting of news.

"Richard, do sit down. You will wear the carpet away. Let me call for some more tea?"

"How can you drink tea, mother. If you had seen Isobella, the pain she was in, I could hardly bear it."

"Darling, we ladies all have to suffer this. And, anyway, if you cannot bear to see it again, then you will have to resist your wife's charms."

"Mother!!" exploded Richard.

"Well, dear, you cannot blame Isobella for the condition she is in. I do think you will have to take some blame," said the Dowager Duchess with a hint of humour.

There was a knock on the door but before he could reach it, it opened and the physician entered.

"Congratulations, my lord, you have a healthy child."

"And the Duchess?" asked Richard fearfully.

"In perfect health. No problems at all..." the physician said, but found himself talking to an empty space as Richard ran out of the door.

Taking the stairs two at a time, he burst into the bedchamber and came to an abrupt halt at the sight before him. He expected to see his wife in a sick state lying in bed but what he saw was Bella sitting up, with hair newly combed and tied with a blue ribbon, and cradling their child in her arms. There was no sign of the pain or sweat that were seen earlier, all he saw now was a picture of serene happiness.

Bella looked up as the door was flung open and then watched as Richard came to a stop. She looked at the expressions passing across his face and smiled.

"Do you intend to stand in the doorway, my love, or would you wish to enter and meet your son."

Her words broke the trance he was in and he strode forward to the bed.

Ignoring the scowl from the nurse, he climbed onto the bed alongside Bella and kissed her. Then he looked down at the small bundle in her arms.

"A son, you say?"

"Yes, an heir," she answered, pulling the shawl down and letting him see the dark haired infant who was lying quietly with his eyes shut.

Richard put out his hand and gently touched his son. "He is beautiful, just like his mother. Do we have a name for him?"

"I thought Samuel Richard might be acceptable, but if you have any other names you would wish..." she trailed off.

"Samuel?" he said, testing the name.

"As you may recall it was my father's name, but if you would wish another I will understand."

"No, I think Samuel will suit him well. Thank you, my love, I do not think I could ever be happier."

"Nor I," said Isobella, resting her head against his shoulder. "But I think you should go and fetch your mother so she can meet her grandson."

"Anything you wish, my love," said Richard, rolling off the bed. "I will be back shortly."

It was much later in the evening when Richard was able to be alone again with his wife and son. The Rothbury family had all been to visit and he had just dined with his mother before she retired for the night.

Going into his own bedchamber he undressed and pulled on a silk robe over his nightshirt. Walking into the adjoining master bedchamber the nurse was still with Bella who was sitting up and feeding their son. Ignoring the looks, he climbed onto the bed and sat alongside, telling the nurse that she could leave them.

Once alone, he put his arm across her shoulders and watched in silence as his son greedily suckled at his mother's breast.

"I am feeling quite jealous, Bella."

She giggled at his words. "Well I do have another breast, sir, if you wish to share with your son. The physician says I have plenty of milk, so I am sure that I can please you both."

"Aah, Bella you destroy me," he said, placing his lips around the rosy nipple she had just exposed for him.

"I hope I always will, my lord," she said with a gasp as his lips gently sucked on her.

Lesley Field

If you enjoyed Dangerous Entrapment, please help spread the word about Lesley Field It's as easy as:

•Recommending the book to your family and friends

•Posting a review on Amazon

•Tweet and Facebook about it

Thank you

Follow me on my website:

www.lesleyfield.com

Facebook

Twitter: and also on Goodreads

For details of future releases

and more!

Or contact me on lesley_field2@btinternet.com if you want to ask any questions or post any comments.

Printed in Great Britain
by Amazon